UNDREAM'D OF SHORES

UNDREAM'D OF
SHORES

BY

FRANK HARRIS

NEW YORK
BRENTANO'S
PUBLISHERS

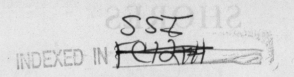
Copyright, 1924, by
BRENTANO'S, Inc.

———

All rights reserved

CONTENTS

CONTENTS

A MAD LOVE

A MAD LOVE

A little more and how much it is;
A little less and what worlds away.

BROWNING

THE scene, Vienna: the time, October in the early eighteen nineties.

I had been studying at the University a couple of semesters and had fallen in love with the gay good-humoured capital. In the Laudonstrasse I had two rooms and a bathroom. I put an Oriental rug or two in my sitting-room and I had to laugh when the maid-servant, the first time she came into the room, took off her boots for fear of hurting the carpet. It was a symbol to me of the contrasts so characteristic of Vienna between the primitive simplicity of a peasant folk and the stately ceremonial of the Court and extravagant luxuries of the nobility. The many-coloured cosmopolitan life drew me from my books; and I am afraid I was a poor student.

One day, seduced by the beauty of the afternoon, I made up my mind to take a long walk. I went down the Prater to the river. The great drive spread before me, tempting me on, but I had started too late; the carriages were all returning to the city at high speed; night was drawing down and there was a premonition of rain in the air.

3

I had walked perhaps a quarter of a mile beside the river when my attention was drawn to a Schutzmann who had gone over to wake a man on one of the benches. He stood before the huddled-up figure, speaking to it but getting no answer. I paused to see what he would do. He said something more; still no reply. Shrugging his shoulders he went off unconcernedly with the easy-going good nature of the Viennese. A glance showed me a man with a greyish beard sleeping heavily. Exchanging a smile of comprehension with the Schutzmann, I went on my way briskly, hoping still to get a walk before it rained.

An hour later a slight wind had arisen, and the leaves began to whirl down from the trees and a slow drizzle set in. The gay scene of the afternoon, with the sparkling river and the stream of carriages and well-dressed people, had all vanished, and as I walked back the desolation of the autumn evening grew on me.

As I neared the town I thought of the wastrel on the bench, and when I got opposite him I was struck by the fact that he did not seem to have moved in the meantime; he was still huddled up in the corner, with his head on his left arm; I could just distinguish the tuft of his beard.

"He'll get wet," I thought to myself; "I had better wake him."

I went over and spoke to him, grasping his shoulder. No response: the sleep was too profound. A vague disquietude came over me. I touched his right hand, which was lying on his knee, and started back; it was cold. Could the man be dead? I pushed his leg and it moved with my hand; he was not dead, but sleeping the sleep of profound exhaustion.

I shook him vigorously, and after a moment or two he turned his head and looked at me.

"Wake up," I said, "you'll catch your death of cold here."

At first he did not answer. His face struck me. The eyes looking at me were not large, but young and unfriendly keen, a light blue that went with his rufous hair and bronzed complexion. The beard was reddish grey and unkempt, but at the first glance I noticed his beaked nose and strong, bony jaws—the face of a man of character, strong and well-balanced. A small moustache shadowed the mouth; the lips were well-cut, sensitive but not sensual. If this man had come to grief, I said to myself, it was not through fleshly lusts. What could be the cause?

He was not badly dressed. His hands were clean and cared for. Why did he not speak?

"It is too cold and wet to sleep here," I attacked again; "wake up; you must feel cold already."

"What is that to you?" he said slowly. "Leave me alone!"

"I was afraid you'd catch cold," I stammered in surprise.

"And if I want to catch an everlasting cold, what's that to you?"

I was nonplussed—the man's language, the

extraordinary resolution in the toneless voice—all
staggered me.

"I happened to touch your hand." I said, "and
found it cold, so I was afraid you'd get really ill
sleeping here in the wet."

"Oh, be damned!" he barked, "I was happily unconscious till you called me back to life. What
possessed you? Couldn't you leave me alone? I
had left all the misery of living behind; now it's all
to do over again. Go away!"

"Will you, an educated man," I said, "allow yourself to die here of cold like a starved dog? Come,
man, have another wrestle with Fate."

He did not move, but simply looked at me. "I
don't want another wrestle," he said, in the same
slow, toneless voice; "I am more than half-way
through. Leave me alone!"

"You are not half-way through," I exclaimed,
feigning a laugh. "You'll probably get pneumonia
and have a dreadful month in a hospital."

"I am cold all through already," he said. "I
have not eaten for a week. Death is at my heart."

I was young and have more than a grain of obstinacy in me; I could not leave him to die.

"If I wanted to die," I exclaimed, "I would take
the pleasantest way out."

He didn't even answer; his eyes closed as if
weary.

I persisted. "I'd go out like an artist, warm and
happy. I'd meet Death rose-crowned like a
conqueror."

His eyes lightened, then his eyebrows went up and he made a motion with his hand as to say: "Have it as you will."

A passing fiacre stopped at my lifted hand.

"Come," I said, "I have a few gulden to spare."

"You will have to carry me," he replied. "I'm stiff."

His immobility struck me. He had not moved all the time we had been talking. I put an arm round his waist and tried to lift him. The driver, with the ready servability of the Viennese, had nipped down from his box and now came across and helped me; with his aid we got the man into the fiacre and I gave the driver my address.

On the way my strange companion said nothing; with shut eyes he leant back in the cab. When we got to my lodgings, the *Kutscher* sprang off the box and came to the door.

"Can I help the gentleman?"

"I wish you would," I replied; "it is only two flights up."

In a few minutes we had got the man into my bed-room and put him in an easy-chair.

"Go to the restaurant at the corner," I said to the driver, "and get me a bowl of hot soup, will you, and some hot water? I have brandy here, and wine."

"Certainly, sir," he said, and hurried off immediately.

I got out some warm winter underthings and tried to get my friend's coat off, but found it very diffi-

cult.   I went and got him a glass of brandy, but the
moment he tried to swallow it he sputtered it all out.

"I'm sorry," he apologised, "it's like liquid fire."

I made it weaker with some water and gave it to
him again and he got it down, but the real help
came when the coachman returned with some hot
soup and bread.   I arranged it on a little table and
the first spoonful brought life back to the half-
starved man.   Meanwhile the coachman busied
himself by taking off the man's boots and putting on
a pair of thick socks I handed him, and after the
soup had taken effect we managed to undress him
and pack him away in the bed.

"You are all right now," said the coachman, rub-
bing his hands; "you'll be asleep in five minutes.   I
wish I had such 'tendance."

The hint was not lost on me.   When paying him
I gave him a glass of brandy, for which he thanked
me by calling me "Herr Baron"! with the instinctive
desire to please of the Viennese.

When he had gone I turned to the bed.

"I am not inclined to sleep," said my friend.
"And you don't even know my name."

"There is time for that," I replied.

"It wouldn't convey anything to you," he said;
"nobody knows me here; but my name is Hagedorn
—Emanuel Hagedorn."

"A long sleep will do you good," I said; "if you
let yourself go, you will soon be asleep.   To-
morrow is another day."

I took his clothes and boots into my little sitting-room and closed the door. The boots, I found, were well made; the clothes travel-stained, but good; they only needed brushing and pressing. Meanwhile I would have to arrange a bed for myself in the sitting-room. I went down to see the landlady and soon got everything in order.

Suddenly I remembered that I had not eaten, so I went out and had a meal at the Friedenhof near by, where I sometimes went when the weather was bad. When I came back my bed was made up on the sofa and a little wood fire was burning on the hearth.

I listened at the door but heard nothing in the bedroom save regular quiet breathing. Reassured, I went to sleep. In the morning I was up early, but I had scarcely moved across the floor when I heard sounds in the other room. At almost the same moment the maid knocked, bringing coffee and bread and Hagedorn's clothes. I called through the door, "Good-morning!" and went on dressing.

Half-an-hour later there was a tap at my door and Hagedorn came in quietly—self-possessed. As I stood up he nodded to me and we were for a moment opposite each other. I caught my breath; he was so calm and completely master of himself, without a trace of humility; there was an air of assured strength about him that was imposing.

I pointed to the arm-chair near me and said: "Won't you sit down? Please throw off ceremony."

He took the chair at once.

"How do you feel now?" I asked.

"Perfectly well," he said; "without a trace of cold or even cough; I never felt better. Fasting must be good for one. My head is perfectly clear and I am fairly strong."

"You will be better after a good meal," I responded. "Where would you like to dine?"

"It is a matter of indifference to me," he said. "I am in your hands in more senses than one, though I must warn you again, sooner or later you will recognise that your help and kindness have been wasted. You see," he went on, "it was not a sudden resolve on my part, but a slowly ripening resolution that still holds, though I recognise the sense of what you said, that if one must kill oneself, one should choose the pleasantest way. Very practical, you English."

"I am not English," I corrected, "but Celt, and not very practical, I fear, but I feel that whoever wishes to swim can swim."

He laughed grimly.

"Women float almost in spite of themselves," he said—"fat hips and small head; they are only pulled down by their clothes—vanity. The athlete or thinker, head and muscles, goes under unless he swims; fat floats."

"What age are you?" I broke in. The night before I thought he was fifty; now he looked much younger.

"Not thirty-four," he replied. "You are astonished. My beard turned grey in the last three

or four months (he had shaved it off, I noticed).
It is hard to make up your mind to leave life; it
costs blood!"

"I don't want even to hear the story yet," I said.
"I want you to have a couple of days' rest and get
quite well and strong."

"As you will," he replied, "but you are warned."

Two or three days passed, and as if by mutual
consent we kept off the topic that was in both our
minds. I did not go to the University, but instead
took long walks with Hagedorn. It happened to
be beautiful weather, almost like an American fall
with its bright sunshine but softer, gentler skies, and
the Viennese were gay and laughter-loving as only
Viennese can be. Hagedorn did not talk much, and
yet he impressed me as a man of real power. We
went to the theatre almost every night. When I
proposed the Opera he shook his head. "I call it
the house of prostitution," he said; "hateful, for
it should be a temple."

"Is it the operatic form you dislike," I questioned,
"or music?"

"Music is only in its infancy," he remarked con-
temptuously, "and opera is a bastard form."

"What do you mean by infancy?" I asked.

He shrugged his shoulders and didn't answer for
a moment, and then began:

"Did it never strike you that other arts, arts of
seeing, like drawing and painting, are universal;
whereas music, the art of hearing, is merely national,
or, if you will, European? As soon as our artists

saw Chinese paintings and Chinese sculpture they
recognised their greatness; Chinese pottery, too,
ranks above our own. Even Japanese colour-prints
revealed to us new decorative possibilities; painting
is an art with a universal appeal. But Music! Let
a Chinaman listen to a Wagner opera or a Beethoven
symphony and he just shrugs his shoulders; it's all
to him a medly of unpleasant or, at best, meaningless
noises. Go yourself to hear Japanese music and you
will find nothing in it that appeals to you. Music
as yet is in its infancy and I don't care to listen to the
babbling."

This was not the first time the man had surprised
me with new thoughts. As he sat there, turned
sideways in indifference, his face, I thought, had the
carved outlines and colour of a Venetian bronze.
Every hour he interested me more; he had taste in
food and wine, I noticed, and the manners of a
great gentleman; he was surely "someone," as the
French say.

A few days later we went to an open-air restaurant outside the town, and after a good meal sat
talking; or, rather, I talked about writing and
writers, in doubt whether I should ever do anything
worth while.

Suddenly Hagedorn broke out:

"Why put off the day of reckoning? I could not
be better than I am, and you ought to know how
hopeless this rescue work of yours is. I may even
be able to do you some good, show you how foolish

the whole struggle of life is, especially for the artist."

Full of curiosity, I acquiesced.

"Let us walk back and talk it over," I said. And back we went to my rooms.

He took a cigar and I lit a cigarette, and we sat opposite each other for what I felt was going to be an interesting talk, for in this week or so of intimacy Hagedorn had made a profound impression on me; his casual remarks were often original, indeed curiously provocative and stimulating. He was a few years older than I, but he had the air of being much older, much more experienced. He had evidently drunk deep of life; I had barely sipped the cup; yet I resented a little the sort of authority that sat naturally upon him.

"I want to tell you the whole story," he began, "because you'll understand it. I am an artist and you are training yourself to be an artist in words. It is we artists who come to the worst grief, not because we are weak, as the Philistines imagine, but because our burden is intolerably heavy—heavy, I often think, in proportion to our gifts."

"What do you mean?" I exclaimed. "The burden should surely be light if the gifts are great."

He shrugged his eyebrows in a way he had of indicating polite tolerance of my ignorance.

"You will hear," he said.

"There are to my mind two sorts of artists. The best artists are great men first and artists after-

wards.   You may have noticed that I did not agree
when you spoke of Beethoven and Wagner in the
conventional way.   These men are both great because they were great men, not because they're great
musicians.   Wagner would have been, in my opinion, an even greater writer than musician, if he had
given himself to literature.   His early libretti are
finer than his music.

"Then you have an artist like Franz Hals, who
is a born painter, or Watteau; his very colours
please you like a child's smile; there is joy and
beauty in the mere tints.   Everyone can see that
Watteau is infinitely more gifted as a painter than
Rembrandt; Rembrandt carries it because he was
the greater man."

"How are you so sure he was the greater man?"
I asked.   "Where do you find the shortcoming in
Watteau?"

Hagedorn paused for a moment, then began:
"Do you know his *Embarquement pour Cythère* in
the Louvre?"

I nodded, and he went on:

"You have the advantage of me.   I have only
seen a print; but the motive is that couples in love
are going to sail to the Isle of Venus.   The first
couples are away up on a hill in the right-hand corner of the canvas; then to the left of them other
pairs, and finally, down by the water's edge on the
lower left side, the boat.   But the procession should
have started from the left-hand top corner and gone
down to the right; our eyes, probably through read-

ing, move more easily from left to right. Had Watteau thought over the matter he could not have made such a blunder in construction. The brain-work in Rembrandt is far higher."

"Of course, of course!" I cried. "A fair illustration."

Hagedorn went on: "I often think a great painter should be able to paint a wonderful picture by merely putting different colours on a canvas without any representment of reality or likeness to the actual."

"Then you're a painter!" I cried.

"No, no!" he said. "I'm nothing. I was a musician with an extraordinary gift. Whether I had any greatness in me, you will be able to judge better than most; but I came to believe that I had.

"My father was a Kapellmeister in Salzburg; pure German, I believe. My mother was a singer who lost her voice with me, her first child. She must have been a Jewess, I think, but I never saw a pair that loved and lived in such unison as my father and mother. No one could have had a happier child-hood than I. When I was six or seven they found out I had a wonderful ear, and they tried to keep me away from music. My father had a dread of pre-cocity and infant prodigies. He always said that Mozart would have lived much longer and done much better work if he had not begun so early. He used to condemn our practice of starting race-horses at two years of age; he thought if we started them at five or six we should have better horses.

And I dare say he was right. He had brains, my father, and my mother agreed with him in everything and always did what he wished.

"They sent me to school, and school was easy for me. I had a quick, retentive memory and learned without trouble. I tell you all this not to praise myself, but to make you understand the tragedy. Then I got to know a shoemaker who lived near us who had a violin, and I used to go round and play with him. I don't know how I learnt, but I did. One day my father, who had been first violin in the orchestra at the Opera, took out his violin and played for us, I forget what. I was about ten. I took the violin from him and began to play. You should have seen his surprise and my mother's pride, and my own gratified conceit. I shall never forget that day! But Fate hates the favourites of Fortune!

"After that they set me free. My father was delighted to teach me instrument after instrument, and I learnt three or four, including the 'cello and the piano."

"Do you know four instruments?" I broke in.

"I can play any instrument," he said carelessly.

"Good God!" I exclaimed, "and you found it difficult to make a living?"

"No, no!" he cried. "I never said that. I've found it difficult to live, but I never had any difficulty in making a living. It's our dreams kill us. It is the heaven we see before us and cannot realise, or the Paradise we've been driven out of, that makes

life disgusting to us and kills us. We artists die of
our dreams as of the plague."

"I do not understand," I said. "Go on, please."

"Let me come to the point at once," he said.

"I am one of the few persons born with an ear for
music; there are not three in a generation; I've never
met another. You don't know why or how Bach
arranged his *wohl temperirtes Clavier,* do you? [I
shook my head.] It would take too long to explain; but the piano is still imperfect. Take C
sharp and D flat. They both sound the same to
you; but C sharp is twelve vibrations faster than D
flat. I can hear them; anyone can hear the difference on the violin. The violin can give you the
true note; the piano doesn't; that's why a great
violinist is often out of pitch with an orchestra, and
why the only good music is that of a string quartet."

"But you," I cried—"can you hear all that?"

"I have absolute pitch," he replied. "You do
not know what that means. It means that between
two notes that succeed each other you hear only an
interval. I know myriads of tones between them.
Our musical notation is all imperfect.

"Now, what does this imply? The painter is
able to give you an idea of any living thing at once
in three or four strokes. He can show you the difference between a woman's figure and a man's; between a cow and a buffalo; between a lion and a
tiger. He can represent anything he sees. Why
can't the musician represent anything he hears?
Why isn't he able to give you the songs of birds,

the sound of the wind in the trees, the long with-drawn rustle of the tide ebbing on a beach? Because music is a half-art, and the sounds of Nature are infinitely too complex for our silly scales."

"But did not Wagner give us a storm at sea in *Der Fliegende Hollaender?* And what of the 'Waldvogel' in *Siegfried?*" I asked.

Hagedorn laughed scornfully. "Talk to me of that storm; it's childish. And the 'Waldvogel'! Why not ask a painter to paint the wood-beast? He'd ask you, 'Which one, squirrel or bear?' The wood-bird is just as ridiculous. Wagner had to use a flute for his bird's note, simply because there is a surface likeness between a blackbird's song and a flute, but the violin can give the tone much better if he had only known it. Don't let us talk of Wagner as a musician!

"Mascagni tried to give the nightingale in *Parisina;* the song went on for forty-five minutes and was intolerably bad; they had to cut out the bird. I gave that opera the name it's known by now in Italy, 'Opera a forbici'—the opera with the scissors. Do you remember *The Creation,* by Haydn, and the beasts in it? Isn't that imitation ridiculous?"

I nodded.

"But can you render the nightingale's song?" I probed.

He bowed his head. "So that any nightingale near will answer me at once, even in broad daylight."

"Good God!" I cried in utter astonishment.

"I can give you the music of the wind in the trees too," he went on, "or of the sea in storm or calm; I can imitate whatever I hear, exactly as a draughtsman-artist can reproduce any form or any scene at will."

"What a gift!" I cried again.

Hagedorn shrugged his shoulders. "That's the alphabet of my art; but the gift made me infinitely conceited, and was one cause of my undoing.

"My parents got so proud of me that they humoured me in everything. I began to appear at concerts and to show off. My father did all he could to hold me back; he kept me on at school till I was about fourteen, but I would not hear of the university. I did not go through even the top classes in the gymnasium. Life tempted me terribly and lessons were intolerable to one who had tasted the heady wine of applause from great audiences. Girls sought me out like moths seek a light, and I was eager to meet them. I got into life too early, and drank too deep with that desperate, unquenchable thirst of youth. I took double mouthfuls, as the French say. . . .

"The only thing except making love and kissing I would practise was my violin, unless, of course, I was learning some new instrument; but that was part of my showing off. I really had only to conquer the little technical difficulties peculiar to each instrument, and almost at once I was master of it. I knew its weaknesses and its powers by instinct, and soon got to the end of them. But a violin—if you get a good one—has hardly any limitations; its virtues are yours and its shortcomings yours——"

"I would give anything to hear you play!" I exclaimed. "We must get a violin. But I cannot afford a Stradivarius," I added lugubriously. "I am quite poor."

"A Stradivarius is not needed," he replied. "I can find a violin as good as any Strad, here in Vienna in a week; the best things have few lovers."

"What would such a violin cost?" I asked.

"Oh! anywhere from fifty to two hundred kronen; it's a matter of chance; I may not find one in a month."

"I will let you have the money," I said. "I want to hear you play so much. But weren't you in request everywhere; weren't you tempted at every moment by big offers?"

"I was in Paris playing on my own hook," he replied, "with an apartment on the Grand Boulevard before I was seventeen. That same summer I played at the Albert Hall in London. I do not need to tell you what my *nom de théâtre* was. It's better forgotten. Gifts don't matter; it is by the soul alone we count."

"But how did you come to grief?" I asked. "You had everything: health, strength, fine presence, extraordinary talent; eminence in an art while still a youth. What brought you to despair?"

"Looking back," he said, "it seems to me that a good many causes combined over several years; but I would prefer, if you are content, to let you find out for yourself. The forces are all there still; they are operating now as before, but I think you ought to be convinced first that I am not bragging or extolling my powers unduly. If you'll buy me a violin, you'll always get your money back for it, and a few days' practice will make it easy for me to show you what I can do."

I gave him the money that same day, and for nearly a week afterwards scarcely saw him, except at an occasional meal; then he appeared with a violin.

"Fortune favoured me," he said. "I've got an Amatis—as good an instrument as one could wish to have; luck has always been with me. Now if you are going regularly to your lectures I will practise here every morning, and you can make any arrangements you like for hearing me play, say, on Tuesday week, and I will try to show you that you did not help a wastrel."

Having started as a journalist in the States, I had formed connections with some newspapers in Vienna and got to know a good many critics. Since meeting Hagedorn I had talked to two or three of my journalist friends about him, and now I told them of his extraordinary powers and got them all intensely interested. I issued invitations for the next Tuesday afternoon, and besought all the journalists I knew to bring any real critics with them. They all told me they would turn up, and one in particular, the best writer on a musical weekly, declared he would have a great surprise for us; he would bring one of the greatest artists in the world to hear my friend. I could not help going in and reading his cordial, and kindly letter to Hagedorn, hoping it would excite him and nerve him to do his very best. He listened to me reading the letter and then said:

"I am glad for you, my friend; your probation won't be long."

"But you don't see!" I exclaimed. "If this great musician takes you up, swears you are extraordinary, anything, everything may come to pass."

He shook his head. "It is not a cancer spot you can cut out," he said, "or a sore to cure. But I shall be ready. You'll see. Only do not let them see me or meet me. Keep them in the other room."

I was a little surprised, but I arranged chairs in my sitting-room so as to seat about twenty-five or thirty people.

When the great afternoon came I was intensely excited. The room was crowded—forty people instead of twenty-five, and all on tiptoe of expectance. Suddenly the musical critic entered, bringing with him Joachim.

"I don't need to introduce Joachim to you," he said, "the greatest violin player in the world."

Of course I insisted on his taking the seat of honour, and I could not help sneaking into the back room to tell Hagedorn that Joachim had come to hear him. He smiled, but his eyes were sad, and I returned a little chilled. He had given me the outline of the programme, and it ran something like this:

1. A young nightingale learning to sing.
2. A nightingale after he has found his love.
3. How he should sing.
4. A Comment on Life.

I announced the first three, and we all sat down to listen in strained attention. After a little pause the nightingale's notes began to fall like golden beads. At the first break in the voice—extraordinarily lifelike—I saw Joachim start, and from that moment I knew Hagedorn had conquered. There was a hush when he stopped playing, and after a moment quiet applause—I had almost said reverent applause—silenced almost immediately by new notes that rang out in a song of desire and joy.

Words cannot describe such sounds; at least I have no words to describe them. I can be excused for not attempting a task beyond Shelley's powers. But as the music ceased Joachim jumped to his feet and silenced the clapping.

"No applause," he said; "let us hear the next; it is most astonishing."

A moment or two later the next song began—what the nightingale should sing. It went from panting desire to throbs of joy, and from joy to triumph, and them came broken wailing notes caught up now and then with faint reminders of the love-ecstasy. Then—abruptly—silence. Joachim started to his feet again.

"He is not only a great master of the violin," he said, "but a great, great musician. Who is he? Please let me meet him."

I stood between him and the door and told him that my friend did not want to be known. The surprise, the admiration of all was manifest. Everyone declared that the performance was wonderful, epoch-making. One after the other found new words with which to praise the unknown master.

Suddenly Hagedorn began to play again. I announced "A Comment on Life." In absolute silence everyone began to listen.

What was he playing? It was all light and gay and hopeful, like a spring morning, the joy mounting rapidly to passion and delight; higher still to rapture, and then—idiot laughter tore the air! A phantasmagoria began of all sorts of emotions mixed together—joy and pleasure broken by dreadful, meaningless chucklings; moanings and imprecations shrilled to shrieks and ravings, only to die away in ghastly mutterings. We looked at each other; plainly the musician was depicting a madhouse. Exquisite moments of joy and sighs of pleasure, ending in howls of rage and ear-piercing screams—appalling! Then a heavy silence!

No one applauded. I looked up. Joachim was shaking his head.

"Dreadful! Dreadfully painful," he said. "Art must not give itself to pain. What a pity! A most remarkable mastery. What a pity!" and he hurried from the room. No wish to meet Hagedorn now. The men vanished as quickly as they had come. One alone remained—a young fellow

I had scarcely noticed, a critic on a daily paper, since famous, then just beginning to be known.

"Great work!" he cried to me. "Let them all go. I have listened to the greatest violinist I ever expect to hear; greater than Joachim, greater than anyone; a great original master; I must meet him!"

"Come and dine to-night and I will see if I can bring him," I said.

"Tell him from me," said the young man, "that I am on my knees before him. He is a great, great man—astounding!"

When he had gone I hurried into the next room to see Hagedorn. He had laid his violin on the bed and was seated in the arm-chair.

"You heard," I said.

"Everything. Your Joachim was characteristic; true to type, as I knew he would be. The limitations pleased him; my mastery of the instrument even. He has some greatness in him; but the moment I showed him a little more than he was prepared for—revolt, resentment—'Art was not made,' if you please, 'to give itself to pain.' Instead of a madhouse I ought to have given them a Jew's view of heaven with golden streets and pearly gates— a childish vision of a tawdry Paradise. But I hope you are satisfied, my friend?"

"More than satisfied," I replied. "Satisfied that everything you have told me about yourself and your art is true; that you are the greatest musician I have ever heard or expect to hear. I believe you are a

great man too, and I am infinitely sorry for you.
You heard what young Neumann said.   Do you expect, out of forty fools, to get more than two to
see you as you are?   I think this is the only city in
the world in which you could find two enthusiastic
admirers!"

He put his hands on my shoulders.

"You are a great boy," he said, "and if anybody
could help me, you would; but it's too late, if indeed
it were ever possible."

That night young Neumann came to dinner and
Hagedorn allowed me to introduce him as the
violinist.   Neumann said everything I have said
here, and said it at far greater length and better, or
at least more enthusiastically.   He admitted with
gay laughter that if he had only heard the madhouse
thing he would not have come back for more, but
he declared that it seasoned the nightingale's songs
and formed the most perfect contrast to them.

"I want you to play me the thing in all music I
love best," he said to Hagedorn.   "It's the——"

"Stop!" cried Hagedorn.   "Don't say another
word; don't tell me what it is."   And he went into
the inner room and began to play.

"He has guessed right," said Neumann, as the
strains floated through the room.   And for a wonderful quarter of an hour we listened to the love
duet in the second act of *Tristan*, marvellously rendered, perfectly, so that expectation was surpassed,
desire sated.

When he came into the room again Neumann took his hands, with tears in his eyes, and said simply:

"I cannot thank you. Words are nothing."

"Let us go and dine," I said, and we went out together. But during dinner we were all very silent. There did not seem much to say, and when we returned to the house and Neumann left us at the door, I could only say to Hagedorn:

"It has been a great day for me, a great day."

He nodded and went into his bedroom without a word, but I noticed now that his face had something Sphinx-like in it; it was as if carved in stone to endurance.

The next morning Neumann called, just as the coffee came.

"I have been up all night," he said, "utterly unable to sleep. I could scarcely wait till it was eight o'clock so that I might come round and say that I put myself at your service. Whatever I can do in Vienna I will do. You ought to have been known ten years ago from one end of the world to the other. Give me the chance of telling Vienna who you are and of showing them what you can do."

Hagedorn smiled. "It is really kind of you," he said. "Talk it over with my friend here and decide whatever you please."

"We must give a series of concerts," cried Neumann in wild excitement; "subscription concerts, half-a-dozen or a dozen, in a large hall, but not too large. I know the very place. We will put the price high and every seat will be filled, and after the first concert every ticket will be worth fifty times its weight in gold. I know Vienna. It is not deaf to genius. I feel sure of a triumph."

"Not a dozen concerts," interrupted Hagedorn. "Say three, if you like."

"I want a crescendo effect," argued Neumann. "Please give me six concerts and write the programmes. I am sure you can do anything you want to. Pick the musicians you care to honour and give their little-known pieces. Only play one or two of your own things in each concert. Match yourself with the greatest. I tell you, man, it will be a triumph!"

It was good to hear him. That was what I felt too. Surely, surely it was possible to save such an extraordinary genius.

We soon found that our task was going to be an easy one. Neumann got the hall and Hagedorn gave me the programmes for three concerts. He had headed them: "Old Masters"; "Modern Masters"; "The Future." Neumann begged for more, but he shook his head.

"I want to repay my friend here," he said. "That's all."

Neumann declared that with six concerts we would make fifty thousand kronen—a sum far beyond our hopes or wishes—but he begged so hard that at length Hagedorn consented. I did not interfere with a word. I had already grown doubtful of my right to interfere: *"The heart knoweth its own bitterness."*

Finally they settled on four concerts. I could scarcely wait for the first one. At Neumann's request Hagedorn had made the programmes very long. He began by playing some well-known things from Bach, and insisted on playing them on the instrument for which they were intended—the harpsichord. In his hands the little tinkling instrument became a wonder, and for the first time in my life a fugue of Bach showed itself as an exquisite thing, a jewel as beautiful as a sonnet of Wordsworth—divine music, impeccably perfect.

Then he played Beethoven's *Sonata* in B flat: we all had heard it again and again. I had never realised it was so wonderful. Then Mozart, grace and sweetness and joy incarnate.

And then Wagner; the famous passage in the *Meistersinger* that is, after all, the great egotist's own trial and supreme triumph.

They were all rendered as I have never heard them rendered before or since, and the audience was enthusiastic as only a Viennese audience can be. For ten minutes the whole programme was interrupted while men stood on their chairs and women clustered together like a flock of doves in front of the platform applauding, laughing, chattering, crying. Really, they seemed to know how great a man he was.

When the women began to crowd into the aisle Hagedorn left the stage. He had insisted upon not even giving his name; the concert was given by "a musician." Only Neumann and I were on the stage, and I went out with Hagedorn.

When the tumult subsided he came in again and began to play on the violin. First a fugue almost like one of Bach's. Then he gave us imitations of various masters, almost as beautiful as the originals. Then a pause, and he began a lark's song. Just a lark's song some summer morning on a sun-bathed down or upland. What a song! The soul of joy was in it; it was simply irresistible. When he had finished and had bowed and walked off the stage, the audience went mad. In two minutes they had crowded on to the stage. They must see him and speak to him. But when I went out to get him I found he had left the theatre. I went back and told the people that it was impossible to find him. The afternoon papers told us that the price of the remaining seats for the next three concerts had trebled. Neumann was more than delighted.

"Let me see him," he cried.

"Go and find him," I said. "You may have more influence with him than I have. I want him encouraged."

"Encouraged!" exclaimed Neumann. "He must need a lot of encouragement if such appreciation is not enough for him," and away he went.

When I got home I found Hagedorn had not yet returned. He came in quietly, about half-past six, and we went out to dinner. I had never known him more depressed.

"All this enthusiasm has made no difference to you?" I asked.

He shook his head, and his eyebrows went up.

"The price of the seats has trebled," I went on.

He shrugged his shoulders.

"But why, why are you so hopeless?" I cried. "Neumann says he has never seen such enthusiasm. The director of the Opera House has written to him, asking for your name and address. It seems his wife and daughter were in the audience and are wild with admiration."

Hagedorn shook his head. "I've had it all before," he said, "ten years and more ago. Praise does not satisfy the heart, my friend. Life to me is like an obscene monkeys' cage: I could give you the gibberings and scratchings, the rages and sensualities; but what good would it all do? . . .

"When I was able to take life seriously, able to hope and enjoy, I failed; the audiences never wanted the best in me, never; but the imitations and childish things. I went on, in spite of the growing conviction that I was born out of due time. Five hundred years hence someone will come who will do my work, and find perhaps half-a-dozen who know him and want him; to-day it is too soon, and I have no wish to encourage or help men; I'm sick of them and their sordid squalor and soulless stupidity.

"Life tests all of us to breaking-point," he went on, after a long silence. "I know now that the road

I trod is the upward road and has been travelled by all who grow. The higher we climb in this world's esteem the heavier our fall. You remember the text in the Bible, *Those whom he loveth he chasteneth*. It is so true, that; divinely true. Those whom he loveth he chasteneth, continually, perpetually, without let-up, to the very limit of their endurance. To those whom He hates He gives everything, lavishly, and then the fall is—fatal. 'Twas here in Vienna I met my fate: you may as well hear the whole story now, though it's not worth the telling. . . .

"I used to send my mother newspaper clippings of my triumphs, and for one reason or another she was always calling me back to her, always wanting me near her. Her mother's heart was full of apprehension; perfect love is one with fear. Well, I came back to her more than once to rest and recruit. But I no longer shared their religious belief (my mother had long before accepted my father's Lutheranism), and that made a coolness. Besides, the hope of the ideal always tempted me away again, and a year or so later I would return again to see her and to brag.

"When I was about twenty-two or three I stayed away some years—a foolish, light love affair in Paris that ripened me—but again I returned just before I was twenty-six with two hundred thousand gulden in the bank. I was rich: I loved horses and drove them in the Prater where you found me!

drove them tandem, drove four-in-hand, and generally had a pretty girl beside me on the box seat.

"When I went to the Opera I used to go behind the scenes and brag to my heart's content. With that charming humour of the Viennese they would push me on the stage to play something in the middle of an opera. No one could have been more favoured than I: and then without warning—my fate.

"One evening I was at a loose end. I did not know what to do with myself or where to go. I had just got rid of a girl who was plaguing me with her love which I had tired of; it was too complete, had no limit, no sparkle; nothing bores like meek adoration.

"I had been dining at a restaurant in the Ringstrasse when a couple of men came up to me, one a journalist named Goldescu, and the other a musical critic on some paper; I forget his name. They were wild to take me to see a dancer—'as great a dancer,' Goldescu said, 'as you are a musician. She will be on to-night for half-an-hour.'

"I had nothing to do and nothing better to propose, so I went with them. It was a little restaurant in the Rumanian quarter—a cellar in fact, long, low and no doubt dark in the daytime. We went down a dozen steps to it. A crowd of common people sat about drinking the sour Rumanian wine, Dragasan. The first phrase I heard was 'Datche me vin'—almost pure Latin. Rumania was a Roman colony under Trajan.

"The proprietor played the Rumanian national instrument, the Kobza, a sort of cross between the guitar and mandolin, and as I got accustomed to the smoke I saw that there was a low stage at the far end of the room. It might have been six or eight feet deep and perhaps a foot high, with a green baize curtain in front of it. No pretence of footlights except two gas-jets in the corners and one in the middle.

"I could not drink the common wine, but the proprietor began to treat us with a good deal of politeness and soon brought me a Tokai which was excellent—one of the great wines of the world.

"My friends talked. Goldescu was a clever fellow and interested me, perhaps because he was of a different race, and too cynical even to believe in virtue, much less seek it.

"After trying to eat one of their strange salads I asked when the show was going to begin, and the proprietor told me he would bring Marie on as soon as he could, but she did not usually appear till eleven o'clock. There was a comic singer who bored me to extinction, and then the proprietor came out beaming: 'She has come and will appear immediately.'

"I drew my chair clear of the table so as to have an uninterrupted view down the middle of the room. The curtains were drawn aside and we saw a small girlish figure on the stage; Goldescu had said something about her being a Jewess; but she was not of the Jewish type, I thought. Her nose was small

and straight; true, her eyes were large and dark and
her hair black; but her lips, too, were refined and
pretty; and with a certain sense of colour contrast
she had thrown yellow veils about her. She was
just pretty, I concluded; very pretty even, but nothing more. I had seen more beautiful women, but
—there was something provocative-intense about
her, besides a dainty aloofness and self-possession.

"The music began—a sort of slow, vague theme,
and Marie began to dance; at first very slowly,
gracefully; and as she danced she discarded veil
after veil. The music took on character. I began
to see that it was a sort of representation of love,
such a theme as you might witness any evening at the
Opera, only there was no pirouetting here, or fast
little runs and poisings on a toe; nothing acrobatic;
simply at first lithe swayings, hesitations and refusals—reserve apparent always and a sort of fugi-
tive grace; then the yielding little by little, the figure
growing clearer and clearer as the veils went, till
she stood outlined before us, and reached complete
abandonment by sinking down and backward on the
stage with outstretched arms while the curtains drew
together shutting her off.

"It was charming, graceful, clothed with beauty
and the modesty of art. The applause was tremendous; they called for the dance again and again, but
no one came. We called too, and applauded loudly,
insistently. At length the proprietor went behind
the scenes but came back disconsolate. Marie refused to do anything more or to come out. She

would bow to the audience when she was dressed and that was all.

"I don't know how it was, but the simplicity of her methods grew upon me. She was a real artist; her form more perfect even than her face. For some reason or other, in my Uebermuth (I was very arrogant), I thought I would bring her out, so I went over and took a violin from one of the musicians. The proprietor, divining my intention, drew the curtains aside and I stepped on the stage and began to play. I first played some imitations of birds and then a love improvisation giving the spirit of her dancing. I had never played better. Still she did not appear. I put down the instrument and went off with my friends, content never to see the place again or the little Rumanian girl.

"The days passed into weeks; it annoyed me to realise that I could not forget the dancer or blot her from memory. Often I asked myself what was the secret of her influence; why did she live with me when more beautiful women were quickly forgotten? I could never find an answer. Time and again I was on the point of asking Goldescu to bring about a meeting and introduce me; but I disliked the cynical effrontery of the fellow and hated even to think of him in connection with Marie's reserved beauty and charm.

"One day I met him walking with a girl. I saw the grace of her before I recognised who it was, and from some way off I noticed how people turned to

look at her. When Goldescu introduced us she
exclaimed:

" 'I hope you don't mind my disappearing the
other evening. If you had stopped after your imitation of the lark I would have come out to meet
you I wanted to tell you how wonderful that
bird's song was; but you rendered the very soul of
my dancing with your music and that broke me all
up. I could not come out in that *bouge* with red
eyes '

" 'Very human, these artists,' cried Goldescu in a
comic voice, and we both had to smile.

" 'He's an artist,' she said, 'but I'm only a half-
artist, an executant; my body's my instrument; it
happens to be a good one, but if it were a poor one
I could do nothing; whereas he doesn't depend on
the instrument at all; his art is in his soul.'

" 'Charming of you,' I protested, 'but unjust to
yourself. You rendered love delightfully. 'Twas
like the *Cherubino* of Mozart; a quality of youth in
it, of freshness and a hint of mature passion as well
—an entrancing mixture.'

"She flushed slightly. 'You don't know how
good it is to be praised by you,' she said simply, giving me her eyes. 'If I could be deceived about myself your praise would do it, but—but——'

" 'What does the "but" mean?' I asked.

"She pointed. 'We women always want perfection; don't praise me then. I am curious about you.
You carry one's soul away by your playing, but who

are you, *you?*   You seem too young to have climbed the heights.'

" 'Age is not a matter of years,' I replied. 'I'm as old as Time.'

" 'A great phrase,' she cried delightedly, 'and true. Oh, if only——'

" 'If you two want to make love,' Goldescu interrupted, 'why select the street?'

"She shrank at that; so I raised my hat and said: 'Please let me know where you dance next and I'll come.'

"I went; her eyes told me she understood that I could not bear our feeling to be cheapened by the Jew's appraisement.

"I've tried to give you a true impression of that first meeting," said Hagedorn, "but I've failed. It was all very simple and I've made it sound highfalutin. I'm not an artist in words, you see. But to me she was a revelation a miracle of frankness, sympathy—charm.

"But ten minutes after I left her I could not help wondering why she went about with that Jew; what was the attraction, the connection. Fishy, it seemed to me; for I knew him, knew that no good thing could live in his atmosphere. I ought to tell you about him but I can't. I'm conscious I'm not fair to him; no human being could be as vile, sordid, soulless, unscrupulous, cruel and vain as I knew him to be. I've heard him boast of things an assassin would be ashamed of. Yet he was big and handsome in a common style, a good writer, a good actor

too, and always carried himself with an assured
mastery in life. He always held the floor wherever
he was. I remember his saying once he could always borrow money from the worldly wise by saying: 'Give me a hundred gulden; I don't promise
ever to pay you back. You should be willing to pay
for my society'; and from greenhorns by insisting
it was a loan to be returned next day. The funny
part of it was, he said, that a second loan was always easier to get than the first; humans hated to
confess even to themselves that they had been
fooled. And he believed as little in woman's virtue
as in man's generosity.

" 'Their refusals,' he used to say, 'are all either
coldness or calculation. Choose the right moment
and——'

" 'And your mother?' someone retorted one evening.

" 'My race tells you,' he responded.

"A common nature and mind sharpened by life.

"When we walked together a dozen girls gave
him the glad eye for one who noticed me. Don't
think I was envious of his gifts or looks; I never
was envious in my life. But though he sought me
out I had avoided him always till I found him with
Marie.

"Two or three days after that meeting on the
street he sent me a 'wire' to say he'd call for me
at seven to take me to a new dance. I was ready
and went with him.

" 'You lucky dog,' he began. 'She's always talk-

ing about you and your playing; it'll be your own
fault if you don't win her, and she's a seductive
little devil. I shouldn't be surprised if it was her
first "affair." Fancy a professional dancer a virgin
—everything's possible in this mad world! And
she certainly has what the French call "the devil
in her body." '

"I could not discuss her with him. The thought
of seeing her quickened my blood and with beating
heart and glad eyes I went to my fate.

"Yet all the preliminaries were hateful to me.
When we reached the concert hall the performance
had begun, so Goldescu took me round to the
stage door and went to her dressing-room as if it
had been his own.

" 'You know the way?' I asked in surprise.

" 'I should think so,' he replied characteristically.
'I've paid to learn it in every theatre in Vienna.'

"I could have struck the dog in the face.

"At his knock she opened—'Come in'—and in
we went, though she was not half-dressed.

" 'The days have seemed long,' she said, turning
at once to me. 'I have thought about you a great
deal.'

"I, too, had thought about her; in fact I had
hardly thought of anything else.

"The stage bell sounded.

" 'I must get ready,' she said; 'forgive me!
You'll come back?'

" 'I shall be delighted! After the show?' I
asked.

" 'After my dance,' she corrected, smiling. I'll need only ten minutes to get rid of the grease paint and change: I'll grudge the minutes.'

"She had voiced my very thought. 'So shall I,' I replied like an echo, and we went to our Press seats in the front row.

"Marie's dance was announced as 'A Joy Dance,' and she appeared all in rose; but the skirt was short and the stuff was so thin and so soft that it clung and drew attention to the beauties of her figure in the most provocative way. My mouth parched while looking at her: I could scarcely draw breath, and heavy pulses hammered in my temples. I was filled with a blind rage of jealousy; all these men seeing her nudity seemed an outrage.

" 'In the beginning dress was mere decoration,' said Goldescu, 'and not clothing, we are told. Marioutza is a true primitive, eh?'

"I could not trust myself to speak. 'How could she? Why?'

"I was all interrogation and revolt; angry beyond control. Yet even in my rage I recognised that she was dancing marvellously; now like a lily swaying in water, now floating like thistledown, seeming to rebound as lightly as she came to earth; and when the music quickened and she sprang from the stage, one really felt that she might go higher indefinitely—

> 'Like an unbodied joy
> Whose race has just begun.'

It all showed such a union of rare natural gifts
and long assiduous practice as only an artist could
appreciate.

"She ended her dance by springing into the wings
and left us with the image of her willowy, slight
figure outlined as distinctly as a figure on a Greek
vase.

"We walked about for a few minutes and on
turning found her at the stage door.

" 'What do you think of it?' she asked with the
anxiety of the true artist. For the life of me I
could not answer as I wanted to.

" 'I liked it, of course,' I said, 'liked it im-
mensely; but I preferred your Love Dance.'

" 'Really?' she cried in such chagrined disappointment that I had to mitigate the rebuff. 'I
mean, love is a greater theme than joy,' I began.
'Don't you think——'

"Goldescu chose this moment to take his leave.
'Don't let him cast you down!' he cried. 'I've
never seen you more entrancing: you're a marvel;
but alas! I've something special on to-night,' he
added. We let him go almost without noticing
him.

"On our way to her rooms the girl enthralled
me. She seemed to divine my secret thoughts and
my jealousy vanished before her outspokenness.
Our talk was confidential and intimate from the
beginning.

" 'Your playing the other night,' she began, 'was
magical, but I was overwrought by it and—and—I

wanted to meet you under better conditions: you understand?'

"Of course I understood. It was my own feeling.

" 'I want you to like my Joy Dance,' she went on. 'I wrote the music for it myself. Often as a girl the beauty of our river and woodland in summer and the song of the birds used to make me weep for joy. Bukarest is so lovely and I wanted to render that beauty that's one with joy and delight. I've a pretty figure and I'm glad of it. We all love beauty; don't we?'

"I felt that I had been a brute.

" 'I know, I understand,' I cried; 'but I'm a man and had already put you apart and above everyone, and when you showed your figure it made me jealous; it was petty of me.'

" 'Let me explain it to you,' she said with her childlike sincerity. 'You know, we dancers look on our bodies as you do on your violin, as our instrument. You love a fine one and know all its good points and so do we. How often we used to laugh at some girl with big shoulders and bust trying to learn to dance; she couldn't: the instrument was not right.'

" 'But do you like exposing yourself?' I asked, all my innate prejudices coming to rationalise my jealousy.

" 'I don't think of it in that way,' she replied. 'I want to express a certain emotion: I try to do it as perfectly as I can; I never even think

whether I am showing a few inches more or less
of figure. . . . Is that immodest of me? You
know, I want you to know me as I am—my faults
even. Others may take the grease paint for my
complexion: I want you to see me as I really am,
heart and soul and all! . . . I think as a girl I
was almost without modesty, in mind as in body.
I used to picture and imagine all things to myself.
I was dreadfully curious, longed to know this and
that. The mind is immoral, isn't it? or rather
it has nothing to do with morality?' And she
looked up at me anxiously. I nodded and she
went on:

" 'My mother used to be shocked at me. She
was a Catholic and religious, and when she found
me studying my figure in the glass (I often wanted
to kiss it) she told me that I must be modest, and
that the body was sinful.

" 'I couldn't believe it. I don't now. I love
the curve of my neck, and my small breasts are
lovely to me; and even my slender feet please me
intimately.'

"I was shaken with delight: she was clear as
crystal, with a woman's depth and a woman's delight in her beauty. I smiled and she continued:

" 'Am I immodest? I don't think so. If there
were anything ugly about me I'd conceal it and be
ashamed of it. I hate my legs because the muscles
show; but I can't help that; it's part of my art
and I'm not modest or immodest about them: I
just recognise the fact——'

" 'You dear!' I cried, 'I've called modesty the fig-leaf of ugliness.'

" 'That's it, that's it,' she crowed with delight; 'that's the truth; the talk of the girls in the dance classes I call immodest; but——

" 'I like your strong, stern face,' she broke off, 'and the boy's eyes you have and your bronzed-fair skin pleases me. Why shouldn't I say so? But most of all, your genius, your wonderful playing, the divine spirit in you——'

" 'You must hear me once at my best!' I exclaimed. 'I'll play for you better than I've ever played. Let me see. On Friday I play at Prince Lichtenstein's. Would you come?'

" 'Goldescu wants me to dance there,' she said. 'Suppose we both perform in public, yet just for each other?'

"She was ravishing and her eyes held mine. Why were they so beautiful to me? Was it the long dark lashes or the brown brook depths? I can't say. For the first time in my life I knew love. I could not help touching her hips as we walked side by side; I was drunk with desire. I knew it was love I felt, love once for all, love that was deathless; this was my mate; the strength of my feeling frightened me. I longed to take her in my arms, but refrained; though the passion of admiration I felt for her and her sacred boldness was clear enough, I'm sure, for now and again her eyes gave themselves to mine.

"At her door she held out her hand and though

I wanted her lips I restrained myself. I had had so much; I did not want to go in. I wanted to drink the divine cup little by little and prolong the ecstasy. But I could not help putting my hands on her shoulders and looking deep into her eyes while I said: 'Auf Wiedersehn! Mein Alles!'

"I'm conscious I've remembered badly; given you no idea of her charm for me.

"I went home as if on air, drunk with the hope that she loved me, crazy with desire sharpened by this and that picture of her slight fleeting girl's figure.

"Next morning I awoke to find a letter from her begging me to send or bring her the music I had composed for her Love Dance, so that, as she said, 'even when dancing I may feel inspired by your spirit.'

"I sat down at once and wrote out the music and took it to her apartment that same afternoon. It was the first time I had seen her in her frame, so to speak. The drawing-room was very simple; half-a-dozen photos of men and girl friends; three or four prints of famous dancers, all sent her by Goldescu, she told me, and nothing more except a piano and the usual furniture. At first she seemed shy; her eyes withdrawn; her hands, I remember, were very cold, but her face was lovelier than I thought; she grew on one; surely her eyes were larger than the night before.

"She made me talk about myself and my tours, of Paris and London and Madrid; 'people everywhere much the same,' was her comment. I had to tell her of my mother and father and my beginnings and all I hoped to be and do.

"Then a samovar was brought in and we had tea, and afterwards I went to the piano and played my Love Dance music for her, and as I ended she put her hand on my shoulder and I could not help putting my arm round her waist, seeking to draw her to me. At first she yielded and I thought she was going to kiss me; but then she grew stiff and looked into my eyes and smiled, shaking her head:

> 'Touch hands and part with laughter,
> Touch lips and part with tears,'

she chanted mischievously, the brown eyes alight. She pleased me so intimately that even her caprices were delightful. She wanted to try my music over before me; she played quite well, I found; and then I had to play it again while she danced. 'Oh, I shall have a new effect!' she triumphed. 'You're a dear, dear magician!' she cried, and for a moment put her glowing cheek against mine.

"I don't know why I record all this, but I want you to understand the full perfection of my love. Whatever she did or refused to do pleased me; her boldness of speech and virginal shrinking from even a kiss delighted me equally.

"That evening at Prince Lichtenstein's was a triumph. She danced divinely and I really think my music helped her. I am sure as she sank back-

ward on the floor, while the music throbbed with
passion and sang with delight, no human figure had
ever shown a more complete abandonment.

"The audience went crazy; you know our Viennese and how they love to show their feelings.
Well, I never saw anything like the enthusiasm dis-
played that night. I suppose there were five hundred guests in the great ballroom, the best names
in Austria, and they were all entranced. They
cheered and kissed their hands to her in wild
admiration.

"She came to me before them all with glowing
cheeks.

" 'O Master,' she cried, 'what music! I felt as
if I were in your arms. Do you really love me?
Can you? Are you sure?'

"For a moment I was tongue-tied and thought-
bound too.

" 'You know I love you,' I heard myself say.
And at once before them all she gave me her lips,
as if we had been alone. I adored her for her
noble courage.

"Love to ordinary people is the event of their
lives; but artists often have a tenfold keener delight. Suppose a sculptor suddenly finds in the
woman he loves the most perfect model he has ever
met; his passion is extraordinarily sharpened. Suppose a woman has tried for years and years to dance
better than anyone else and suddenly finds her
powers intensified by a musician who gives her sur-

prising melodies, her æsthetic ambitions are all
realised beyond hope; if she's inclined to love the
musician you can easily see how her passion will be
heightened. That's how I explain the bursting
forth of Marie's love. As for me, well, from the
beginning she had been to me perfection perfected.
At last I had found the ideal we all long for, and
my very soul was ravished.

"I looked up and the men and women were all
smiling, as I thought, maliciously or disdainfully.
(What were we to them after all but a musician
and a dancing-girl?) I had an inspiration. Taking her by the hand I led her over to Prince Lichtenstein and bowing said: 'Prince, you have often
been kind to me, but never so kind as to-night; for
in your house I have found my bride.'

"Everyone applauded and shouted, and Lichtenstein swore they must celebrate the betrothal of
the two greatest artists in the world; and indeed
we did celebrate it all night long, for the early
morning sunshine was gilding the house as the
Prince took us to the door and sent us home in his
state carriage with outriders, if you please, and
all his guests cheering on the steps. And even then
he would not let us go till I had promised to celebrate the marriage in his palace.

"I took my love to her rooms and she would have
me go in with her; so I sent the carriage home and
stayed. And there with shining great eyes she told
me she had loved me from the first and only wanted

to make me happy, and as I kissed her holding her in my arms I was more than happy, drunk with pride and joy, delirious with desire.

"Next week my father and mother came to Vienna and I took a house and began to furnish it, and Prince Lichtenstein sent me some pictures and others of the nobility followed suit. The Gross-Herzog Rudolph, who called himself my first admirer, gave me the whole drawing-room furniture —pictures and all—from one of his palaces.

"Our marriage was an event, but the part I liked best was that my mother had taken a great fancy to Marie and told me at the wedding she hoped to be a grandmother in a year.

"They say happiness has no history and I found it true; I could tell you little or nothing of the next three years, except that as I learned to know my wife's nature I loved her more and more. Positively she had no faults and a myriad of high qualities, all set off by gaiety and sweet temper.

"After the first season in Vienna I took her for a tour through Italy and the second year through Spain. We learned everything together, languages and all. I found it easy with a few performances each year to increase our fortune; the only drawback to our joy was that we had no children, but neither of us missed anything; at least I certainly did not, and my wife assured me she was content. But she was always encouraging me to write an opera or an oratorio to show how great I was! *The Passion of St Matthew* by Bach was her favourite: I ought to do a great oratorio! I didn't want to face the work; I was continually plagued by the idea of making first a new and scientific musical notation. I wanted to go to China and Japan and learn their music and then build up a music which should include theirs and be as effective in Peking or Kyoto as in Paris or Vienna. Meanwhile I worked constantly in my own lazy way and made up my mind to spend the next summer in Shanghai. Marie consented.

"But that season in Vienna, for some reason or other, perhaps to excite my ambition, she took up her dancing again, and got Goldescu to get her engagements and play publicity manager. I wrote several new themes for her and she certainly embroidered them superbly.

"I don't think our passion had lost its keen edge; I found Marie a wonderful mistress, with an extraordinary congeniality of taste and desires. It was she who first taught me to love pictures. If I proposed to go into the Carpathians in mid-winter to hunt bear and wolves, or in summer to go to the Lido at Venice for a week's bathing, she clapped her hands and crowed joyful acceptance. Never was there such a joyous, eager companion.

"I often wondered what her own intimate wish was: had she desires apart from mine?

"I had bought a little country place twenty or thirty miles from Vienna and I went there frequently, sometimes without her, to put it in order.

"Once or twice I had been annoyed by her liking

for Goldescu; she always told me she had known
him as boy and girl together, and had never even
kissed him; his cynical effrontery, she insisted, disgusted her; but she had no good reason to give him
up; he was so serviceable; she used him for this
and for that and I believed her. I would have
believed whatever she chose to tell me. I was
too happy even to work at my art, too happy to
measure how happy I was when the blow fell.

"I had gone out to our country place one Saturday and found the water-tank that supplied the
bathroom had burst and overflowed everywhere.
I wired to Vienna for skilled help and stayed to
set them to work. I wrote my wife I should not
be in Vienna before Wednesday or Thursday and
returned on Monday afternoon to get fifteen feet
of piping that was urgently needed. I got the piping and I saw that I had half-an-hour before I could
catch my train. Naturally I drove to my home and
went upstairs. The drawing-room door was ajar;
hearing low voices, I pushed it half open. On the
sofa opposite was my wife nestling in the corner
and leaning over her, half behind her, was Goldescu. As I was about to speak he leaned forward,
lifted up her chin and kissed her on the mouth. I
was petrified; literally unconscious that I drew the
door to; suddenly I found myself at the stair-head,
yards away, shivering with cold. Like a sleep-
walker I passed down into the hall, picked up the
coil of piping, went out the front door, found a

droshky and drove to the station—mechanically!

"I gave the coil of piping to the overseer, who told me I must have caught a chill and following his advice I went to bed. He gave me a hot rum. I fell asleep and four hours afterwards awoke to a tempest of rage and hate that altered my whole nature.

"The rest can be told briefly. In the morning I wired my lawyer, who was also my father's; I told him the truth and begged him to tell it to my parents. I made over half of all I possessed to my wife, asked the lawyer to tell her the truth if she pressed for it and that evening took train for Venice. Since then I have been a wanderer over the face of the globe. I buried myself for two years in China and think I know their music now and their language and the spirit of that great people as well.

"I went all through Japan time and again and understand, I think, their music.

"But I've never done anything: the truth is I've never recovered from the shock of that afternoon. I used to hate her when I thought of it; often feared I should go mad with hate; but now I'm just cold to it all; it might have happened to someone else for all I care; but with my love I lost my love of life; all the uses of living became stale, flat and tedious to me.

"Three months ago I returned to Austria after six years of wandering, and went down to Salz-

burg. My father and mother were both dead. I
came to Vienna meaning to make an end; what
was there for me to live for?

"You saved my life; for a brief space I've
warmed myself with your inexhaustible strength
and vigorous love of living, but it can't go on. . . .

" 'Everyone,' says the Russian, 'gets tired of
holding up an empty sack.' You'd get tired in
time, my friend, or if you did not, you must feel
that I am tired already; I have travelled the path
before, know all the toils and triumphs of it, and
therefore it all says nothing to me—nothing! I
got the best of life too easily, too early; I can't
struggle; I won't; it's fat that floats," he added
disdainfully.

"Did your wife never write to you or seek to
see you to explain?" I asked in amazement.

"She wrote," he said, "and the lawyer forwarded
it; but I never read the letter; I would not reopen
the wound; the cicatrice was painful enough; why
should I let her torture me again?"

"But you can't tell anything from the act," I
insisted; "one might kiss and nothing more."

He shrugged his shoulders impatiently.

"You haven't followed my story with full sympathy," he said. . . .

"Surely you know without my telling you that
I went through all the tortures of hell. At first
I wanted to go back and kill the Jew, and when that
madness left me the memory of her beauty and her
kisses drove me crazy. She had made me feel more

intensely than anyone: her body was always before me, in its slim beauty; I'd see it, touch it, get drunk with the odour of it. A thousand times I said to myself: 'I'll go back. What does it matter to me whom she kissed so long as she'll kiss me, give me the illusion of love?' My body ached for her, man; a thousand times my mouth parched and desire choked me.

"And my maimed, lost soul cried for her day and night incessantly. I was lonely always and missed her as the blind man misses his eyesight. . . . Time and again I found myself in the train, once at least I got to Vienna and then went back. . . . I could not face the ruins of such perfect happiness, such divine bliss. . . .

"Don't think I blamed her! No, I quickly got over that. 'She may have kissed him,' I said to myself, 'for any one of a thousand reasons; the flesh is faithless in woman as in man; she may even have loved me best, nay, she must have loved me best, else why did she marry me and not him whom she had known all her life?' . . .

"But the heart does not reason, my friend; it aches and contracts in agony, or it triumphs and grows big and joyful. My heart bled and my life-blood drained away. Day and night I cried: 'Why? Why? Oh, my soul! Marie! why?' The pain choked me and I lived without living, without joy or hope or interest, till gradually, years later, away off there in China, I found myself taking a faint interest in music; but my heart was dead and my interest in life was no longer living, vivid, but mere curiosity. . . .

"They say that cells in the body can outlive the body's death for years; my music cells will outlive soul and body in me; but the little corpse-light of life is not strong enough to do any good; I'm finished. . . .

"Are you answered, my friend?"

"I understand," I said. "But, nevertheless," I persisted, "it's your duty to write a great piece of really new music, music that shall appeal to every human ear. Think, man, of the fame to be won; immortal reputation as the *Bahnbrecher,* the Road-maker to a new Kingdom of the Spirit. You owe a debt to Humanity; pay it first; your life's not your own."

"How often I've said the same thing to myself," he began slowly; "if you only knew how much I grew in those happy years. I had divined nearly everything I learned later in China; the music of the future is clear to me from the tom-tom of the savage to—— But I can't write, man; I can't; the love of my art is dead in me; she killed my very soul.

"All the music I've played here for you is old, old stuff; it has all been memory music, every note of it. You surely know that you must be alive, in-tensely alive, before you can create anything! It's the life in you that you impart. I'm dead: the heart is cold in me; the soul a corpse. I can do nothing worth the doing——"

"Don't say that," I protested. "Think how much nobler your work will be if you do it without joy and without hope; but do it; make a beginning at least that the world will never forget——"

He shook his head. "I can't. You will not understand. The bad alone survives in me. What good would it do to picture a madhouse or a wild beast's cage? Your Joachim was right; art is there to cheer, encourage, console, warn even if you will; but never to horrify and disgust and discourage. And I see nothing but beasts, lunatics, idiots; the posturing, gibbering apes are loathsome to me!"

"Thanks for the compliment," I exclaimed, laughing; "but you don't dislike Neumann or me, do you? Well, another concert or two and you'll find hundreds like us to love and admire you, and our love will inspire you to do the new work."

He shook his head. "What an optimist you are! You see you had the knocks first, the training first that hardened you; I had the triumphs first that left me soft and weak."

"At any rate give yourself time," I pleaded; "do nothing hastily; don't go off at half-cock, as we Americans say; another triumph or two will make a difference; you know the French proverb, 'L'appetit vient en mangeant'—the appetite grows with eating."

He smiled. "I owe you that; at least I won't do anything till I must"; and forced therewith to be content I went off to consult with Neumann, whom I brought back with me to dinner.

The second concert was a far greater triumph than the first; all the best music-lovers in Vienna were there and prepared now to welcome a great master. As he stood bowing on the platform at the end and the audience cheered and cheered and the women even came up in crowds to the stage, I made my way to the side door that led behind the stage. As I got there a young woman addressed me:

"Are you Herr ——?" Then, without waiting for an answer: "I am his wife, take me to him!"

"I would, so gladly," I exclaimed, "but is this the right moment?"

She looked at me with wide frightened hazel eyes. "What do you mean? I must see him. Explain. . . . My God, speak, man! will you take me to him?"

She was quivering with excitement; she caught my arm in her hands as if I were about to evade her; she was certainly very pretty; I tried to persuade her for his sake.

"I'll do whatever I can," I said impressively; "but now and here you won't get a chance of a quiet talk; he'll probably have left the place as he did last time before I can catch him; but he lives with me. I'll get you a good opportunity, madame, where you can use all your persuasiveness. I want you to succeed and save him, I promise you——"

"Oh, now, now," she interrupted; "please,

please, for God's sake. I've waited so long, all these weary years; please," and the tears poured down her cheeks.

"Come," I said, unable to resist, "we'll find him if we can," and hurriedly I took her through the passage to the waiting-room, but Hagedorn had "left two minutes before," as Neumann told me, looking intently at my companion.

"Go to my rooms at once, Neumann," I cried, "and if Hagedorn is there keep him till we come, or keep with him at least till you bring about a meeting. For the love of God, don't lose sight of him till we all meet. If you don't understand, please believe I have good reason, and don't tell Hagedorn I was with a lady; just say I must meet him, see!"

"I understand," replied Neumann. "I'm off; and if he's not in your rooms I'll wait there for you. What a success, eh?" And the next moment he was gone.

"Now," I said, "madame, we can go quietly to my place. Should we drive or walk? It's only ten minutes' drive."

"As you please," she replied quietly. So I took her outside and got into a fiacre with her and gave my address.

"Shall I explain to you?" she began as soon as we were alone. "I feel that you know the story, know it perhaps better than I do. Why did he leave me? Why didn't he answer my letters? It wasn't because of one kiss?"

"I fear it was," was my answer. "I'm not defending him or accusing you; but that's what he says. He must have always been an idealist."

"That's why I loved him," she cried; "but, good God! how unjust, how cruel of him! I can hardly explain how it happened; perhaps you won't understand. We women do so much out of pity, for pity's sake.

"I had told Goldescu that his cynical way of talking disgusted and pained me; it did him harm too; he was growing coarser, worse, and I was so happy. I wanted to help him; so I told him he must stop jeering or I'd have to cease seeing him.

"He didn't speak for a little while and I thought I had been hard on him.

"Then he began in a strange, passionate voice:

" 'You blame me for being cynical; it's too much. I'm cynical because I was a fool, lost my chance. Are you stone-blind? I might have won you, was near it years ago and waited thinking you would come to me, waited too long, and he won you in an hour. That *Musiker!* And now you blame me for being cynical—you! the cause of it! you!'

"I was thunderstruck, shaken.

" 'I'm sorry,' I muttered. 'We women are always sorry, you know, for giving love-pain!'

" 'Don't be sorry,' he cried, 'I couldn't stand that. I never meant to tell you; don't be sorry; I'm the only one should grieve, but say you forgive me.'

" 'Of course I forgive you,' I cried.

" 'I'll try to be better. We'll never talk of it again,' he said. 'One kiss of forgiveness,' and before I thought he lifted my face and kissed me— a long kiss.

"As soon as I felt how he was kissing me I pulled away and started up hot with rage.

" 'A poor comedy,' I cried, 'but even you can only play it once with me,' and I went to the door; it was open.

"Vaguely I wondered why; after Goldescu had gone I wondered, but then forgot all about it till I got that awful letter from the lawyer.

"I couldn't believe that; it all seemed too monstrous to me; it does now! Like a horrible nightmare turning sweet sleep to horror.

"A thousand times I cried: 'Why should he leave me? Goldescu kissed me without my will; I was as if hypnotised; the next moment I stopped him. I've never seen him since; wouldn't see him. I loved no one but my husband, no one, ever! Oh! Oh!" And again the tears drowned her face and voice.

I pitied her so that I could not help trying to console her:

"Don't fear, please; it will all come right, it must"—the usual inanities.

When we got upstairs Neumann met us.

"He's not been home yet, but he's sure to come before dinner. You'll not forget you're both dining with me; this lady too, if she'll come."

"We may be late," I said, "but we'll come if possible."

Neumann took the hint and left.

As soon as we were alone Madame Hagedorn began to fidget. "I feel misfortune in the air," she repeated. . . . "You know I feel sure if I can talk to him I can convince him that my love never changed. And then I'll love him so, he'll have to love me again. Don't you think so?"

Then she began again graming and grieving: "I've been so unhappy, and now so fearful. Are you sure he has not been here? Is this where he sleeps?" and she pointed to my sofa-bed.

"No, no," I replied; "he occupies the bedroom in there," and I motioned to the door.

"Let's go in and see if he's been in," she cried.

I went first and opened the door; the bed, the chairs, his clothes—all in the usual order. "You see," I said, turning to her, "he's not been here"; but even as I spoke she pointed to the head of the bed and there, pinned on the pillow, was a sheet of paper.

I took it and read:

"I knew she was in the hall; I felt her presence; I saw her speaking to you; I fled.

"It's no use, man. I will not renew the intolerable anguish; I dare not. I prefer to—— Good-bye. You did all that could be done. . . . I forgive, but there is only one way to forget.

"E. H."

AKBAR: "THE MIGHTIEST"

AKBAR: "THE MIGHTIEST"

IN the heart of Asia, in the great Temple of
Samarkand, are three tombs: one to Timour,
the first of the Mughal Conquerors who over-
ran Asia; one to Akbar, his descendant, who as a
youth won India and established an empire; and
one to Akbar's master and counsellor, Abulfazl.
Akbar's tomb, erected by himself, is quite a small
and insignificant one, and there the Conqueror rests
quietly enough these three hundred years and more
now at the feet of his teacher. The simple gran-
deur of the great sarcophagi, the humility of the
invincible emperor quickened my curiosity, first
awakened by the name given to him of "Akbar,"
which means the "Mightiest" or "Highest," and is
generally used as an attribute of God. Was he
really a great man? Who gave him the astounding
title? How came it to stick to him? Why was
he the only conqueror in recorded time whose empire endured for centuries after his death?

Samarkand, too, interested me. It is one of
the oldest cities in the world: even the stones of
the strong houses are eaten into by the centuries
and coloured with the patine of time, and its chief
citizens are tanners now and goldsmiths as they
were two thousand years before Christ, when it was

called Marcanda. But again and again I left the
bazaars and dark shops, with their silk praying-
rugs that take a generation to weave, and barbaric
jewels—sky-blue turquoises as large as filberts,
carved amethysts as big as hens' eggs, and sapphires sold by the ounce—to return to the Temple.

One day, in an Armenian's den in the bazaar, I
found a Crusader's sword, and a suit of chain
armour that must have belonged to one of the
knights who followed St Louis to the Holy Land.
The owner of the shop talked the Levantine jargon,
which is based on modern Greek, and so I could
make myself fairly understood. In his cautious
way he took a polite interest in me, as a customer,
and when I explained to him that I was interested in
the cathedral, and especially in Akbar and his life,
he told me he would send a compatriot of his to
the caravanserai, a learned Sunni, who would give
me all the information on the subject I could desire.

The next day I found a Sufi waiting for me,
who looked the priestly part, whatever his practice
may have been. He was of middle height, yet
impressive by reason of impassivity. The slow
quiet ways of the immemorial East seemed to have
moulded his gentle, deferential manners. I have
never seen so expressive a face that changed so
little. It was of the purest Persian type: a narrow oval, the features almost perfectly regular,
though the nose was slightly long and beaked, the
eyes long, too, and dark brown, almost the black-
brown of strong coffee; he might have been any-

where between thirty and forty-five. He introduced himself as having been sent to me by the merchant, and placed himself at my disposal. I told him that what I wanted to know was the story of Akbar—how he came to power, why he built himself a small tomb at the feet of his teacher. Was there any reason for his humility, any spiritual significance in it? Had he no woman in his life, but only a man-friend?—a host of questions.

The Sufi bowed and told me he would do his best to answer me: would I care to hear the popular story? I responded eagerly that was just what I most wanted. Then he was afraid his knowledge of Greek might be insufficient: would I mind if now and then he availed himself of a dictionary? And he pulled a little shabby, dog-eared booklet out of his pocket, which was issued in Leipzig, and contained words in Persian, Hindu and modern Greek.

I assured him I was chiefly curious about Akbar himself. Did the great fighter really become a sort of religious teacher and put forth a new religion? He assured me he would tell me everything as it had been told to him when a boy. I thanked him; that was what I desired.

"Everyone knows," he began, "that Akbar's real name was Jelàl-ed-Din Muhammad. He was born at Amarkot in 1542, when his father was fleeing to Persia from Delhi. In 1555, when the boy was thirteen years of age, his father died. Jelàl gave the control of his kingdom to Bairam Khan as regent, and occupied himself with games and physical exercises. Bairam Khan set to work to subdue the provinces that had revolted from Jelàl's father. He carried out his work with such relentless cruelty that his name became a byword from the banks of the Ganges to the Caspian. He brought peace, it was said, the white peace of death!

"Till he was about eighteen Jelàl gave himself to sports and poetry like other youths, and thought little about governing. He was the most enthusiastic polo player of his day, and one story told about him depicts his strength of body and impetuous intensity of character better than pages of description. He was surprised once by nightfall in the middle of a close game; he resolved to go on till he had gained the victory. Accordingly he had balls made of palás wood that burns a long time, and with these fiery balls he continued the game till his side had won.

"I always see Akbar, in my mind, galloping furiously in the dark after a ball of fire; that seems to me symbolic of the intense spirit of the young conqueror. When he was sixteen or seventeen he began to listen to criticisms of Bairam Khan. He even made some pertinent suggestions; and the Minister-General, jealous of his power, looked out a lovely girl for him and persuaded him to take her to wife. With the cunning of the East Bairam Khan knew that the best way to lead princes was with such silken strings.

"A year or two later the king had his first real shock: one evening he was poisoned and came near death—only recovered, indeed, because he took violent emetics on his own initiative before the doctor had time to come to his assistance. Who were the culprits? The king knew intuitively. There must be a conspiracy between two, he said: between the chief cook, who alone prepared his food, and his wife, who had cajoled him into eating it without waiting to have it tasted. He had the chief cook before him, and in five minutes wrung the truth out of him and found that his suspicions were correct. His dismissal of the wretch was equivalent to a sentence of death. The culprit was strangled before he left the ante-chamber. While that was going on Jelàl strove to compose his spirit by writing a sonnet, but he could hardly please himself even with the first verse.

"He could not shirk the question: What was to be done with the girl? At length Jelàl called her before him and asked her simply why she had conspired with the cook. What had he done to make her hate him?

"The girl shrugged her shoulders disdainfully and kept silent.

"'Do you love cooks better than kings?' asked the monarch at last; and the girl burst forth:

"'We women love those who love us and care for us. When did you ever care for anyone but yourself? You think more of winning a chaugan game than of winning love. A woman to you is

a plaything. How can you expect love when you
never give it?'

"The king was shaken with surprise and doubt.
After all, the girl was right enough and what she
said was true. He had always treated her as an
instrument of pleasure. Why should he expect
gratitude and affection from her?

"What was he to do with her? . . . this woman
he had loved and trusted?

"He was utterly at a loss till a thought struck
him. In spite of his diabolic cruelty, or because
of it, Bairam Khan had been successful in life. He
had conquered provinces and subdued cities; he
should know how to deal with a faithless woman.
So Bairam Khan was summoned to the presence
and asked by the king for his advise. The old
warrior pronounced himself decisively.

" 'A great ruler should be beloved by his friends,'
he said, 'and feared by all the rest of the world.
The Emperor Jelàl is already beloved by all who
know him. He must make himself feared so that
whoever in the future dares to think of revolt shall
have the cold of death in his nostrils. The girl
should be hung up in public and sliced to death with
a sharp tulwar. That is the most lingering and
most painful death that can be inflicted on a woman
It might be so managed,' he concluded, 'by beginning with the hands and going on to the feet, that
the agony would be prolonged for more than an
hour. The emperor himself should preside at the
ceremony.'

"The young monarch heard him attentively to the end and then:

" 'What would the pain of the woman profit me?' he asked sharply.

"Bairam Khan answered: 'The punishment of the wrongdoer is the protection of the powerful.'

"The young king stared at him. 'The powerful need no protection,' he said; and, after a pause, added in a loud, severe voice:

" 'You have taught me, Bairam Khan, that what men say about you and your cruelty is true. Hitherto I have lived for my pleasures and left the care of my kingdom to you. Now I'll take the rule into my own hands and allow you to make the Holy Pilgrimage.' (This was practically an order to Bairam Khan to make that pilgrimage to Mecca which ensures salvation.) And the young king, with that generosity which was always a marked trait in his character, added:

" 'A suitable jaghir out of the parganas of Hindustan shall be assigned for your maintenance and transmitted to you regularly.'

"Thus dismissed, Bairam Khan stood stock still for a moment and then salaamed till his forehead rested on the floor before he rose and backed out of the hall.

"Jelàl then called the defiant girl before him again. 'You can keep the jewels,' he said, 'and all the other gifts my love bestowed upon you.' The girl glanced aside indifferently, as if she had not heard. 'I cannot punish where I have loved,' the king went on slowly, 'nor give you pain who have given me pleasure.'

"The girl looked at him still in suspicion, unconvinced.

" 'What are your gifts to me?' she snapped. 'I shall be killed before I leave the palace.'

"And the king answered: 'You shall go in peace, still keeping the name and honour of the king's chosen.'

"On hearing this the girl cried aloud: 'The king is indeed the king.' And, falling on her knees, bowed herself before him.

"And the king continued: 'One of these days I shall come to Agra and there build you a house, and you shall live in it and speak to me freely.'

"And the woman looked long at him, as if seeking to divine his meaning, and then turned and left the Court without a word and went to live in Agra. From her the king has learned many things only known to women. . . .

"When the rule was taken away from Bairam Khan he rebelled, but was quickly broken in battle by the king, and then as quickly forgiven and sent on his way to Mecca. On the point of embarking he was stabbed in the back by one he had wronged, and died with all his sins unpardoned. Jelàl continued the promised jaghir to his children. . . .

"Ten years later the young king had overrun all India north of the Deccan and subdued it, spreading his fame the while from Delhi to the Dardanelles—indeed from end to end of the civilised world as the civilised world then was.   Men began to wonder at him, and his constant successes awed them; some even passed from praise to adoration, calling him 'Akbar.'   But he would not use the name: didn't deserve it, he said; his victories had all been easy. . . .

"It was after he had subdued Kashmir that the first severe trial of his life took place.   The king of distant Khandesh had sent an embassy to him, congratulating him on his conquests, and, according to custom, the emperor sent him back a firman, thanking him and saying that he would take one of his daughters to wife as a pledge of enduring amity.

"The king replied that he felt himself greatly honoured by the proposal, and with the letter dispatched his youngest daughter with a great retinue and many gifts.   She turned out to be a beautiful girl, as those Northern women sometimes are, but very proud.   The emperor, being only thirty-two at the time, fell to desire of her at the first meeting. Strange to say, she held aloof from him; would not go into the harem even as a queen, and was not to be won by prayers or promises.

"When the king in a moment of passion threatened to take her by force she plainly told him he could take her body perhaps, but her spirit and her heart were her own, and he would never gain them by violence.

"The king then tried to win her by gifts and kindness, by rich jewels and great shows staged in her honour—shows in which hundreds of wild beasts

fought for days, such shows as had never been seen
before in the world. The girl was flattered and
pleased in spite of herself. One combat in especial
interested her. When she saw a pair of wild stal-
lions fighting with superb pride and fierceness she
cried out with delight and admiration, for the wild
desert horses fought standing up on their hind legs,
striking with their front feet and ever seeking with
open mouth to seize the adversary by the crest and
hurl him to the earth. This conflict pleased the
girl much more than the deadlier, bloodier strug-
glings of tigers and bulls which the emperor staged
for her amusement.

"But when it came to love-making she withdrew
into herself and again and again denied the monarch, now passionately, now sullenly.

"One day the king threatened to send her back
home, and she retorted that nothing would please
her better; and when he questioned her further he
confessed boldly that one of the young nobles about
her father's Court had attracted her. It appeared
that the courtship had not gone beyond glances, the
girl admitting ruefully that her father would never
allow her to marry a mere subject, as he believed
himself to be directly descended from God. This
new and unexpected difficulty enraged the emperor.
He was at a loss, too, irritated by his own indecision
and fear of taking a wrong step.

"Fortunately good counsel was at hand. An
Arab, named Mubárak, whose ancestors had settled
in Rajputana, was renowned for wisdom, and as his

two sons grew to manhood they became famous as having inherited their father's genius. Shaik Faizi, the elder, was known everywhere as a doctor and poet. He had composed many books and won popularity by always attending the poor for nothing. His younger brother, Abulfazl, was an even greater man. When only fifteen years old his learning was the wonder of the district, and by twenty he had begun to teach in the mosques. The Persian proverb says that no tree grows very high which comes to maturity quickly. But Abulfazl was an exception to this rule. Jelàl induced him to abandon his intention of giving himself up wholly to a life of meditation at twenty-three, and took him into his own suite. Though eleven years older than Abulfazl, the king grew to respect him more and more, and their intimacy developed into a mutual understanding and affection. At his wits' end to know how to win his proud wife Jelàl turned to Abulfazl.

" 'In love and war,' he said, 'no one should ask for counsel. But in this absurd difficulty I'd like to know whether anyone can find a way where I see no sure outlet.'

"After some time for thought Abulfazl told him there were many ways and they all reached the goal —with time.

" 'I'm faint with desire,' cried the king; 'wild with impatience.'

" 'Is she wonderful in beauty, or in mind, or in character?' asked Abulfazl.

" 'In all!' exclaimed the king. 'She's without a peer in the world.'

"Abulfazl smiled. 'The madness of love speaks through you. Such desire is mere ignorance. Enjoy her once and the glamour will be gone.'

" 'But the joy will be mine,' cried the king, 'and the memory. The illusion of love and desire are the chiefest pleasures in life. Bare us of them and what would life be worth?'

" 'More than you would believe now,' said Abulfazl. 'But what is her real power over you?'

The king thought in silence. 'Her courage,' he replied, 'and, to tell you the truth, her disdain of me and, of course, her loveliness.'

" 'It is a great opportunity,' said Abulfazl, 'to win the great fight with one blow. The only course worthy of my lord is that he should conquer himself and subdue his passion.'

" 'Impossible!' cried the king. 'She is in my blood, in my brain, in my heart. If I don't win her I shall have lost the world.'

" 'So it seems to you now,' rejoined Abulfazl, smiling, 'and were you anyone else I would advise you to go into Persia, far away from her, and there give yourself up to other beauties and lose all memory even of this one woman; but my lord should take the high way. If you can conquer such a passion you can do anything. It is not the food that gives the pleasure, but the appetite. Restraint will increase your desire and any new girl will seem wonderful to you.'

" 'Do you know what you are advising?' asked the king, turning on him with hard eyes.

"Abulfazl nodded his head.

"With one movement Jelàl was on his feet.

" 'So be it,' he said quietly, after a pause. 'If you have made a mistake you shall be impaled. If by following your advice I lose my joy of life and my delight in living I shall see you die with pleasure; but if you are right, and by conquering myself I win content, you shall be master in my kingdom and I shall be second to you.'

" 'You would not be my master,' replied Abulfazl quietly, 'if you could thus punish your best friend.'

" 'I am my own best friend,' retorted the king gloomily; but love is surely a madness and there may be some wisdom in your consel.'

"For a month the king went in and out and paid no attention to the girl or to Abulfazl. He then started off suddenly to Agra, and when he returned he sent for Abulfazl again:

" 'You were right in one thing,' he said, 'and wrong in another; fasting does sharpen appetite amazingly, but you were wrong when you said any dish would give pleasure. I want nothing but this one girl: no other can tempt me, and I am mad with longing for her.'

" 'I have thought, too, while my lord was absent,' said Abulfazl, 'it may be that the princess is indeed the king's complement and meant for him. In that case seek her out, get to know her soul and body, and give her time and occasion to know you. As

you are greater than she is she will be drawn to
you—that's the law; the greater draws the less; besides, she is already curious about you. She will
love you. In this way you may both win love and
make love your servant.'

"The king broke in:

" 'The woman at Agra told me to hide my desire
and make the girl fear she had lost me. Women,
she said, all want what they can't have or what is
above them.'

" 'All men too,' said Abulfazl, meeting the king's
eyes and smiling as he spoke, for he saw that the
master was again at one with him; 'the woman's
counsel is wise.'

"Jelàl then began what he always afterwards
called his 'discipline.' It was a long struggle and
only one or two incidents in it were decisive. Each
day the princess was told to attend the king while
he listened to complaints in the morning and gave
judgments in the Great Hall. Now and again in
difficult cases he would ask her advice, but he seldom took it, and soon the girl had to admit to herself that the monarch knew life and men better than
she did. But just when she was getting impatient
under cumulative evidence of her inferiority, the
king with fine wit took care to praise her for some
mental quality or grace of spirit she did not possess,
and this appreciation pleased her greatly.

"In spite of his passion Jelàl pretended to take
only a mild interest in her and showed himself always engrossed in affairs of State. Still the girl

would sometimes smile to herself, as if she saw through his acting. But when she let her eyes rest on him or encouraged him by smile or word, and he would turn away to talk to some Minister, she would grow thoughtful, and the women of the harem said her temper was not so even as it used to be.

"As soon as the woman at Agra learned that the king had aroused the girl's interest and made her doubt her empire over him, she advised him to send for her lover and offer to marry them, and the king consented, for the counsel pleased him. He himself had noticed from time to time an uncertain humility in the girl's manner and in her eyes a sort of appeal. Others noticed that she had begun to drape her tall figure after the fashion of the women in the harem, and now swathed herself so closely that her shape could be seen through the soft stuffs just as if she had been coming from the bath.

"It was in this mood that the lover of her girlhood appeared to her. Half unconsciously she had idealized him and exaggerated his charm to herself, and now she saw that the attraction he had had for her had completely disappeared, and to her consternation she realized that he was much more concerned to win the emperor's favour than her love. He seemed to her paltry and immature; yet she could not bear to admit her mistake to the great king. What was to be done? She resolved to carry it through.

"In full Court the king came to her, leading the

Khandesh noble: 'Here, lady,' he said, 'is one who loves you, and your father consents to your marriage.'

" 'Only if Akbar wishes it,' added the unfortunate youth, bowing low.

"As the girl flushed with anger at her suitor's obsequiousness, the king turned away and shortly afterwards left the palace.

"Next day the girl heard that he had gone again to Agra and the women of the harem assured her that he had gone back to his first wife, for men visited a woman for only one thing. It was noticed that the girl seldom spoke of her betrothed, and when the king returned she prayed him to see her.

"Schooled by Abulfazl the king replied that he would surely see her as soon as he had concluded some urgent business, and he kept her waiting nearly a week. By this time the girl had grown sick with fear lest she had lost the monarch's love. When she was admitted to his presence she could only cry:

" 'My lord, my lord.'

" 'What can I do to pleasure you?' asked the king. 'Will you be married to your compatriot at once?'

"The girl saw that his eyes were laughing and took it that he despised her.

" 'As the king does not want me,' she retorted proudly, 'I wish to be sent back to my father."

" 'But you said you didn't want the king,' persisted the monarch, and you loved this young man. Why have you changed?'

" 'I was young,' she said, gulping down the lump in her throat, 'and knew no better.'

" 'And now?' asked the king.

" 'There is only one man in the world for me,' she said, 'and that is the king,' and she lifted her eyes to his and gave herself in the look.

"Though his heart thrilled with joy, the king kept his control: 'Go to the harem,' he said, 'and wait for me.' And she turned, glowing, and went like a child.

"In the harem the king found her another woman. After he had convinced her of his love she broke into praises of his looks and strength, and when he said that there were many handsomer and stronger men she wouldn't listen, but covered his mouth with her hand and declared that there was no one in the world like him, and that he was the most splendid man in the Court, though he was only a little taller than the average.

"Because she was very fair, with skin like ivory and eyes as blue as sapphires, she praised his black eyes and hair and his loud, deep voice, and even the small wart on the left side of his nose; he was her god, the 'Most High—Akbar,' she exclaimed, and she would never call him by any other name.

"But when he told her he would have to earn it first, and thus recalled to his ambitions made ready to leave her, he found another woman still.

" 'You shall not go!' she cried boldly; 'the cook's mistress at Agra calls, you shall not go!'

"And when he said that he went to Agra for

counsel and not for love, for the woman was cunning and had taught him much, she wouldn't have it.

" 'You shall not see her,' she panted, 'not yet—not till you know me better—promise, not till I give you leave!'

"She was so passionate in her pleading that the king promised and caressed her, and then she burst into tears and said he might go if he liked, but it would break her heart and she was very unhappy and—— Her tears set off her beauty better than her pleading or her pride, and her quick changes of mood charmed the king, who could not help showing his astonishment. He had thought her proud and reserved at first, he said, and at that she smiled deeply, saying love was a magician and fashioned a woman to her lord's desire.

" 'But you did not love me at first,' he said; 'it was only by feigning indifference and holding off that I won you.'

"At that she looked up at him from the divan, smiling. 'It was the wise Abulfazl, was it not, who gave Akbar that counsel?'   And she said this though she knew in her heart the counsel came from the woman at Agra, but she would not keep her memory alive by making mention of her.

"The king was astonished by her intuition.

" 'How did you guess,' he asked, 'that I went to him for counsel?'

"She pouted and said carelessly: 'If I had not loved Akbar from the beginning, no holding off would have won me.'

" 'But if you loved me why did you plague me so at first by pretending coldness and aversion?'

" 'Because I loved,' she said. 'I saw that all things came to Akbar too easily and so I held away, though when he took me in his strong arms and kissed me in spite of my resistance I almost yielded.'

" 'Akbar blamed himself afterwards for forcing you,' said the monarch.

"Again, unexpectedly, she laughed aloud:

" 'You child!' she cried, 'you child! You would never have tasted my lips had I not let you; the resistance, like the coldness, was all feigned. There! I've given my secret away. We women are all traitors to ourselves.'

"In wonder the king exclaimed:

" 'I believe you know more about women than even the woman I have called "wise" at Agra!'

"The smile left her face and a change came over her: 'All women know women,' she said, 'but she is a vile creature, fit only for the bazaar.'

" 'Why do you say that?' asked the king, and the girl responded: 'If anyone killed my lover I would never forgive him, never. When he put his hands on me I should feel the blood sticking on them; hate would be in my heart for him, and I'd curse him by day and by night.'

" 'He was only a cook,' said Akbar.

"But the girl wouldn't have it.

" 'If I had stooped to my lover, still more would I have felt his loss: it is our sacrifices for you that endear you to us!'

"Suddenly the king turned on her, for he was curious:

" 'Why did you resolve all at once to yield to me?'

She answered quietly:

" 'When Akbar brought that man here and offered me to him before the Court, my heart was as water lest I had lost my lord's love: I had enough of the struggle or'—and she took his head in her hands and kissed his mouth—'I wanted you——'

And she sighed in content.

"That first communion with his love showed the king that the instinct of his desire had been right and that he had an extraordinary mistress—as changeful as the sky in the monsoon and charming with all the gaiety and liveliness of girlhood; but he was soon to find that she was more.

"Almost from the first day she made up to Abulfazl, and not only won his admiration and affection but found out from him quickly sides of the king's character which she might otherwise have been years in discovering. From this counsellor she learned that the deepest motive in the king was his ambition, and not ambition merely to conquer, or even to consolidate his empire, but to grow himself, to become wiser and better than any man on earth. Her lover was indeed a king of kings.

"She even found out from Abulfazl without his knowing it the true explanation of the kindness shown to the woman at Agra.

" 'The king doesn't keep her now for counsel,' he

said, 'but to remind him of what he first learned by
forgiving. He wishes now that he had forgiven the
cook. I believe,' he added, 'that if the cook had
lived the king would long ago have sent him to his
love at Agra.'

"At that the girl gasped; for such magnanimity
was beyond her. But she had learned the chief lesson, that Akbar, like all great and generous natures,
was to be moved by an appeal to the highest much
more easily than by tempting the animal in him or
by urging his own self-interest. And with this key
in her hands and her woman's intuition that everything is to be done with a man by praise, she became
a real companion to her lord and an inspiring help-
mate. She pleaded for the gentler virtues, and
Akbar, having already begun to realize that a great
man should have a good deal of the woman in him,
was ready to listen to whatever was wise in what she
said and to profit by the new insight."

And here the Sufi stopped, as if he had come to
the end of the story; but I was too interested in
Akbar to let him off so easily.

"You have told me half the tale," I began, "and
have told it fairly well for a learned man; but you
have left the more important part unexplained. I
understand now why 'Akbar' honoured Abulfazl
and why men honoured Akbar; but I don't see
yet why Abulfazl wrote Akbar's deeds and words
and showed such unfeigned admiration of his
master."

"Jelàl was not called 'Akbar' for nothing,"

replied the Sufi: "he was the first Conqueror whose
empire survived him, and it survived because it was
built on sympathy and not on suspicion, on love and
freedom and not on fear and hate."

"What do you mean exactly?" I asked.

"Previous conquerors," said the Sufi, "held down
each province they subdued by a standing army.
Akbar not only allowed each province to govern itself, but gave the peoples greater freedom than they
had had before, while insisting on complete religious
toleration. Personal ambition even found scope and
security under his rule. That was why his empire
lasted till the white traders conquered Hindustan
two hundred years later."

And again the Sufi paused.

"You have yet to tell me," I persisted, "when and
why he took the name of 'Akbar': was it pride
or——?"

"The best Mussulmans," said the Sufi, "blame
him for taking the divine attribute—'The Highest,'
but if ever a man deserved it, he did. His mind
was never at rest. When there were no more foes
to conquer he invited to his Court Lamas from Tibet
and Padres from Goa, and was the first to declare
that Jesus was not only a great prophet, as Mohammed had said, but greater than Mohammed
himself, the greatest of all. Jesus and Mohammed, he used often to say, were like stars in the
heaven, and greater and brighter luminaries would
yet come to throw radiance on the ways of men.
He even went so far," and the Sufi whispered the

words as if in dread of some eavesdropper, "as to assert that every man might be Mohammed and Jesus besides being himself, for he too had come from God as they had come."

"Interesting," I said; "and so Akbar lived as a god, 'happy ever after.' "

"No, no," cried the Sufi with Eastern wisdom; "happinesss is not for wise or great men: Akbar was tried beyond the ordinary. His two favourite sons drank themselves to death, and the son who ultimately succeeded him in the empire revolted against him and got his friend Abulfazl murdered. That grief and disappointment changed all life for Akbar. What good was vengeance and what profit was there in anger when he knew by a sort of instinct that wild envy and jealousy had induced his son to kill a better man than himself.

"Akbar saw he might as well forgive his son, for nothing he could do would bring Abulfazl back to life or put light again in those kindly hazel eyes which were always warm with love for him.

"The murder of Abulfazl, who was too gentle to have any enemies, brought the nothingness of life very close to Akbar. From the afternoon when the sad news reached him he resolved to live as if every day were to be his last; that marked his conversion to the ideal life. . . .

"In maturity he had been gross of body, as strong men often are who carry the appetites of youth into middle age; but after this Akbar became an ascetic and lived altogether on rice and fruit."

"Did he ever take the title of Akbar himself?" I interjected.

"It was given to him very early," explained the Sufi, "by many when he was only thirty; but he never took it himself till after Abulfazl's death. We can see how he came to it," the Sufi added, as if in apology, "for he was always frank and sincere as a child. His studies of various prophets had taught him that they were all alike in some qualities, and recognising in himself in later life the same characteristics of gentleness and lovingkindness, he came to believe that he, too, was divine and sent by God as His vice-gerent on earth, or khalifa."

"Very interesting," I could not help interjecting. "Did he then speak of himself as the khalifa?"

"He did," replied the Sufi solemnly, "and in this conviction he put forth a new creed, Din-i-Ilahi—'The Divine Faith'—which contained the best in a dozen religions, and so long as he lived it was adopted and practised throughout the empire."

"You amaze me," I cried; "what was this new religion?"

"Akbar," replied the Sufi slowly, "took the ceremonies of it from the Parsees and the spirit from Jesus, and he built the Ibadat-Khana or palace-temple at Fatepur-Sikri for men of learning and genius; and there he gathered about him prophets from Persia and painters from Francia, and allotted pensions to writers and saints and men of talent of all kinds, and his fame spread abroad throughout the world. All over his empire he built roads and founded schools, for there was peace in his time, though men said he had 'forgotten how to punish.' . . ."

"But was his religion followed?" I asked. "Had he any real converts?"

"Myriads of disciples and hakim," replied the Sufi, "for in love of his wife he took Mohammed's heaven into his gospel and said that perfect happiness was only to be found in the love of women. . . ."

"What was his end?" I asked.

"Alas! alas!" exclaimed the Sufi, "it came all too soon. He worked too vehemently, always galloping in the dark after that flaming ball, so that he died worn out when he was only a little over sixty; but he had the consciousness of having lived a great life and left a noble example. Some of us still believe," added the Sufi, as if speaking to himself, "that he was indeed a son of God, the true Khalifa, and the faith he set forth was worthy of the name he gave it—'The Divine.'

"Toward the end of his life, though he always passed much of his time in the harem, it was for counsel chiefly, and there it was said that he was happy, for he would have no other companion but his wife, the king's daughter, though she was childless, and she was at his side when the darkness took him."

A FIT OF MADNESS

A FIT OF MADNESS

EVEN specialists in mental aberration had rarely met a case like that of Rambeau.

Henri Rambeau was a very strong fellow, nearing forty years of age. He loved to laugh and eat and drink, was possessed of a considerable fortune, and appeared to be gifted with an extraordinarily healthy and strong body and mind. He never used his mind much and certainly exhausted neither it nor his body.

Each morning he spent an hour and a half on horseback riding in the Bois; he devoted the afternoon now to visits, now to golf; in the evening he either went out with his wife to some social party or to the theatre. Latterly he had become accustomed, when his wife did not want him, to spend an evening watching the gambling at the club while smoking a cigar. He disliked all excessive emotions, and the few affairs of the heart that he was supposed to have had were not very absorbing. In fine, he led a most useless but healthy and pleasurable existence.

He never read or studied anything exciting; he had no ambition except to appear just what he was —a gentleman rather well off, well-fed, well-bred, well-dressed, up to date in every respect.

Curiously enough he went in for athletics more than an ordinary Frenchman. He was a little stronger than the average and looked like an American; always shaved completely, and had a well-balanced face lit up by ordinary blue eyes. He always tubbed in the morning and went in for half-an-hour's Swedish gymnastics. He had been an idle, playful little boy; a young man of all the virtues; a husband of perfect respectability—the last person in the world to go wrong in any way! . . .

Madame Rambeau could never get over the surprise she felt one morning when she came into her husband's room and found him in his pyjamas kneeling on the bed, holding in one hand a small English flag and in the other one of those little playthings in the shape of a wheel which make a creaking noise. As soon as he saw his wife he cried out: "Go away! Go away!" and hid himself under the clothes.

"What is the matter with you?" cried Madame Rambeau; "it is midday and you are not up yet, Henri—that is why I came in." He looked at his wife in absolute fear, and to her amazement replied: "What does this lady want of me?"

"Do, do be sensible," said the wife. "It is me! me, Germaine!" But after trying in vain for a quarter of an hour to make him realise his position, his wife had to say that Henri Rambeau had been struck by a fit of madness.

Curiously enough, he talked sensibly in a wrong-headed way. "I am not well!" he said. "My head's clear and I would willingly drink my coffee, but I cannot remember where I am or who I am, or who this lady is who speaks to me so familiarly. It's quite funny. I'm thirty-eight years of age, yet everything appears to me to be new; this apartment, this furniture, this pretty woman who pretends to be my wife and the servant who tells me he has served me since I was a child.

"It seems to me as if I have had a sleep for years or had died and come to life again: a strange life! . . . Please do not cry, madame; I am willing to admit that I married you. You are really charming, neither too fat nor too thin and very dark, and I have always liked dark women. You call yourself Germaine—I like the name too, but I cannot call you 'Germaine' like that, straight off; I ought to say 'madame' or 'mademoiselle.' Do I frighten you? I am sorry! You tell me that my name is 'Henri Rambeau,' no title, no distinction. . . . I do not mind this place here: it seems comfortable and I am perfectly at my ease.

"That old servant came in; he says he saw me born; smiles because he thinks I am drunk. I am not drunk. Perhaps I have had a little accident of memory. You will please go into the next room to let me get up; I cannot dress before you!"

After he had dressed and had come into the sitting-room he consented to see the doctor. The doctor took numberless notes and recommended Madame Rambeau to keep him as quiet as possible and humour him in everything.

At one o'clock they had *déjeuner* together; he became very affectionate to his wife in the course of the *déjeuner*. He said to her: "You please me infinitely, you know, my dear lady. I discover all sorts of beauty in you I had not dreamt of. Your voice awakens all kinds of feelings in me. I believe we are going to be very happy. Will you allow me to kiss your hand?"

In fine, he made love to his wife as he had done fourteen years before, and he was so charming, told her so many flattering things, that she began to blush as she had blushed in the days of their first meetings.

"I am so afraid," he said, "of annoying you with my affection."

"Do not be afraid," replied Germaine, speaking with an eagerness she could hardly explain, "I, too, have a feeling as if you were partly unknown to me, but I do hope you will go on liking me. What are we to do this evening, because you know the Delaroches have invited us to dinner?"

"The Delaroches," he repeated.

"Your cousins, you know," said his wife.

"Oh, do not let's go. Let's stay here, and when the twilight comes I will read you some verses. . . . I never noticed before what a pretty foot you have. Please let us be together and keep the foolish world out; you know how I love you!"

It was evident that he only thought of his wife and had fallen as intensely in love with her as he had done fourteen years before. His desire, his admiration, his flatteries troubled her, moved her and finally won her as they had won her before.

He followed her with all sorts of little attentions, with a passion that seemed to know no respite and yet was always respectful. The poor woman did not know what to make of it, but the doctor had told her to humour him in every way, and really she found it easy to humour him! Without sharing his madness she became the young wife she had been fourteen years before. Henri's devotion was so complete that it really won her heart as she had never been won.

After the first twenty-four hours he would not let her out of his sight; she had to insist in the morning and lock herself in her own room in order to get up and dress in peace. At midday she knocked again at her husband's door. As soon as he saw her he cried: "Oh, here is the delightful lady! Who I am I do not know; I am not even curious, except that I am perfectly well and very happy, and will take my coffee if that old fool of a servant will bring it to me; then, mademoiselle, I am going to make love to you as soon as I get up; I will not allow you to leave me again."

After a week Madame Rambeau declared that she was the happiest woman in France; she had no idea, she said, that a man could be so charming and so wonderful. And when the doctor returned, bringing other doctors with him, and had a long consultation, she was frightened almost to death. They proposed that Rambeau should be sent to an asylum, but she would not hear of it. To lose her husband and lover together was too much. No! no!

She was determined to take care of him herself, and not trust him to any other hands.

The family doctor shrugged his shoulders; he could not explain such conjugal devotion, but he could see that Germaine was absolutely content and happy; it shone from her face and manner—she was delighted.

As for Henri, he seemed to begin his life again every twenty-four hours. He had no curiosity, he did not seem to want to go out, he absolutely refused to meet anyone who called on him; he wanted nothing but Germaine, and from morning to night and from night to morning they lived for each other.

This happiness continued nearly five weeks and then one morning Madame Rambeau, who had dressed herself with great care, came and knocked lightly at the door of her husband's room and went in as usual; but now he looked at her coolly, carelessly: "Oh! it's you!" he said. "What have you come to disturb me about?" . . .

Germaine could not help it, the shock was too dreadful; she burst into sobs, crying: "My God! My God! It's terrible to think you're cured—so soon!"

A CHINESE STORY

LA CHINESE STORI

A CHINESE STORY

IT was my second visit to Shanghai after a long interval. I had only a vague idea of the old walled city, though the European settlement seemed fairly familiar. But now the old Chinese city drew me in spite of its gloomy, stinking streets and swarming verminous life. What lay on the other side? What was the soul of China, and that Chinese civilisation which speculated in transcendental philosophies and practised impressionist painting when Rome was still mistress of the world? Could I get any glimpse of the tantalising mystery in spite of the veil of language?

An English student-interpreter put me on the way: "There's a Pole here named Shimonski," he said, "who is called in in every difficulty; they say he knows more about China than the Chinks themselves: he'd be an ideal guide. I'll send him to you to-morrow morning, if you'll be in."

I agreed gladly; but no Shimonski appeared next morning or the morning after, and the appointment was gradually blotted out of my memory by the rush of new and strange experiences.

One morning I had been accosted in front of the hotel by an old Chinaman, who talked to me with many genuflections in a tone and manner of profound humility. While I was trying to understand his expressive face and mimicry he suddenly flourished a large knife, evidently not with any evil purpose, for as soon as I turned away, the knife disappeared. I went about the hotel trying to get the matter explained to me, and about eleven o'clock returned to my room.

To my astonishment a man was seated in my particular arm-chair at the table, smoking my cigarettes. He did not get up as I entered, so I said to him: "Have you not made some mistake?"

"I think not," he replied, in a quiet voice and excellent English. "I was told you wanted to see me."

"And your name?" I asked.

"My name is Shimonski," he replied, negligently knocking off the ash from his cigarette, and looking up at me.

"Oh!" I cried, "you are the guide whom Lawrence spoke of?"

He nodded merely. Rather interested by his casual way of taking the matter, I drew up a chair and sat down beside him.

Shimonski was tall, almost six feet in height, and spare of figure. He seemed about forty, but might have been five years more or less, for his whiskers and moustache and hair were all of that straw colour in which grey hairs scarcely show. His features were very irregular, almost like a Tartar's—the forehead low, the straw-thatch growing down into it and making two bays, so to say; the eyes small

and grey; the nose, the prominent feature, long and
thin, pinched, indeed, on top, with very broad nostrils that vibrated with every emotion, and in anger
grew quite white. The dominant erpression of the
face was sharp temper, inclined to suspicion. I was
not pleasurably impressed.

"They tell me," I began, "that you know more
about China than any foreigner."

"That would *not* be high praise," he answered
quietly. "Here, as in India, the natives speak of
the whites as savages, and with good reason."

"I wonder," I went on, "whether I could learn
anything about China without knowing the language.
All that I hear is so strange to me. I am told that
all of the great mandarins and governors are appointed according to their literary achievements. I
wonder how that works."

"Do you think it would be preferable," he asked
sneeringly, "to have them appointed by money, as in
America, or by snobbery, as in England?"

"You've got me there," I laughed. "I am prepared to admit that rulers everywhere are a poor
lot, and I dare say they are no worse here than
elsewhere."

"Better here," he retorted, "though not much;
there is a good deal of human nature everywhere."

The man's way of talking interested me. He was
evidently free of prejudice and used words scrupu-
lously.

"You think I may learn something even without
the language?"

He nodded.

"How much do you want to be my guide and teacher?" I asked.

"If I am to do you any good," he said, "it ought to be forty or fifty dollars a week."

"All right.   Shall we begin from to-day or to-morrow?"

"As you like," he answered; "but I think you ought to give me a cheque now; not that I have any claim on it, but I want it."   The remark was made in the air.

I could not associate cheating with this nonchalant, thoughtful person, so I wrote him a cheque for the larger amount and handed it to him.   He put it in his pocket.

"How long are you going to stay in Shanghai?" he asked.

"Two or three months," I replied; "but I am not limited to time if there is anything of value to learn."

"That depends on you," he said, and his little eyes bored into mine.   "Well, so long!"   He turned abruptly and went.

As soon as I was alone I began to reproach myself for not asking him to explain the old Chinaman, but I told myself that it would be time enough next day.

But next day there was no Shimonski, nor the day after, nor the day after that.

One evening I spoke to an American merchant who had been in Shanghai twenty odd years and asked him if he knew Shimonski.

"A queer fish," he replied.

"Is he honest?" I asked.

"Oh yes," said the merchant. "I say he is queer, because he lives like a Chink; his eyes are getting to look like a Chinaman's, don't you think? And you even see him in their dress."

A day or two later I was told that someone wanted to see me.

"Send him up to my room," I said. To my astonishment a little Chinese girl came in and gave me a slip of paper on which I read: "Please give bearer my week's money; I shall see you soon. Shimonski."

I hesitated. It seemed to me the height of insolence.

"Can you take me to Mr. Shimonski?" I said to the girl.

She shook her head: "He isn't in Shanghai."

"When did he give you this?" I asked.

"Before he went away, a week ago," she answered.

It was curious, but the man's personality was so impressive in its entire sincerity, in its absence of pose, that I wrote out a cheque and handed it to the girl. As she put out her hand to take it I noticed that her skin was lighter than the skin of the majority of Chinese women. "Maybe Shimonski's daughter," I said to myself.

A couple of days passed and I heard no more of the matter, but I was again accosted by the old Chinaman with the knife.

Then one afternoon the door opened and Shimonski came in.

"Good-day!" he said.

"So you have turned up at last," I replied.

"Yes. I had something to finish that took me out of town, but now I am at your service, and from to-morrow I think you will find me fairly punctual. I suppose you will be up about nine o'clock?"

I said I would, and the next moment, without a word of excuse or explanation, he had left the room.

The next morning at nine o'clock I was up and dressed. Again he came in without knocking. "Shall we go out?" he said.

I took up my stick and hat and went with him. At the door I was once more approached by the old Chinaman.

"What does he want?" I asked Shimonski. "He has bothered me three or four times."

Shimonski spoke to him and then turned to me.

"His proposal," he said, "is to kill himself any way you like for ten dollars!"

"Why should I want him to kill himself?" I asked.

Shimonski shrugged his shoulders. "He says he will do it according to the Japanese way, which is the most painful, or he will go across the street and cut his throat there, or do anything you please."

"What good would that do me?" I asked.

"Good?" said Shimonski carelessly. "I don't know; it would be an experience."

"One that I won't buy," I said. "What does he want ten dollars for?"

"He has an only daughter," said Shimonski, "and he can get her well married for that dowry."

The old Chinaman had stood listening to us with his head on one side, looking from face to face. He seemed so eager that I took out ten dollars and gave him the bill. He pressed it against his heart and then again took out the great knife and made remarks.

"Tell him to put that knife up," I said, "and go off to his daughter."

Shimonski said a few words and the Chinaman disappeared.

"What an extraordinary creature," I remarked, "to be willing to kill himself for so little."

"Life is cheap in China," said Shimonski; "they all recognise that life to the poor is worthless."

"Does that explain, I wonder, our shootings in Western America?"

"Sure," replied Shimonski. "Where life is easy and pleasant it becomes precious."

"But men in Western America are free," I went on.

"Nothing like so free as they are in China," snapped Shimonski.

"What do you mean?" I asked, in surprise.

"That old Chinaman could have killed himself in the street and no one would have interfered with him; some days would probably have elapsed before the corpse would have been taken away. No country in the world is so free as China."

"Really!" I cried.

He looked at me, smiling. "What countries did you think freest?" he asked.

"I have always thought England and America," I replied.

"Surely," he retorted, "you know that the Greeks and Dalmatians are infinitely freer. In England, it is true, there is a little sense of personal liberty; in America there is none: it has been completely lost. America has a small sense of equality; here there is no sense of equality; no sense at all, but an extraordinary sense of liberty. Freedom is a religion in China.

"I am taking you now to the execution of some pirates who were caught the other day at the mouth of the river," he went on, "that will teach you what we mean here by freedom," and he led the way over one of the bridges. In ten minutes we came to a sort of yard, at the other side of which was a poor-looking temple structure. We had been there only a few moments when there filed into the yard eighteen men, all with their arms tied tightly behind their backs; their legs were tied too—in fact so closely haltered that they could only totter with short steps.

In a little while the executioner appeared—a gigantic man from North China—the biggest Chinaman I had seen up to that time, six feet three or four inches in height, of superb breadth and strength. He was flourishing an enormous sword as he came to us; it was scimitar-shaped and fully an inch thick at the back: it must have weighed thirty pounds. When he spoke the pirates all knelt down and he stood in front of them and made a short speech, which Shimonski translated.

"He says that he is the greatest executioner in the world, and that if they will only keep quiet and push their heads well back and their chins up they will never know that death came to them nor feel the stroke. See, he is shaving hairs off his arm to show them how razor-sharp the sword is."

As the executioner stepped smiling towards the first man in the line I stared round me and noticed that half the wall looking on to the street had been broken down, but of the people who were passing not one even paused to look at the tragedy.

The executioner said a word or two to the first man and lifted his chin in the air with his hand. Then stepping to the side, with one slice, he cut off his head, that rolled in the mud. I was horrified; but again the executioner stepped in front and said a few words.

"What is he saying?" I gasped, with dry mouth.

"Simply asking them to notice how perfect the stroke was; that the man has gone into the other world without knowing it. Look at his head; you will see the features are quite composed," Shimonski replied coolly.

Again and again and again the tragedy took place, accompanied each time by the boasting of the executioner. It was the fourth or fifth body that remained upright after the head had been sliced off, the poor torso spouting blood two feet high in a stream.

The executioner pointed with his sword to the body and said: "That's the way I do my work; all you have to do is to keep quiet, chin up, head back."

To my astonishment the remaining pirates nudged each other to look at the headless trunk, and laughed.

"I must go," I said to Shimonski. "I cannot stand this; that laughter and the cold cruelty are too horrible."

"It may be interesting," he said. "Wait."

But I could not wait, and hurried outside to get the wall between me and the ghastly spectacle. It was ten minutes before Shimonski rejoined me. "You might as well have waited," he said; "nothing happened."

"Do you call the murder of eighteen people nothing?"

"Nothing," repeated Shimonski, shrugging his shoulders. "Thousands die every day in China that no one cares about."

"Fancy," I said, "not one person outside even turned to look; in America there would have been a crowd."

"Yes," replied Shimonski, "you are interested in your neighbour; in China we mind our own business; that's all."

.   .   .   .

Chinese contempt for human life was made plain to me by this execution, but Shimonski seemed determined that I should learn something more about the

judicial system in China, for the next time we went
out he took me to a court.

One or two cases were decided, not by argument
of any sort or an appeal to law, but simply by the
sense of justice of the judge, a peculiar-looking little
Chinaman, with eyes that were mere slits and a low
monotonous voice that was, somehow or other, impressive.

The first few cases were decided with a sort of
rough justice, I thought, and then came a more important case. A merchant, it seemed, was com-
plaining of his manager or chief assistant. He was
a stout, rather large man, very voluble. He declared that his assistant had recently married and
was living in a better way than his salary justified.
This excited his suspicion. He took a sort of inventory and found that certain silken garments were
missing. He believed that his assistant had stolen
and sold them and made use of the proceeds; how,
otherwise, could he have got the money to live as
he was living?

The complaint seemed to me absurd and un-
founded, but the little mandarin on the bench said a
word or two, which Shimonski translated: "The
judge says he wants to hear the assistant."

So the assistant came forward, one of the finest-
looking young Chinamen I had ever seen. His face
was almost Caucasian, the eyes large and frank, and
the expression honest and intelligent; he was, besides, a fine figure of a man, taller even than the mer-
cant and broader, but carrying no fat. He

showed no fear or anger, and told his tale quite simply. Shimonski translated for me as he went on:

"He says the accusation is absurd: if the merchant will take an inventory he will find that nothing has disappeared that has not been paid for; he has never taken any garment outside the shop; he makes much extra money by going to the European Hotel in the evening and carrying baggage to the steamer or doing anything they want him to do, and his wife, too, works."

Again and again he was interrupted by the merchant. When he had finished the judge said a few quiet words and Shimonski chuckled.

"What is it?" I asked; "surely he will dismiss the case."

"The judge asks him what became of the silken garments that the merchant says were in the shop. The judge is in favour of the merchant. The employé is too bold. We shall see some fun."

The young man answered the judge at somewhat greater length now and with much greater emphasis, and when interrupted by the merchant he turned on him and spoke indignantly. Again the judge peered through his slits of eyes and said something and there was a commotion in the court; two or three Chinese police went out by a side door.

"Now you will see something," whispered Shimonski excitedly. "This is getting interesting."

"What is it?" I asked.

"The judge is going to make him confess," said Shimonski. "You'll see."

A moment more and two policemen came back with the most curious-looking affair I had ever seen. It was a high pole, as thick as one's leg, with a very large basin-looking thing at the base, a bar stuck out horizontally at the top, with a pulley attached. In the basin was a huge cannon-ball of stone that must have weighed two or three hundredweight.

"What on earth is that thing for?" I asked.

"You'll see," replied Shimonski curtly, with gleaming eyes.

Again the mandarin on the bench said something in his slow, monotonous, quiet voice. Two policeman took hold of the young man and dragged him to the machine. Two or three others pulled the cannon-ball about six feet high by the rope. A policeman shoved the right foot of the young man into the basin and held it there. A word from the judge and the ball fell with a thud on the young man's foot and turned it into mere blood and pulp. I never heard such a cry as he uttered. I was fascinated with horror. "Good God!" I kept repeating. "Good God!"

I turned to Shimonski. He was smiling, with his eyes fixed on the mandarin, who was speaking again, evidently addressing the young man, who was being held up by the policeman.

"What is he saying?" I asked.

"The judge is asking him if he remembers the silk

robes now, and he says 'No. He can only repeat what he has said already.' "

The merchant came forward and even his face was white. He made some remark and Shimonski translated: "He says now he may be mistaken. Won't the honourable judge please let the young man go?"

For the first time the judge used a few short sentences: Shimonski translated: "He says that as the merchant had pleaded for the young man's life he may go, but he hopes the punishment will be a lesson to him to keep from stealing in the future."

The little old mandarin then got up and disappeared through a door at the back. The policemen took their hands off the young man, who pulled himself together and limped to the door, a long stream of blood pouring from his right leg to the floor.

"Good God!" I cried to Shimonski, "give the poor fellow some money and see if he cannot be carried home and his leg attended to."

"Why give him money?" asked Shimonski. "In a couple of hours he'll be dead. Why waste money on a corpse?"

"But can't they put a tourniquet on his leg," I said, "and stop the bleeding? He will be a cripple, but he may live."

"What good is life to a cripple?" replied Shimonski. "Give your money to people who are sound, if you want to give it."

"Let us get out of this," I cried, appalled. "I cannot stand your Chinese justice."

A day or two afterwards I cross-examined Shimonski about the matter. "Is there no appeal in such a case?" I asked. "The merchant evidently lied and the young man was murdered for nothing at all."

"No, no," said Shimonski; "he was impudent."

"Innocence," I retorted, "is always impudent."

"Wealth is the only thing in China that dares to be impudent," said Shimonski. "If you are independent you can be impudent; if you are not, you had better be respectful."

"So," I said, "this is the way your boasted liberty is bounded: freedom for the well-to-do; torture and untimely death for the poor."

Shimonski shrugged his shoulders. "As long as I am one of the well-to-do," he said, "I do not bother."

There was no doubt he took pleasure in cruelty, and when I asked him he admitted it quite coolly.

"You have a childish idea," he said, "that pleasure in life is only to be got from love and liking and such roots, but I think as much joy in life comes from gratified hatred, and there is keen pleasure in punishment that falls on another."

"Justice has nothing to do with it, then?" I asked.

"Nothing," he said. "You do not ask whether you deserve to be kissed or not; you take pleasure in the kiss. The wise man gets all the pleasure he can out of life."

"But can there be any pleasure in cruelty?" I asked.

"Of course," he replied with a sigh, as if tired of such foolish questions, "the very sharpest."

A little later he took me to another Chinese execution, but before I tell of it I want to say that his cruelty had begun to interest me. I wanted to find the reason for it, the explanation of it. After all, he couldn't have been born with that fiend's nature.

The second execution which Shimonski brought me to see is certainly an institution peculiar to China and throws a grim light on Chinese judicial proceedings. It, too, was in public, but this time a crowd had collected in the half-paved yard, where bloodstains could still be seen from the execution of the pirates.

Against the wall, underneath the temple, a wooden staging had been built, and the back of the staging was planked right up to the top of the wall. The executioner was a man of ordinary size, but of considerable muscular development, and he was stripped to the waist. He was abrupt in movement and vibrant with energy.

A large basket was at his feet and he had two assistants. It took them perhaps a quarter of an hour to tie up the criminal to big nails let in on the wooden hoarding at the back. When they had finished the victim was spread-eagled against this wooden background, but standing more or less at ease on his own feet, though he could not move his hands or head

or limbs, because he was trussed like a fowl and tied
everywhere to the hoarding like an advertisement.
The victim was a man of perhaps forty years of age,
but of an extraordinary emaciation; he looked more
like a skeleton than a man. It appeared he had entered the house of a rich man to steal, and had been
arrested after killing one of the policemen.

"Want drove him to it?" I remarked to Shimonski.

"Probably poverty," he replied; "he looks like
it."

Shimonski was not as interested as usual. "They
are not going through with it," he said discon-
solately. "The man has some girl children and they
have curried favour with a rich mandarin and I hear
the executioner has been bought; if so, we shan't
have much fun."

"Justice, then, can be bought in China?" I said.

Shimonski looked at me. "Justice is bought
everywhere; sometimes with popular applause, as in
America, sometimes with money, as in France, and
sometimes with titles and snobbery, as in Great Brit-
ain; but everywhere justice is bought. In China
money is the purchasing power. The Chinese are a
matter-of-fact, realistic, sensible people."

Scarcely had he finished speaking when the executioner turned round and made a speech. Shimonski
translated it for me. He began by saying: "In
this basket at my feet are fifty knives. I do not
know what is written on the handles. I pick them

up and read, and act according to the instructions. It is all a lottery and our lives are at the mercy of our masters."

"Fifty knives!" I cried.   "What on earth does he want fifty knives for?"

"You will see," said Shimonski.   "Wait and see."

Suddenly one of the *aides* drew the cloth away from the basket with a flourish and immediately the executioner stooped down and picked a knife out of the basket: there was a label on the haft.   He read it out: "Through the arm," and whirling round at once he pinned the man's left arm to the wood by driving the knife through it.

The victim did not utter a sound nor move, but his head bent further forward on his chest and his yellow face became grey; he appeared to be on the point of fainting.   Another knife was taken out and read: "Through the shoulder," and it was thrown in the most marvellous way, just catching the skin on the shoulder.   The grey face became livid, but not a sound.

The executioner lifted up the third knife and read: "Through the heart," and whirling round drove it through the heart of his victim.   There was a roar of hatred and rage from the crowd, who evidently expected that the pleasant performance would be prolonged.

"I told you so," said Shimonski.   "I heard the executioner had been paid; that is the proof; otherwise he would have shown off his skill, using every knife to the end, and the man would have been squealing before the tenth, like a rat whose legs have been cut off."

I left the ground while the executioner was still trying to tell the mob that he had simply to take the knife that came first; that he could not say what was on the label: in fact he was trying to justify himself as if he had been an Anglo-Saxon politician or profiteer.

"And can judges also be bought in China?" I asked Shimonski.

"Of course," he said; "but the price for judges is higher, and they are usually bought from above by the governors or the State."

"And for the three hundred and fifty millions of Chinamen," I said, "there is no justice and no law?"

"None," Shimonski answered. "But for the hundred and fifty thousand or so who can make some money and live independently China is the best country in the world. You can buy whatever you want in it and everything is very cheap. Did you ever get such good service before? Isn't the food excellent? the fish and chickens wonderful? the climate healthy? perfect freedom? What more can a man want?"

"The whole thing is a horror to me," I said. "What is there for the soul here?"

"Ah!" said Shimonski, "that is another question. You will find greater paintings in China than anywhere in the world—an art that grew and blossomed through two thousand years. Every school of painting imaginable can be found in China. Have you have heard of the painter who said that it was no object of the artist to represent life or even to give you the effect life produced on you, which is the object of the modern European schools, but that the true aim of the great artist should be to represent the rhythm of life itself—not progress, that doesn't exist; but the ebb and flow, the movement and rhythm of life?

"In the same way our poets always try to give us new emotions, and the moderns want to catch the most evanescent feelings, the fancies that break through language and escape.

"Our vases and cups are the finest in the world: common household things with a glaze on them of priceless beauty. Carpets, too, we have which make all other carpets look like rags."

"I know," I cried. "I have admired turquoise blues and camel-hair effects. I think them wonderful."

"You will never know what a carpet is till you see an old Chinese carpet two or three hundred years old, for, unlike all other carpets, its beauty increases with age; as it gets worn down a gloss comes upon it that can only be compared to the bloom on a peach or grape. I could show you carpets three hundred years old that are as lovely as any picture—beautified, indeed, by the patine of the years, the unimaginable touch of Time."

"But the religion?" I asked. "Can there be any religion in a people where justice is bought and sold and cruelty is a passion?"

"Oh yes," replied Shimonski. "Man is a complex animal; he unites in myself many contradictions. The religion of China is the highest and most abstract in the world."

.   .   .   .

My memories of Shimonski are becoming unduly voluminous; I must bring them to an end.

I have dwelt on his delight in cruelty and on his originality of thought, for those were the qualities in him which excited my curiosity and admiration; naturally he possessed dozens of other virtues and vices, but these two in eminent degree. It was especially his epicurean pleasure in cruelty, his savouring it as a titbit and dainty, that intrigued me, for after some months of acquaintanceship I found that the Chinese girl whom he sent to me as a messenger was an orphan whom he had picked up, educated and cared for. He had another girl in his house who looked after his clothes and books, though she was blind of one eye, and an old woman who cooked for them, and all three he had rescued out of pure pity, and they all adored him as a sort of god.

As I got to know and like him he grew more communicative. We went up country together that summer to see some old porcelain and on the journey he gave me the key of his strange nature. I'll try to tell the story as he told it, but without the interruptions and wanderings of his narrative.

One thing was peculiar in his confession. He

never tried to justify himself or to moralise his conduct in any degree. He was certainly above good and evil, in his own opinion at least.

We had been away about a fortnight and had stopped for the night in a walled town, three hundred miles from Shanghai. He had been explaining to me how curiously free and independent these towns are in China. The Imperial Government, it appeared, sent down annually a requisition setting forth what amount the town would have to contribute in taxes to the Imperial revenue; but the method of taxation was left to the town itself.

I told him that the same municipal power existed all over Germany, and was one of the chief reasons why Germans could stand an extreme Imperial despotism, because in their village and town affairs they were their own masters.

He shrugged his shoulders indifferently. He had no great liking for the Teutonic races, he said; the Germans and English, and even the Americans, were all tarred with the same brush—a self-sufficient greed varnished with hypocritical righteousness or sentimentality which he thought ridiculous. He preferred the Latins to the Teutons, but reserved his special admiration for the Slavs and the Chinese. In China, he said, we have had the "general strike" for a thousand years now which you are only beginning to think of as a protest. If the Government does something we don't like, we all strike and the Government soon gives in. Despotism, like democracy, is only a word. . . .

It was a beautiful morning in early summer and a beautiful scene. The river ran through an ever-narrowing valley; the banks were thickly wooded and the trees were all blushing in the light, warm air of May.

Rounding one turn we came upon a strange procession—coolies in front carrying clothes and provisions, two or three palanquins, and more servants bringing up the rear. We asked what it was, or rather Shimonski asked, and was told that it was a girl being brought down to be wedded to a Chinese general in the town we had just left.

"My fate came to me like that," Shimonski remarked.

"Tell me about it," I said.

"It is ten years ago now," he began. "It was far up country I met just such a procession. A handsome youth was in charge of the bride, his sister; he told me he was taking her, as the loveliest girl in the whole province, to be wedded to the Governor of Szechuan, then the most powerful of provincial rulers. I was mildly interested and a little curious, so I told him where he ought to stop next and gave him various pieces of information he wanted; then I praised his looks and bearing just to get his confidence, so that when I said I'd like to see his sister, he took me to the palanquin at once and drew the curtain. Never have I seen anything so wonderful! Her eyes held me and fascinated me, and it was some time before I could throw off the enchantment

enough to realise the different traits that constituted
her exquisite loveliness.

"Oh, the flower face! Well was she named the
Morning Glory. Her face had only enough of the
Chinese type to give it a strangeness that enthralled.
At first glance she might have passed for a Russian,
only no Russian was ever so beautiful. How shall
I describe her? When I have said her eyes were
very large, a dark hazel in colour, lit and warmed by
golden points; when I've told of a straight nose and
perfect oval of face and rose-leaf skin, and lips a
little too full and ripe, I've said nothing. Other
girls have these. But her eyes, besides being beautiful, were nobly serious, with a brooding expression
that came from depth of feeling; there was a question in them and an appeal and trust that enlightened
the face to a smile; and then I saw the slender arm
and the dimples at the elbow and the budding
breasts, and my mouth grew dry as in a parching
wind.

"Do you realise at length that in China we know
more about beauty than any other people; we have
studied it more curiously, more intimately than any
other race. Have you ever noticed that our haw-
thorn jars are moulded after the curves of a woman's hips, and that the magical powder-blue vases
are copies of the lines of some slight girl's body?
The glaze itself has the smooth gloss of a child's
flesh and the radiance on it is of our wonderment. I
have shown you marvels in material things; you must
just trust me when I tell you that this girl was per-

fection perfected, her body a rhythm, her face a flower. . . .

"I turned and went with them—made myself a guide and protector. Both the brother and sister trusted and liked me, and I did all I knew to increase their liking. I told them all sorts of strange stories: tales of heroes and fightings for the youth and of romantic love and despair for the girl. I ransacked my memories of Russian and Polish and German and French history, and I used to love to have their eyes fixed on me and feel her breath catch. . . .

"The halts for the midday meal grew longer and longer and our daily journeyings shorter, while they listened enthralled to my stories. I told of sinner and saint, of St. Elizabeth of Hungary and of Ninon d'Enclos of Paris, and she drank in everything I said.

"And always the youth wanted to learn and the girl to feel; but I think she grew even more quickly than he did. I remember telling him once of the great Chinese Emperor Shi Hwang-ti. Do you know the story? He came to the throne at thirteen and while still young abolished the feudal system, divided China into provinces, built roads, canals, and at length the Great Wall. The feudal princes revolted; writers and pedants held up to the admiration of the people the heroes of feudal times, and the advantages of the old, worn-out system. To break once and for all with the past, the great emperor ordered the destruction of all books having reference to the past history of the empire, and many scholars were put to death for disobedience to the 'edict.'

"I can still hear her sighing: 'What a pity a great man could kill innocent people! Is no great man at once strong and wise and gentle?' The divine sweet spirit of her!

"You don't know how wonderful our Chinese girls can be," Shimonski went on, "but at least you realise now that Chinese art is the finest in the world, and soon you will be able to see that our old Chinese religion, too, is the highest at once and most rational ever held by man. And when you acknowledge this you may be ready to understand that Chinese men and women are the noblest human creatures of whom Time holds any record.

"At any rate I would like you to believe that it is not the blindness of passion makes me put this simple Manchu girl higher than any other human being I have ever met. If I am not utterly depraved it is because of her; whatever good there is in me comes from her; my soul is merely an emanation of her divine passion and pity. . . .

"But I must get on with my story. I had been with them nearly a fortnight when one day the brother went away to see a famous temple and I told the sister the story of Jeanne d'Arc. It had a tremendous effect on her, an effect I never anticipated. She grew paler and paler, and tears fell from her eyes. When I told her of Jeanne's martyrdom I expected her to break down weeping, but it had the

contrary effect on her; her whole face was trans-
figured; and when I told how Jeanne acknowledged
that she had lost her 'voices' through her own selfishness and her woman's wish to do what her king
desired, my girl's eyes glowed with enthusiasm and
she exclaimed: 'What a great end! What a noble
girl!'

"She fell silent while I told how the Catholic
Church, centuries later, canonised Jeanne as a saint,
and how she was loved and revered now wherever
her story was known.

"Glory, as I called her always, got up from her
couch and suddenly leaning forward took my head
in her hands and kissed me on the lips.

" 'Thank you, thank you,' she cried, 'for the great
story; it will be a part of my soul for ever.'

"It was not passion with which I kissed her, for
a great reverence was upon me and I was enthralled
by her emotion; but afterwards passion woke in me,
for I had held the round firm figure against my body,
and the supple grace and litheness of it got into my
blood and the desire of her shook me like a fever.

"What a day of days it was! Fate is sometimes
good to us. The brother did not return and we
spent the evening together, and when she rose to retire I kissed her hands, one after the other, for she
was sacred to me; but she drew me to her and offered her lips and I put my arms around her. I
kissed her and kissed till she pushed my head back
gently, saying: 'Dear, you take my breath'; but

really she had flushed crimson for the first time, I think. Conscious of her body, she had yielded for a moment to a man's passion.

"The days after went by on wings; her brother liked me so much that for a fortnight he did not notice the intimate terms we were on. But one evening he had said 'Good-night,' and gone, but returned quickly and found me kissing her. She said simply: 'I love Shi,' and put her hand on his shoulder with a caress and left us.

" 'How will it end?' was all he said after a pause, and then: 'I must leave it to you both. 'You,' he went on to me, 'will, I'm sure, think of her safety.'

"And I answered him that I would and told him the truth, that our caressings had all been innocent and I would not engage the future lightly; but even while reassuring him I knew that I had come to the extreme verge and uttermost limit of control, and was ripe for anything, with no more self-mastery than a child.

"Women, I often think, are far braver in such matters than men. Next day Glory wanted to know what we had decided, and walking beside her palanquin I told her we had arranged nothing; but he had left it to us. She nodded and said nothing.

"That day her brother did not stay with us after the midday meal, but made some excuse and went out, leaving us together, and at once, I don't know why, I took her in my arms and began kissing and caressing her. And she yielded to me; but in a moment her lips grew hot and she drew away.

" 'Have you really decided—at last?' she asked, and there was a challenge in that added 'at last' which stung me.

" 'For myself—yes,' I replied; 'but for you—how can I decide to bring you and him into danger?'

"The deep eyes held me, and without a word she put both her hands on my shoulders and studied me.

" 'Your Jeanne d'Arc,' she said after a moment, 'gave her life for her king. Do you think I am afraid? To lose you would make me afraid; with you I fear nothing in the world. I am proud you want me, happy you have chosen me, my man of men; with you I am content and my heart's at peace,' she added like a child, and gave her mouth.

" 'I want to have a talk with your brother first,' I said. 'We must get rid of all the servants and I must arrange to get you and myself to one of the treaty towns, where we shall be safe. But the risk is appalling and the chances of success small, for the Governor is as powerful as a god and the news of your beauty will have reached him.'

" 'Do men want beauty so much?' she asked. 'You know he has never seen me; he can't care much if he loses what he doesn't know.'

" 'You are wrong, you dear,' I cried. 'Men desire beauty more than anything, and you are so wonderful that he will have heard about you and be inordinately curious to see and possess you. Then for a strong man with power to miss something he desires, to lose it to an inferior is very bitter, and I'm afraid he'll do his uttermost against us.'

" 'Then take me,' she said, 'as long as I am yours and you are mine—me I mean,' she corrected, nestling to me; 'I am content, happy.'

"Ah! the sacred boldness of her whose law was love.

"There's one verse of your English poetry comes into my head when I think of her, and only one:

'Teach me, only teach, Love;
     As I ought
I will speak thy speech, Love;
     Think thy thought—
Meet, if thou require it,
     Both demands,
Laying flesh and spirit
     In thy hands!'

"It was Glory who showed me the heights of Chinese thought. Till I met her I believed that the practical teachings of Confucius and his rules of conduct constituted the religion of China. She introduced me to his master, Lao-tse, whom he called 'the old philosopher.' Confucius was a mere moralist, but Lao-tse was the deepest thinker who has yet arisen among men, and his religion is the earliest known to the Chinese as Buddhism is the latest.

"Lao-tse wrote his *Tâo-Teh-King* in the sixth century B. C. The title even is almost untranslatable, but may be called the *Way of Virtue*. No foreigner has ever yet grasped what the *Tâo* means, and even students are put off by apparent differences. Glory, however, was the daughter of a great thinker and she made the *Tâo* clear to me.

"Lao-tse went far beyond a belief in God or in man; the childish dualism of body and spirit, this world and the next, the Devil and God were ridiculous to him; both flesh and spirit seemed to him equally unimportant. What he saw was the unfolding of life, the mingling of life and death; the Becoming; and this perpetual Becoming is the rhythm of Life itself—the rhythm, mark you, and not the progress or development, the world of thought and deed and Being as it is in constant unfolding. That is the *Tâo,* and a study of it shows how to live in harmony with it. Glory had all the master's best sayings by heart and she taught me many of them.

"'Those who are skilled in the *Tâo* do not dispute,' she said; 'but they know some things. They know "there is nothing softer than water," as Lao-tse said, "and yet nothing can resist it." They know that "he who inflicts death is as one who cuts wood; soon or late he cuts his own hands." They know that "trees and plants and men at birth are soft and easily bent, and at death hard and firm, and the sage therefore keeps the innocent softness of the child." They know that "when a people does not fear what it ought to fear, its great dread shall come upon it." They know that "the Sacred Way I call the *Tâo,* unlike the way of foolish men, diminishes where there is abundance and increases where there is deficiency.' "

"Somehow or other her spirituality intensified my

passion and gave me the sense that what was so far above ordinary life or ordinary thought must be enduring. But every now and then facts broke in and disturbed my dreaming.

"One day her brother said to me: 'We are within a fortnight's journey of the capital, you know, and though we may take a month over it, still—the Viceroy may send to meet us. And your passion is being talked of by the coolies. Even the *Tâo* prescribes foresight . . .' and he smiled.

"I was struck to the heart. Should we try to escape at once: there was no sense in drifting. I was like an opium-smoker, lost to everything but my exquisite dream-life. And how wonderful it was can never be told, for Glory was all sorts of women in one. At first a child, afraid that this or that might not please me; then so filled with joy when she found that whatever she did delighted me; shy now and now curious; frank as a boy, and wise as only a woman's love is wise.

"I went to her. 'What are we to do?' I cried. 'I am yours. Decide!'

" 'Is there a chance of escape?' she asked.

" 'Yes,' I replied; 'just a chance.'

" 'One week, one day with you is life to me,' she said; 'do you feel that too?'

" 'Sure,' I replied.

" 'Then let us try at once to escape,' she said. 'First of all let the coolies return to-day; pay them in full; content them without overdoing it: my brother will see to that. He will probably prefer to return himself and take up my father's business. Then you and I will go into the—appointed—whither you will.'

" 'Are you afraid?' I asked with shrinking heart.

" 'No, indeed,' she replied, smiling; 'but it is impossible, says Lao, to live long on the heights. Yet such life, even for a day, is better than years on low levels.'

"All was done as she had outlined.

"I planned to break to the west, for the frontier tribes there were in partial revolt, and it would take an army to get us; but this was only a blind. I intended to double back and get to the river, which leaves no trace, and if possible reach the sea before the chase grew close. Any foreign steamer, English or German, would then bring us easily to safety and a new life. After forty-eight hours of forced marching west and back we were on board a *sampan* on our way to happiness.

"But happiness was with us on the boat."

Shimonski paused: "Often I tell over to myself those golden hours, each one filled with its own joy, a delight in living and in memory. In that week I learned all a woman could give in passionate tenderness, and with what treasures of gaiety and courage she could crown her love.

"The moment we went on board, Glory took up her new part. European girls often make good wives and mothers; but she was an incomparable lover first and at the same time a companion of infinite variety. It was impossible to be dull or depressed in her company; she drew the best out of me and then declared that the wisest or wittiest sayings were all mine. She flattered me outrageously; but then who does not love to be praised by the woman he loves? The more I studied her body and face the more beautiful I thought her. She had no need to bind her feet, whether to make them look smaller or to increase the obsession of love by sedentary living; and the more I learned of her mind and spirit the more I had to admire her. She never pretended to be well-read, but she had been brought up by a wise father, who encouraged her to think for herself. She was astonishingly original in thought and ingenuous in feeling—a girl's body and a woman's soul. While loving me and telling me all sorts of things about China and her own bringing up, she managed all the time to watch the boatmen and make them her friends and protectors.

"Thanks to her mainly we hadn't a single hitch— no trouble with any of the towns or villages we passed through, no sign of any pursuit. As we neared the great harbour I allowed myself to hope, for I had planned to reach the port in the small hours of night, and knowing the Chinese ways I felt sure we should be able to evade even watchful eyes.

"Everything happened as I had foreseen; it was black night when we ran alongside the German mail steamer. I had already promised the men a large reward, so taking Glory in my arms for a long kiss I begged her to cry out if she saw anything suspicious, then ran up the ladder to see the German captain. He received me in bed, told me he would be glad to take my wife and myself as passengers, and I returned, knowing that Glory's beauty, if there was any difficulty, would be my best advocate.

"As I sprang on the deck of the *sampan* I was surprised not to see my love; but before I had time to think, I was struck down from behind, and re-member nothing more till I awoke in a Chinese house, with Chinamen about me and a pair of Chi-nese eyes boring into my dull consciousness. In a moment or two I found I was cold and wet; they had probably thrown cold water over me to bring me to. And Glory! My hand and feet were bound. I was caught—but Glory? Glory! Could she possibly have escaped? If so, I'd pay for both gladly.

"I can hardly describe what followed. I soon realised that the mandarin watching me was the Governor. I lay on a sort of couch in the middle of a room, two men on each side, while he questioned me. He wanted to know whether the brother was in the plot. I said 'No. I had persuaded him I was coming straight through.'

"The Governor told me that if I lied he would torture me so that I should beg for death as a re-lease. No bodily pain could have added to my misery and remorse.

"I grew to fear and hate his cold eyes. I thought we had only one chance and I took it. I told him if he would give me Glory I'd serve him all my life as no man yet was ever served. I begged with all my soul. He told me he would give Glory to his servants before my eyes. . . .

"I don't remember much afterwards; it is like a dream in fever, half-reality, half-mists of pain. But one moment is clear; when she fainted I heard some-one laugh. It was I. From that moment I lived for revenge.

"They tortured me too—did something to me they thought would give me a lingering death in agony, and threw me into the street. I crawled to a coolie's hut and got a girl to fetch me a German surgeon. A timely operation saved my life, and that same night I learned that Glory was dead.

.   .   .   .

"The rest's a long tale, but I can cut it short. I went to Peking and got a place in the household of the empress; in time she took a liking to me, and I thought and plotted and planned till at length she sent for the Governor and told him to come without a retinue.

"I had made my arrangements. He was taken outside the town, brought in by my servants, and bound in the cellar of a house I had bought. . . .

"He was a month dying.

"Every day I went to my duties at the palace; every evening and morning I spent an hour with those cold eyes. He used to beg me to kill him; that made me laugh. . . .

"In that month I learned the keen delight there is in torture.

"Do you know," Shimonski broke off, "I never see a punishment now or an execution without seeing that man in the place of the victim. His pain thrills me. What a month it was! I soon found out what parts of the body hurt the most when you tweaked off pieces with red-hot pincers. You'd never guess.

"He grew old in a week. . . . As I pulled his nails off, his hairs fell out. . . . With his tongue and teeth gone, his beard turned white and the yellow skin of him shrivelled as I . . ."

I put up my hand to ward off more, and Shimonski turned and went across the room muttering to himself. "Glory, Glory!"

Had suffering turned his brain—or passion?

ST. PETER'S DIFFICULTY

ST. PETER'S DIFFICULTY

ONE day Peter was greatly disturbed. He wanted to leave the Gate of Heaven and his duties there for a few minutes, so he called his brother Andrew to take his place.

Andrew was very willing to play guardian, but Peter was afraid to leave him in charge.

"Mind now," he cautioned him, "don't let anyone in who is not entitled to enter. Don't act on your own judgment. Ask the Recording Angel and go by his assurance only, and remember that those who have a right to get in will always get in, and a little delay will not harm them, for son of man or daughter of Eve was never too humble. Take care now and make no mistake."

Andrew assured Peter again and again that he would follow his directions to the letter, and at length Peter hastened away towards the Throne, his business brooking no delay.

On the way he met Jesus, and after some hesitation could not help unburdening his heart to Him:

"A dreadful thing has happened, Master," he began, "and I want you to believe that I am not to blame. I have been given charge of the gate and have never left it for a moment till now, and I pledge you my word I have never let a single person

141

inside who has not a perfectly clean sheet. No one can be more grateful for all the privileges of Heaven than I am. You believe me, don't you?"

Jesus bowed His head with smiling eyes.

"I am sure, Peter, you have been an admirable guardian," He said, "but what is troubling you now?"

"The other day," began Peter, looking up at Him with sidelong intent eyes, "the other day I met a little blind girl whom I certainly never let into Heaven. Oh, Master, Master, someone is admitting them; I can do nothing and I shall be blamed for someone else's fault."

Jesus put His hand on Peter's shoulder: "We do not blame easily, do we, Peter? But who do you think is letting them in?"

"I cannot sleep or eat for thinking of it," replied Peter evasively; "please help me."

"How shall I help you?" asked Jesus.

"Come to-night at eleven o'clock when all is quiet and I will show you everything."

Jesus looked at him in some surprise, but answered simply: "I will be with you, Peter."

That night Peter took Jesus and guided Him by the hand all along the rampart to the first great bastion; then he whispered to him to wait in the shadow and he would see. And lo! a few minutes later they were aware of a woman's figure close to the battlements. They both saw her unwind her girdle and let it down over the wall; in a few moments a little hunchbacked creature climbed up, took one or two halting steps and then cast himself down on his face before the woman and began kissing the hem of her garment.

At once Jesus drew Peter away, and as they went towards the gate, out of earshot, He said: "My mother!"

"Yes, it is Mary," Peter began, "and what can I do? Those she lets in are all deformed like that wretched hunchback; she helps only the maimed and the halt and the blind, and some afflicted with bleeding, putrid sores—dreadful creatures; they would shame even an earthly city. But what am I to do, Master?"

"Peter, Peter!" said Jesus, and the luminous great eyes dwelt on him, "you and I had not even deformity to plead for us——"

one or two halting steps and then cast himself down on his face before the woman and began kissing the hem of her garment.

At once Jeanne drew Peter closer, and as they went towards the gate, out of earshot, he said: "My mother?"

"Yes, it is Mary," Peter began, "and what can I do?" Those she had in arm-... turned like that wrapped him tightly; she helped only... he moaned and the bath and checked ... and some affected with bleeding, natural when ... glorified loveliness, they would shame even an earthly star. ... But what am I to do, Master?"

"Peter, Peter!" said Jesus, and the luminous great eyes dwelt on him, "you and I had not even dreamt of glory for us——"

LOVE IS MY SIN

LOVE IS NO SIN

LOVE IS MY SIN

MANY years ago now I was staying at a certain castle in Scotland. I didn't like the country; it rained without ceasing, and the rain was bleak and cold, like the harsh, Doric accent of the people, utterly unlike the soft Irish rain and the caressing slur of the brogue.

The host and guests went out shooting or fishing every day, usually taking the ladies with them, and I was left to my own devices, for I had already come to loathe the taking of life for mere sport.

The library hadn't a modern book to boast of, so in the intervals of sunshine I usually walked about the Italian gardens, where the lilac bushes stood glittering like queens bediamonded.

One day, at a loose end and lonely, I resolved to explore the great house, and went up and down stairs and along endless corridors till, in the north wing near the roof, I heard something, and glancing into a bare loft-like room saw a man seated on the floor with a picture on his knees, while others stood about on easels and propped against the dais.

"May I come in?" I asked out of sheer curiosity.

He nodded his head, intent upon his work, and in I went and stood beside him, looking down on an *Infanta* of Velasquez.

"My name is Symonds," I began, smiling. "I'm interested in painting and art as a journalist. I hope you don't mind my looking on at your work?"

"Not a bit," he replied, smiling pleasantly out of hazel eyes. "You won't know my name," he went on; "it's Ronden; wholly undistinguished," he added.

Was it fancy or did I catch a shade of bitterness accentuating the last two words? In any case my curiosity was sharpened.

"What are you doing?" I went on, noticing at the same time his curious pallid complexion and the long sensitive fingers manipulating a sort of palette knife.

"It's rather a long story," he began, "but it may interest you.

"In painting, as in all the arts, I imagine, there have been curious changes in taste. In the eighteenth century Murillos in England fetched a large price, while Velasquez was little thought of. Of course there were amateurs who knew better even then, but, as a rule, Velasquez, with his seeing eyes and poignant realism, was not much esteemed, and his pictures were often banished to the garret, or even to the outhouse, whereas Murillo's fashion-plates were throned in the chief places of the mansion.

"Now all that's altered. Murillo has sunk in our esteem and Velasquez has risen, so that Velasquez paintings have been dragged out of their hiding-places and the Murillos have been relegated to bedrooms or sold to sentimental millionaires.

"But many of the Velasquez have been damaged by exposure. Canvases rot quickly in damp. Consequently a new trade has sprung into being.

"Was it possible to transfer a Velasquez painting to a fresh canvas? Could that be done without injuring the original? I thought it could, and went to work at it. I soon found that this sort of craftsmanship, the art of transferring paint bit by bit to a fresh canvas and fixing it there with a thin paste or gum, was more lucrative than any work I could get, so I have been doing it for a good many years now.

"I sometimes think it is like a writer condemned to journalism to earn a living."

"How interesting!" I exclaimed. "Are you really able to transfer the whole of that picture to a fresh canvas without injuring it? You might drop a little piece of paint on the floor, might you not, and it would all crumble into dust, wouldn't it?"

"Surely," he replied, and as he spoke he flicked off half a square inch of paint on to the floor, where it immediately fell to dust.

"I have studied the painting," he went on, smiling shrewdly, "and I can reproduce every tone exactly."

"Good God!" I exclaimed, "what an astonishing mastery. You almost persuade me that if that girl's head had come to grief you could paint it in correctly."

"If I had ever seen it," he said, "and studied it, I think I could reproduce it so that Velasquez himself would hardly know where his brush ceased to work and mine began. Mark you, I am taking the whole of the inspiration from Velasquez. I profess to be merely a copyist—a craftsman, but a competent one, I hope."

"But if you can resuscitate Velasquez," I said, "you must earn enormous sums."

"A good living, at least," he replied casually. "I'm told that journalists often earn more than men of letters, and so we craftsmen often earn more than great creative artists."

"Intensely interesting," I cried. "You must be able to solve one of my difficulties. Of course I know hardly anything about painting, but I have often wondered whether Rembrandt painted all those brown portraits of his. Ever since the so-called *Night Watch*, which is really the *Day Watch*, was cleaned, one sees how he loved brilliant colours for their own sake. Could he have used those umber tones so exclusively?"

"Nearly all painters," replied Ronden, "even the great masters, bought their colours and used them without thinking much about the composition of them; many of the paints were mixed with bitumen, and in time bitumen conquers all the other colours and degrades them to a dull brown. The so-called Cornish school in England have begun studying the matter and are trying to use pure paint, just as the best Frenchmen now are all using pure colours.

But the painter's art, which is the only universal art, is more transitory than other arts—I suppose by way of compensation"—he spoke as if to himself; "all colours fade or get brown in a couple of hundred years, and the magic of the artist's conception is lost. You have to read the master's message by faith and not by sight."

Excited as well as curious now I probed further.

"How did you come to all this knowledge and this mastery?" I asked.

He looked up at me and I seemed to sense something pathetic—sad—in the long brown eyes.

"That's another story," he said, "too personal to be interesting, I'm afraid. This world forces nearly all of us to do things we do not want to do. But how comes it that you take such an interest in painting?"

"I take a sort of amateur interest in art," I said; "in fact, I am on *The Standard* as art critic and Jack-of-all-trades. How is it I've never seen you downstairs?"

"I keep away from the society crowd," he replied casually; "they've nothing I want and what I've got doesn't interest them."

"We're in the same boat then," I remarked. "The host and I are old friends, but the others leave me quite cold." . . .

A little later the bell rang for tea and I went downstairs out of politeness; but not before I had engaged Ronden to go for a walk with me on the morrow before lunch. The man attracted and interested me peculiarly; he was very handsome, with the regular features, fine eyes and olive skin of the best Latin type; but he was something more than handsome; there was an air of thought about him and—why shouldn't I say it?—a suggestion of sadness.

Next morning we met and strolled into the park. The walk didn't amount to much, for in ten minutes Ronden had to confess that he suffered from fallen arches in his insteps and could not walk far, in spite of the supports in his boots.

"That's why I am so pale," he explained. "I've good health," he hastened to add, "but, like a galley-slave, I'm not allowed to get about freely."

Bit by bit I came to understand that this disability, to which I paid little attention at first, was the determining factor in his life, the infirmity making him curiously shy and introspective, while sharpening also his faculties of observation and deduction. But at the moment I was enthralled by his talk; attracted, too, by the morbid beauty of his face and by something thoughtful and aloof in his personality. He would go for minutes at a time without speaking; he did not always respond to my talk, as acquaintances do out of courtesy. He was unaffectedly simple and sincere always, always himself with a suggestion of underlying melancholy.

We sat, I remember, for half-an-hour that morning under a great bell-like chestnut, and I learned a good deal from him incidentally about painting and the trade in the old masters. He had wide and profound knowledge, and what I liked most about him was a large catholicity of taste. He could get as enthusiastic about a Botticelli as a Greco, and the old ladies of Franz Hals appealed to him as intensely as the *mayas* of Goya. He had no prejudices, no inhibitions, and his personal feelings were veiled, so to speak, by his impartiality. . . .

Time and again I sought him out and gradually learned a good deal about him. He told me he had two boys of twelve and fourteen, who were at Dunstan's famous school in Somerset, and one day he mentioned his wife; and when, out of courtesy, I asked about her, he took out his watch-chain and showed me a miniature of her that might have been painted by Cosway. It was a pretty face: a fine oval, with good features, set off by red-gold hair and long grey-blue eyes.

"No need to say 'beautiful,' " I exclaimed, "with such features and such colouring. Is she tall or——?"

"I might say the height of my heart," he reddened as he spoke, "but really she looks as tall as I do; she's about five feet six and I am five feet nine nearly."

The more I knew of Ronden the more he interested me. One day I found out that his boys were stepsons, his wife's children by a previous marriage.

He was rather reticent and hardly ever spoke of himself or his surroundings. Still, in the course of a fortnight or so I came to know him and his surroundings. He was employed steadily by a Bond Street dealer, who paid him on the average from three thousand to four thousand pounds a year— "just enough to live on," he added with a touch of bitterness.

"Lots of good writers," I retorted, "would look on such an income with envy; in fact I scarcely know a single author in London who makes as much."

"I dare say that's true," he replied; "you see the painter's appeal is universal whereas the writer is limited to those of his own tongue."

Everywhere I tested him I found he had thought for himself.

Recalling the fact afterwards I couldn't understand how a man and his wife in a Knightsbridge villa could be pinched even with a couple of thousand a year: his wife, I inferred, was probably a bad manager.

Ronden knew most of the current plays. His wife, it seemed, liked the theatre, but never went to the opera. The majority of plays, he confessed, bored him, and he often let his wife go out alone with friends.

"She's a great favourite in society," he confided to me once, "while I'm half a recluse," he added ruefully, "all but lame, you know."

One day I asked him if I could see any of his original work, and he admitted that he had done very little. "I have all I can do to keep the wolf from the door; but some day, when the boys are off

my hands, I shall paint half-a-dozen pictures I
have had in my head for years. The masters all
seem afraid of brilliant colours," he went on; "I
love colours. I want a picture to stab the eye
with contrasts. Is there any colour more gay than
scarlet or more joyous than gold, yet what painter
has ever used them freely?"

I had set him off.

"Colour is to me pure magic," he continued, his
eyes glowing. "I often go to Covent Garden on
a spring or summer morning to see the flowers. A
bank of primroses forty feet long and ten feet high
takes my breath, hyacinths by the yard make me
shout aloud with joy—masses of colour singing to
the eyes. None of the old masters knew colour.
What do I care for form or story? I love colours
—colours only, colours in contrast, colours in harmony; fair ears of corn and blue flowers; green
grass and golden buttercups—the splendour of
earth's raiment—God's, if you will."

This rhapsody taught me that Ronden might
prove as interesting an artist as he was a companion.
Our intimacy, however, was cut short by my recall
to town, and, once in London, the old life so en-
meshed me that Ronden and his curious personality
faded from my mind. It was fated, however, that
I should come across him again years later and get
to the heart of his mystery.

.   .   .   .   .   .

Everyone knows the Empire lounge in London,

where the prettiest of the half world move about
and watch the audience or the stage, and some
provincial ladies, too, come there, enticed by the
colour and movement and weird variety of the
show.

I seldom went: the slave market, as someone has
christened it, did not interest me. Life had a more
picturesque variety show to offer than could be
found on any stage.

Almost immediately after we went in we saw all
eyes directed at one of the women, who was walking
with a man. When she turned I was struck by the
rare beauty of her face. I looked at her rather
scrutinisingly; I don't know why. She was tall, five
feet six or seven, with a fairly good figure, but a
face that once seen was difficult to forget. It really
more than pretty, set off as it was by red-gold hair,
the nose small, well formed, the eyes grey-blue and
large. The man with her I knew slightly, a lieu-
tenant in the Guards,—Wyndham.

My companion seemed even more struck than I
was.

"A good-looking woman," he cried as they passed
quite close to us. "I wonder where Wyndham
found her. Splendid colouring, isn't it? I wonder
who she is. Should we go over to Wyndham and
make him introduce us?"

"As you will," I said, "but I would like to talk that
matter out with you first. There is surely no haste;
they are going to be here for some time."

So Chesterfield and I had our talk out. But all

the time I was wondering where I had seen that face,
for I had seen it somewhere, I felt sure; it reminded
me of something, I could not quite make out what.
Again and again the two passed before us, talking
very earnestly—at least Wyndham was very much in
earnest, but the lady was perfectly self-possessed and
her eyes were taking in everything that was going on.
She had evidently noticed my companion's admiration, for she certainly flashed a look at him as she
passed that was quite significant.

At length Chesterfield stood up and went over to
them, and I followed in his wake.

"Oh Wyndham," he exclaimed, "I haven't seen
you for an age. Won't you introduce us, and can't
we have supper together or something?"

Wyndham flushed, a little embarrassed. "Delighted, I am sure," he said. "This is Mrs. Ronden, Lord Chesterfield." I was introduced too, and
Wyndham went on, half shyly:

"I persuaded Mrs. Ronden to come here, though
she said she thought the Empire was barred, because
Sims Reeves is going to sing to-night for the first
time in ten years."

"Do you care for music?" Chesterfield asked the
lady.

"No," she replied, "I don't; but Reeves had such
a reputation as a singer and lady-killer that I wanted
to see him."

Mrs. Ronden! In a flash the country house in
Scotland—everything—came before me again. So
this was the goddess of Ronden's idolatry! I recog-

nised even the features, curiously alike and curiously
different, as a photograph always appears when compared with the reality.

But what was Mrs. Ronden doing in the Empire
lounge with young Wyndham? Mrs. Ronden had
two boys, so Ronden had told me, by a previous marriage, boys twelve and fourteen years of age—and
that was three years ago. She could be no chicken
—thirty-eight or forty at least—and going about
with a young Guardsman of twenty-three or four!

A fisher of men?

Clearly Chesterfield was very much interested.
He asked her quite boldly for a meeting, and then
and there made up a party for an early dinner at the
Savoy three nights later and afterwards the theatre.

"May I bring my husband?" she asked.

"Of course, of course," said Chesterfield. "I
shall be delighted to meet him. Won't you come,
Wyndham? And you?" he added, turning to me.

I excused myself. The enigma was interesting to
me; but I had liked Ronden and so I seemed to be
approaching it from a wrong angle, so to speak.

When the party separated I went my way con-
siderably intrigued.

Mrs. Ronden had the manners of a lady—yet—
every now and then her speech betrayed her. As
soon as she was at her ease a little Cockney twang
came into her pronunciation—a common twang—
and she was evidently much flattered by Chesterfield's admiration, responding very graciously with
nods and becks and ingratiating smiles.

What did it all mean?

I was fated soon to know more. Three or four weeks later I passed through the great waiting-room in the Savoy Hotel on my way to the restaurant, when I saw Ronden and Mrs. Ronden. Ronden called to me and I went over immediately. "My wife," he said, and I bowed as if I had not seen her before. But she took up the ball boldly:

"I met this gentleman the other night," she said, "with Lord Chesterfield." And Ronden asked no further questions.

Mrs. Ronden went on to tell me that they were waiting for a Mr. Stone, who was to be their host at dinner and afterwards take them to the theatre.

"Allan Stone!" I exclaimed, "the Jew financier?" He was widely known in London and I knew him particularly well.

"The same," Ronden replied.

"Curious," I went on, "that we should meet two or three times running like this, not having met before in the three years."

At that moment Stone came up and insisted that I should dine with them and go to the theatre afterwards, but I had other fish to fry. I could not but notice, however, that he seemed on the very best terms with Ronden, and especially with Mrs. Ronden. Once, indeed, he put his hand on her bare arm and I saw Ronden's face change. I wondered how much he understood, for, knowing Stone well and something about the lady, I had grown slightly suspicious. But I had to secure a table for my party and therefore rose to go. While excusing myself Ronden was sincerely kind, as always:

"I had hoped to have seen you at our little house in Knightsbridge. I have not forgotten our meetings in Scotland."

I promised to call on him shortly, and before I left I had arranged to lunch with Stone the next day; he had something very important to say to me, he said, about a great enterprise in which he thought I could help him.

The next day I met Stone at the Savoy and we had our business talk; then the conversation drifted to other things.

"A curious pair, the Rondens," he began. "I never could understand Ronden, but she is all clear enough; rather a nuisance, too. I suppose he is one of those poor painters who can never sell his daubs?"

"On the contrary," I said, "he makes a great deal of money; he is one of the best craftsmen in the trade; knows more about the old masters and about modern paintings, too, than anyone I know. You are underrating Ronden."

"No one has a right to be mean with a pretty wife," Stone went on; "and he must be very mean with her."

"I don't believe there is a mean bone in Ronden's body," I said warmly. "I think he makes a large income and lets her spend it royally."

"Good God!" Stone exclaimed, "she must be like

royalty then, for a good many of us contribute to her income."

The Jew's tone was ineffably common and suggestive, and I could not help taking it up.

"You ought not to speak like that from guesswork," I said. "I know Ronden pretty well and feel sure that he's straight."

"I have paid for my knowledge," retorted Stone curtly. "I think I am justified in talking. I can assure you that even if you have paid that lady, and paid her pretty liberally too, she has no hesitation in asking you for more if she wants it."

"I'm surprised," I exclaimed. "Ronden makes three or four thousand a year and I feel pretty sure she gets most of it."

"Oh, well," said Stone indifferently, "that doesn't go far when the lady wears fifty-guinea hats. Fifty seems to be her price," and he laughed loudly.

"Can one really spend fifty guineas on a hat?" I asked.

"If you had seen the hat she was wearing yesterday you would know she had spent more than fifty on it, and she gets them by the dozen, I believe.

"I have studied her," he went on. "She's a type. She cannot resist a pretty thing that suits her, whether a piece of lace or a hat or a pearl; she simply has to have it. It is the colossal vanity of the woman. She would not only do anything to get it, but if she had to do without it she would be ill. I remember praising her once for fun as the loveliest

woman in the world and she drank it all in and asked
for more.   I have noticed that many pretty women
when they are about forty are like that.   Their
looks are leaving them; they notice quicker than anyone that they are not getting more attractive with
the years and they become crazy for adornment.   If
what you say is true about Ronden's income, Mrs.
Ronden is crazed with vanity.

"The last time I took her out," he added, "I told
her plainly that I did not feel inclined to give her
any more fifties just for the asking."   Stone evidently did not think highly of the lady, thought he
did not seem to have noticed her Cockney accent.

A little later I met Mrs. Ronden in Sloane Street.
Thanks to Stone's teaching, I noticed that she was
beautifully gowned and beautifully hatted in a great
picture hat of filmy black lace with one black-and-
white ostrich feather.

"A wonderful hat," I said.

"I am glad you like it," she laughed delightedly.
"I like these big hats too."

"I think you would set off any sort of hat," I replied.   "I should like to see you in a small toque."

"Would you?" she said, and stopped dead in the
street.

"Certainly I would."

"Really?"

"Really!"

"Wait here a minute," she said, "and I will be
back.   I have got a dressmaker here."

She went into a quiet little shop in Sloane Street

and in a few minutes came out with a ravishing green toque which set off her henna'd mane of hair magnificently.

After praising the hat I noticed her dress and at once she became very cordial to me.

"So few men notice a woman's dress," she said, "and it is so important, don't you think? I dislike men who are so wrapped up in their own affairs that they cannot think of anybody else—like that silly husband of mine."

"I thought Ronden suited you," I said. "You look so well together. He is very good-looking, too, you know, in his dark way, as you are in your fair beauty."

"I know," she said; "his face is good-looking, but I don't think we women care for good looks in men much—not nearly as much as men care for looks in women. Then he's a cripple. I did not know that or I would never have married him."

"A cripple!" I exclaimed in astonishment. "Surely not."

"He has flat feet," she went on, "so flat that he cannot walk; he has to stay in the house all the time; he is a home bird, if you like; can scarcely walk at all without pain."

"I did not know," I said rather dryly, "that walking was a necessary marital accomplishment."

"That's unkind of you," she answered. "No woman wants a man stuck round the house all day long. I think those home birds are more jealous and suspicious than other men. I hate jealousy, don't you?"

"I don't really know," I said. "I don't think I have ever felt very jealous."

"It's a 'orrid vice," she said, and the "h" scarcely sounded; quite at her ease now, the Cockney twang came into her voice.

"I love a bit of fun," she said, "change and excitement. To stick at home all day and talk art ain't living: I'd most as soon be dead! You men have the best of it: you go out and make up to girls, and if one don't please you, another may, while we women have to stick at home and mend stockings and put on buttons for our husbands. I can't darn and won't; not for my husband; he's jealous if you like, always nagging at me. You don't know how mad he can be."

Perhaps I looked disbelief, for suddenly she cried: "Look!" and stripping off her glove she showed me her thumb. "He bent it back that night we went out with Stone till he almost broke it, the beast"; and indeed the whole base of the thumb was black and blue. "He is a jealous brute, and goes mad as those quiet brutes do. I hate such men. I don't believe any woman can care for them really."

I said nothing. The self-revelation was pretty complete.

I wondered vaguely whether matters would drag on in this way or whether there would be a catastrophe.

"I do not expect you often get hurt," I remarked; "you are far too pretty to be hurt much by any man."

Her appetite for flattery was absolutely limitless; she smiled at once, perfectly happy, and I think we separated at her own door without an idea entering her head that I was more sorry for her husband than for her.

. . . .

One day I got a note from Ronden from Hampstead asking me to come to see him. I could not make out why he had suddenly transferred his household belongings from Knightsbridge to Hampstead. I had not seen either him or his wife for some time, so I went out to see him gladly. He had got a little house in Hampstead right up on the Heath, but I could not help noticing that his hair was all silver above the ears and he looked looked ten years older.

"I wanted to see you," he said, "because I have cut loose."

"What do you mean?"

"I have got rid of Helena. Her real name was Ellen, but she called herself Helena," he added bitterly.

"I am sorry," I said, not knowing what to say and waiting for him. I saw he was primed to the muzzle.

"Good God!" he said, "what fools men are. I was trying to make myself a painter when I met her. She told me that she must have more money for her boys, and so I did journeyman's work, as you know, leaving the artist in me for a more convenient season. I thought she was satisfied with the three or four thousand pounds a year I gave her; she had all the dresses—everything she wanted. Yet she took money on all sides, I am sure, and from all sorts of men. The shame of it! She must have asked Chesterfield for money."

"I know nothing about it," I answered, "though I have been his friend for years."

"Englishmen are not good at intrigue," said Ronden, flaming, "as Jews are and the other men she gets. Chesterfield sent her two pearl ear-rings. She told me they were false, so I thought nothing of her having bought them. Then I got a letter of his one day; just a note; I had opened it and looked at it before I realised what it was. He excused himself, saying that the pearls had cost him eight hundred pounds, and he could not send her any money at the moment.

"She must have asked him for money shamelessly. And I had given her my whole life, minted my heart, my blood, my artist faculty—everything, to give her all she wanted.

"She cares for nothing but herself—not even for her children; she was quite willing to hand them over to me, give me full care and control of them. She has no natural affection at all. . . . She used to cry with rage, but would stop herself quickly because her eyelids swelled and got red and remained inflamed a long time in spite of her bathing. I

never saw her cry with sorrow except once when
her hair began to come out in handfuls; then she
cried so that I thought she would be ill till I told
her she would only lose more hair by doing that,
and then she stopped quick enough. . . . She's all
vanity!

"I came away from Knightbridge; I could not
stand the place though I loved it. I took this
house away from everyone. Fancy, suppose I
had met Stone! I know that she has had money
from him. He would never have dared to touch
her in public as he did if she hadn't prostituted herself. The shame of it! I am afraid to go out for
fear of meeting anyone I know. Everyone I know,
I seem to have known through her—and from all
of them I feel sure she has had money. Oh, damn
her, the——!"

I was silent for a moment. Then I said: "Look
here: why not turn round now and give yourself to
your art, do your real work as you ought to have
done long ago? You are still a young man."

"You're right," he said, his despairing eyes
searching mine. "I must do my work. That is
why I wrote to you. I felt you would help me.
We all have to bear some burden, I suppose."

"Sure!" I broke in; "and the heavier the burden
for the artist the more he is able to reveal afterwards. You remember Shelley's

'Our sweetest songs are those
That tell of saddest thought.'

Turn your anguish into soul-beauty. That will be your consolation and ultimately your reward."

"That's it," he cried; "that's it. I knew you would help me. I'll get to work, though I'm nearly out of my mind with grief and rage and shame. I loved her," he said, lifting despairing eyes to me. "God! how I loved her. Why? Why?" And he fell to graming.

I got away by promising to come again soon, and in a week or so I went back, hoping he would have at least begun a picture; but no—he was as wild as ever, or worse.

"I've done nothing," he replied bitterly to my questioning. "She has ruined me. What do you think of that for a bill?" and he took a bill and threw it across to me. It was for hats for six months—eight hundred pounds.

"I have paid a dozen at least of those," he added. "They must come to an end soon for I'm bankrupt. Why are such women allowed to live? We kill snakes that are harmless and let such creatures live——"

There was madness in his eyes. I grew anxious for him.

"Get to work," I cried, "and stop thinking of the past. You are doing yourself harm; you must stop resolutely and get to work." I insisted and persisted till he got out a canvas and stretched it and promised me to get to work on it at once—Ruth, a Biblical subject that had been in his mind for years.

Before I called again to see how Ronden was get-

ting on the Greek-Turkish war had broken out and
I was sent to Turkey by *The Manchester Guardian.*
It was one of the great experiences of my life, but
I must not stop now to draw the moral of it.

When I returned to London some six months
later I found two letters from Ronden: the first
written shortly after my departure, thanking me for
my encouragement, telling me how well he was getting on and asking me to come to see him when my
occupation permitted. The second was months
later; in it Ronden just asked me to call. Its reticence puzzled me; what had happened?

As soon as I had a free afternoon I went up.
Ronden received me in the old friendly way, but now
nothing could disguise the change in his appearance.
He was an old man; the hair grey, the smooth skin
all lined and, worst of all, the brown hazel eyes
were only half alive; the whole face had changed,
lost colour, brightness, hope.

He received me pleasantly, and I explained my
absence and silence; he had guessed that I had been
called away.

"But what have you done meanwhile?" I asked.

"I'll show you," he replied quietly; "not very
much, I'm afraid"; and he led the way to the studio.
As we passed through the drawing-room I was
startled by a still-life of astonishing beauty: an
arum lily in an apple-green vase with primroses—a
glory of colour. "First-rate," I cried. "I was
sure you'd make good; I'm so glad."

Ronden nodded his head half sadly and went on;

on an easel in the studio was a portrait of his wife,
very frank and straightforward; but it left one with
a doubt of the woman; it was like a head by Titian
for richness of colour and veracity; near it a great
picture of *Ruth in the Alien Corn,* Boaz in the middle distance and far-off hills framing the scene.
What was the matter with it? The Ruth was
plainly a Jewess—black hair and brows, large dark
eyes and lips a thread of scarlet, and yet——

I felt puzzled: the landscape was really good,
the corn wonderfully rendered, the shadows pools
of purple on the ground.

What was the matter?

I turned with a question in my face: Ronden without a word drew up another easel and showed me
the head of a well-known star actress: Miss Jay's
face was unmistakable: yet?——

Suddenly the truth flashed on me. Both portraits
had a look of Mrs. Ronden.

I turned to Ronden just as he gripped me by the
arm. "You see it too," he exclaimed with savage
intensity; "it's *her* face, always *her* damned soul that
looks through brown eyes or black, always *hers*——

"Has she cast a spell on me or am I crazy?" he
raved on. "I've tried everything. The first figure
pictures I did I destroyed; they were all plainly
Helena; damn her! So I got models and copied
the models religiously; all to no use, still *she* looks
out of every canvas at me—the beast——

"She's got into my blood," he whispered, "and

I shall never get her out"—and his face went grey
with despair.

"Oh yes, you will," I cried. "Your landscapes
are lovely; that still-life alone is worth any labour
and this *Miss Jay* has less of her look than the *Ruth*.
Stick at it, man, and you'll work yourself free——"

He shook his head. "It's worse than you think,"
he began. "I got a model a month ago for the
figure; the girl was beautifully made, but as I drew
her—thighs, breasts, all her lovely outlines—beside her I saw more distinctly than the real figure,
the lines of Helena; I couldn't draw the model,
man; all the while I was seduced by the other; her
memory is stronger than reality; I am her slave;
yet I loathe her and her prostitute's soul. Was
there ever such degradation?"

"Stick at it, man," I cried. "Ten years of passion cannot be wiped out in six months; but you'll
get free—why, one of these days you'll be falling
in love with some model and that'll be a final cure;
you're young yet, not forty?——"

"Thirty-five," he replied. "Perhaps you are
right; your courage does me good; I'll go on. I
was nearly giving up——"

"Do some more flower work and vases," I said.
"Set yourself tasks; put a rumpled damask cloth on
the table; throw white roses on it and red cherries
and gold oranges—make it all flame with colour:
call on your real talent all the while; and work,
man, work; don't think; work is the cure."

"I knew you'd help me," he remarked quietly. "I believe you're right; I'll get at it again; I'll do a flower piece that'll astonish you. I promise. I'll work."

"I want to live and get free," he added, "work myself free. Thank you, thank you!"

I left him on this in good heart, as I thought, and resolved to visit him again in a week or so; but my own work pulled me, and one day a month later when I came into my rooms I was surprised to find on my mantel-shelf a flower piece superbly painted. It was my thought realised. There was the crumpled tablecloth and a vase and cherries thrown about and oranges of red-gold and among them a broken nutshell showing a little dried-up kernel—all marvellously rendered.

"Who sent it?" I had asked my servant before I saw it and remembered. "When did it come?" I added.

"This morning, sir," he replied, "a messenger boy brought it, just like that, so I put it up there."

I nodded. 'Twas too late to go Hampstead that evening; on the morrow I'd go.

The morning after when I opened the paper the first thing that struck me was:

DEATH OF AN ARTIST: FRANK RONDEN.
SUICIDE SUSPECTED.

And the journalist went on to tell how Ronden's wife had left him and how he had grieved for her and tried to get her to return—the usual rigmarole of romantic lies.

To say I was shocked doesn't convey an idea of what I felt then and for weeks afterwards. He had taken, it appeared from the inquest, a whole handful of trional—taken it purposely; he had paid his servant the night before and cut up and burnt all his pictures.

If I had gone to see him as I intended, could I have saved him? Who can tell? We men are so ignorant, so short-sighted, so selfish.

A month later I ran into Stone. "The very man I wanted to see," he shouted. "You know Ronden killed himself for that b——[I nodded], but you don't know that she's got hold of Lord Haliburt and he's adopted her two sons: she's Lady Haliburt now—what do you think of that?"

"Never!" I cried.

"It's true," he grinned; "she came to me and begged the money for the wedding dress, and though I only half believed her story, I risked the fifty— fifty was her figure, you know—and by God she brought it off. She's a marvel—that woman!

"I'm glad I don't like your cold women," he added: "they must love the game if I'm to be interested. Lord Haliburt has made a bad bargain."

I took no interest in the outcome. Poor Ronden's flower piece will always be with me, teaching that a too great love is a mortal malady.

AS OTHERS SEE US

AS OTHERS SEE US

THIS is a story I heard told by the hero of it,
if hero he could be called, Raoul de Reval.
When I first met him Raoul was a handsome and charming man, in the early twenties, of
good medium height, with upwaving golden moustache, noticeably fairer than his brown hair and
hazel brown eyes; he had good teeth and very red
lips. He was well made too, slight, but better looking because of his slightness, and finished perfectly
even to his hands, with their small wrists and long
tapering fingers. Before he got his degree as a
lawyer in Paris he had begun to write, and his
stories were curiously like himself: elegant, sympathetic, attractive, charmingly finished. I used to
praise them to him, and he sought me out time and
again, soliciting my praise almost like a girl.

I could not tell him the truth, that his stories and
articles—all he wrote, in fact—were of light weight.
The characters he selected were French characters
of ladies and gentlemen of the better class, and they
were not deeply realised nor their circumstances
deeply etched in, yet the dialogue in his stories was
excellently conventional, but true to the convention.
I told him one day in a fit of frankness that if he

ever had a great passion or a soul-searing, tragic experience he might become a great writer.

I left Paris and did not return to it for many years. After three or four years of absence I got a letter from Raoul asking me to send him, if I could spare it, five or six thousand francs, as he was in sore need. The letter was almost incoherent, pencilled in great haste: the address given was in the rue Ramey, up in Montmartre somewhere—a common, out-of-the-way little street. Nothing less like a begging letter could be imagined. It was even a poorer specimen of the art than the worst of his stories. I happened to be in funds and sent him the money, and, strange to say, did not hear from him again, no acknowledgment even, which seemed to me curious; but as I had registered the letter I shrugged my shoulders and promised myself if I ever met him again to find out what had happened—what hole he had fallen into, for he had always seemed to me to be well off.

Curiously enough, I did not get to Paris to stay for twelve or thirteen years: my work in London had been engrossing and I only passed through Paris without stopping long enough to look up any of my old friends. One day, however, the taxi-cab I was in nearly ran into, in fact did graze, a splendid limousine. An angry face was thrust out of the window of the limousine and the owner of it told my taxi-cab driver what he thought of him in picturesque French. The voice screamed, and it was from the thinness of the voice that the thought

flashed across me that this was Raoul. I called him
by his name, and the next moment we were shaking
hands on the pavement at the corner of the rue de la
Paix—shaking hands and grinning as old friends
met by happy accident.

He wanted to know where I was staying—when I
could come to see him—a dozen questions; finally
we fixed a rendezvous for the next day at dinner.

He was living in the Parc Monceau, and he presented me to his wife, who seemed to me older than
Raoul—a good deal older. They had no children,
though they had been married six or seven years.

As I sat at table with them I could not help wondering at the changes wrought by time. Raoul had
got much stouter, his face had lost its character of
handsome elegance. He was still good-looking, but
the flesh about the jaws was sagging into a double
chin. There were the beginnings of gummy bags
round the eyes: in fine, he was a man who had not
got better-looking with age, but commoner, coarser.

The apartment was splendid, looking out on the
Parc Monceau and beautifully furnished.

After dinner Madame Raoul had coffee served in
her husband's study and left us to ourselves rather
prettily, saying she knew we would have lots to talk
over: she had heard so much about me from Raoul
that she was sure I would have nothing but a good
influence on "Toutou," as she called him, the pet
name usually given to a little dog in France.

"Well, Toutou," I said, smiling, "you seem to
have landed on your feet. You never answered my

letter from that place in the rue Ramey. It is seven years ago now."

"No," he said, "but your help saved me at a critical moment. I shall be delighted to send you a cheque in return."

"Won't you tell me about it?" I asked. "You were not a wild adventurer in life," I added, giving my surprise words.

He hesitated a little while and then began:

"You used to say that I might be a great writer if I had a great passion. Well, the great passion came. I fell in love with a girl on the *Bouffes* (Les Bouffes Parisiennes, a theatre for lightest comedy). She was pretty(but what took me was her perfect figure: you know I was always a lover of sculpture rather than of painting; then, too, she was impudently vivacious, with a curious understanding of life and pert shameless speech. Talk about *argot!* she was born in the gutter and really used the language of the *Apache* with most extraordinary verve.

"Is it our opposites that tempt us so in life, attract us so desperately? I was *pincé,* by her naked vulgarity!

"I took an apartment for her and put her, as we say, *dans ses meubles,* and treated her as I would have treated a wife. I wonder now I didn't marry her; I was crazy about her. I had a little patrimony my father had left me, a couple of hundred thousand francs, just enough for me to live on with my stories, but Augustine was terribly extravagant (yes, that was her name; it suited the little grig by contrast). Money slipped through her little claws like water, and at the end of three or four years I found I had spent everything. I had not written much in the forty months, so I had to try to get work on a paper. I had a bitter year: I fell as one might fall through a tree, clutching branch after branch that broke away with me and let me down lower, but Augustine stuck to me until our apartment was to be sold up. Then I discovered that she had been deceiving me for the last six months or so, and she told me quite coolly she was going to live with my friend Levallière, who had arranged to take over the furniture and the apartment and pay the debts."

At this Raoul got up: "It nearly killed me, you know," he said. "I had no idea one could suffer so intensely, and as time went on the ache of loss seemed to increase. I could not write or work; but I had a dear student friend who lived in the rue Ramey, and I went there and he took me in. I had a sort of brain fever, and it was when I had recovered from the fever and had made up my mind in my weak state to take up life again and not be beaten by a *gourgandine* that I wrote you that letter and you sent me the money, which practically saved me, gave me a chance anyhow to go home to Brittany and get quite sane again, and there on the *plage* I met my wife.

"She was a Mademoiselle Pousset, daughter of the great grocer and rich. She fell in love with me, and I saw that the sensible thing to do was to fall in love with her as far as I could and marry her, which I did promptly. She has many good qualities, my wife, and the Augustines teach you how valuable goodness is: a little heart is worth a lot of body—in anyone.

"We went to spend our honeymoon in Switzerland, in Lucerne, and the honeymoon was extended to three months because my father-in-law and mother-in-law were arranging our apartment for us."

I interrupted him by saying: "At any rate, they have treated you very well in that respect."

He burst out laughing.

"Oh," he said carelessly, "this is the price of *The Wingless Victory*." He pointed to a statue in the corner, an original from the Acropolis. "You know my story of that name?" he went on.

I replied politely: "Oh yes, I have heard of it."

"You have not read it, then?"

I replied: "No, I have had so much to do in England."

"Then I will give it to you to read, because it explains my life, or a good deal of it. I shall never forget the disappointment and depression of my marriage. I think I will tell you the real truth. My wife has a habit of falling asleep, and she slept in the train as we neared Paris. Very few women look their best when they are asleep. That little beast of an Augustine used to, but Madeline, my wife, doesn't, and she slept all the way to Paris, I remember, as we returned. Every now and then she would wake herself with a loud snore and go to sleep again, and I was feeling woefully depressed: life seemed trivial and worthless: in fact I had a bad taste in my mouth, so to say.

"No one met us at the station, though I had told my father-in-law when we were due to arrive. My wife found nothing extraordinary in it; she yawned and said it was very kind of her mother to leave us alone the first day, and we drove straight to the apartment they had prepared for us.

"You never saw such an apartment! It was ugly and it was prim, business-like, and while my wife tried to go into ecstasies over it, I yawned myself stiff and thought of how to find some way to alter it.

"Pousset, my father-in-law, was proud of me as a writer, and when he came round next day he showed me how he had arranged my study with books of accounts and a proper desk to write at, and he hoped I would begin to work as soon as possible! And Madame Pousset pousséed, so to speak—very worthy people in their way. Next morning I found that my wife had arranged my desk, put out pens and paper, everything; like her father, she urged me to sit down to work.

"I don't know whether it was the spirit of contradiction inherent in humanity or some ebb after the flood-tide of the honeymoon, but I could think of nothing but Augustine and the way she used to flit about the room, often in a chemise or less, and come and curl up on my knees and coax me not to write, but to come out for this, that, or the other piece of fun. So I let myself go and began describing her. She really had the prettiest figure I have ever seen in my life. She was just like one of the little Greek statuettes on the famous balustrade of the temple in Athens; she might even have stood for that statuette there of *The Wingless Victory*. I began eagerly, passionately, to write the whole story of our relations, and especially I tried to picture her slim loveliness and make it vivid by her crude bold speech and gutter phrases."

Again he laughed.

"What are you laughing at?" I asked.

"I am laughing," he replied, "because my wife got hold of the chapter where I described the girl's perfect figure and her comment was characteristic:

"'It is wonderful, you know, Touton,' she said, 'but everybody will recognise that you are sketching me, and, though I like the picture enormously, I'm afraid your heroine wasn't a good woman.' Good!

"I stood in the room when she went out and held my head in my hands and asked myself was it possible that she could see herself in this lovely figure I had described. After all, you know, my wife is a certain weight.

"Ah, women are funny creatures. I went on with the book and it had an enormous success, and my father-in-law, when I told him I was going to have this new apartment on the strength of my first big cheque, was good enough to double the cheque, which enabled me to buy that little statuette of *The Wingless Victory* there in the corner and furnish this flat."

"I must read the book," I said; "but you have written some others, notably that wonderful study of a *gourgandine,* which can be compared only to the *Odyssée d'une Fille* of de Maupassant."

"Really? You think that, do you!" he cried. "I know I have no genius," he went on; "you made that clear to me years ago, but that book of mine is a book of pure observation."

"Where on earth did you observe an ordinary woman as closely as that?—the little passing tempers of her, the funny view of life that such a woman has got, the extraordinary calculation in her and the everyday little phrases by which bit by bit she reveals herself—commonplace phrases that yet light up the character in a most extraordinary way? Where did you get all that?"

Raoul rose and stretched himself, smiling:

"To you I can tell everything. Well, all those sayings were taken down absolutely after little talks and quarrels with my wife, taken down absolutely from her lips—her very words. It is merely a close study of married life."

"Good God!" I exclaimed.

"The curious part of it is," he went on, "that she thought *La Gourgandine* a poor book. 'It may be like some common girl,' she would say, 'but now only a year after our marriage you have left me out of your pages: I shall always prefer *The Wingless Victory*, where you described my very figure.'

"My wife has never recognised any likeness to herself in the exact portrait and that's the key to her contentment: our mortal happiness is all—illusion and self-deception."

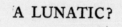

A LUNATIC?

A LUNATIC?

I HAD gone down to the forest heights beyond Tunbridge Wells to rest and recruit, and one day I found a road across the common, where I used to walk undisturbed by passing motors.

It was a heavenly morning—one of those English August days which show how lovely summer can be in the foggy island. The air was like warm fresh milk, the walking pleasant, and I sauntered for an hour or more amid patches of purple heather and golden gorse. Away to the south I could see the rounded bare outlines of the Downs like the backs of galloping hounds and about me the good smell of warm earth perfumed by clumps of canary gorse and beds of shy violets.

I had walked farther than I intended, for suddenly I came out on the highroad and noticed on my left a pair of ornate iron gates leading to a broad gravelled walk into private and well-kept grounds.

A man was standing almost in the gateway, a quietly dressed man of good height. A second glance showed me that he stooped a little; his face was thin, rather narrow too, with a short brown beard and moustache. Our eyes met and I was interested at once by something interrogative in the quick glance of his lively brown eyes.

"A beautiful day," I remarked.

"Beautiful indeed," he bowed courteously; "warm enough to sit in the open without fear of a chill."

It was half an invitation and I had nothing to do.

"I don't see any seats," I replied, "or I would sit willingly, for I must have walked four or five miles, and am just a little tired."

"There is a seat over there," he answered invitingly, pointing to the right, "by the little wood. I often sit there." We turned and walked together.

"I came up here for rest and change," I said by way of introduction. "I'm a writer."

He responded immediately:

"A writer? How interesting! Do you write essays or stories or——"

"Both; but I prefer stories and pen portraits of important contemporaries."

"Portraits!" he repeated, pursing his lips reflectively. "The painter makes money by them; but I don't much care for mere presentments of life. I prefer works of pure imagination."

"You can put as much imagination into a portrait as you like," I replied.

"True, true," he exclaimed, "and I have no right to criticise."

"Merely to love imaginative work," I said in response to his courtesy, "is to be one in a million of our time."

He shrugged his shoulders deprecatingly.

"I wanted to be an artist, but they wouldn't let

me, and now I do nothing—am no good to anyone, no good at all. Merely an observer."

"Lucky man," I replied. "Work is apt to dwarf one or deform. The labourer is bent and old at forty, and his hands are as insensitive as his soul."

"Do you think so?" he questioned. "I have always regarded any artist's work or writer's as a sort of mental exercise."

"It should be, I suppose," I answered; "but once you have created a character that people like, they pay you to go on repeating yourself so often that it grows mechanical, tiresome."

"I see," he said, nodding his head. "New thoughts," he went on meditatively, "are not appreciated by the common. But won't you be seated?" and he motioned with his hand.

It was an ordinary bench placed in a sort of bay in a small pine wood. Brown needles under our feet made a thick slippery carpet and the air was fragrant with the strong scent of the pines.

"So you think the world hates new ideas?" I began.

He smiled and lifted his hands as if amused.

"So do you, I'm sure. We all know only too well how the world treats its guides and leaders; in exact proportion to their value they are punished: to Spinoza and Cervantes the world gave poverty and contempt, perhaps because they would both have used money nobly; to Jesus shame and torture —the crown of thorns—probably because He was a little proud and very sensitive to pain. Did you

ever think of that?" And he twined his thin hands
round his knee and looked up at me with his head
on one side—all question.

The man interested me peculiarly.

"That's probably true," I exclaimed. "But who
are you?"

"No one; just an onlooker at life," he replied;
and then as if in explanation: "I have no books
down here, and I hate newspapers, and having nothing to read I am forced to think and think all by
myself; but most people are offended by new ideas."

"There are some of us," I broke in, "who would
give more for new thoughts than for anything else
in the world."

He smiled, and the smile lit up his whole face;
he took off his cap at the same time and I was struck
by a certain breadth of forehead I had not noticed
before and a fullness over the temples outlined by
the greying hair.

"Who can he be?" I asked myself, a little surprised.

"Do you really care for new thoughts?" he went
on, with hasty eagerness, "or is it only your own
glimpses of truth that interest you? I find so few
who care to follow another's mind. I am a recluse here, have been for years, and so have a store
of thoughts which seem to me, I confess, valuable.
If I did not bore you I should like to develop to
you some of my ideas. They are not taken from
others anyway. Books are the grave of originality."

"You could not please me more," I cried; "fire away."

"When I was a young man," he began, "Darwin and his new moral law, 'the survival of the fittest,' had just begun to affect thought, and at first I tried hard to believe that the fittest were, other things being equal, the best. Like most other men I wanted to find a moral purpose and meaning in life, but bit by bit I was forced to see that the fittest were often morally the worst." And he paused and looked at me as if to mark how I received the bomb.

I contented myself with nodding; the line of thought was familiar to me, and I was eager to learn whither it had led him, and how far he had gone on the untrodden path.

"Who are the fittest in our society to-day?" he went on. "The most greedy, the most sordid, the most unscrupulous; those who desire money, and more and more—the millionaires—the wolves who prey on their weaker fellows. They are the fittest; they survive and propagate their kind.

"Of course we try to believe that it is only the weak and the wastrels who come to grief and are being killed off in favour of the sharks and wolves; but we soon find out that even that consolation is denied to us. It is not only the weak and the wastrels who are 'unfit,' and are therefore condemned to disappear. Our present industrial civilisation inevitably kills off the best as well as the worst. It murders the artists, the saints, the lovers of their kind still more implacably than the idle and improvident, the drunkards and the vicious. That's the truth, the awful truth. If you doubt it, ask yourself which the millionaire is inclined to help— the drunkard or the saint, the vicious dope-fiend or the man of genius who despises him and his golden calf? The rich man often helps the worthless with his gold, the genius never; that's the truth. The best and the weakest are the unfit.

"And that way dejection came upon me and I fell to despair." . . . He paused for a moment: "I am not a lively companion, am I?" he asked with a short laugh.

"Go on," I said. "I am not frightened, though I've never heard it put so forcibly; but do not forget that some of the wisest and best are strong also, and can beat the wolves at their own game; and some of the wolves, thank God, are noble and fight against their kind to protect the helpless. I hope everything from the wolves who become watch-dogs."

"Pshaw!" he exclaimed excitedly. "That is how you cheat yourself. I used to gull myself at first in that way, but now I see clearly.

"What is the purpose of the world? You can judge God by His acts. Is it not true? Let us do it; let us read Him by His deeds.

"I will now take Nature where from one end to the other the strong prey on the weak; from the tiger to the beetle there is no law but force and cruelty and desire; sympathy even is a form of fear.

You will give me Nature I suppose? Even Tenny-
son did that!"

I nodded, smiling. "Yes, yes, I will give you
Nature—'red in beak and claw.' ''

"Then let us go to man, where God is seen at
His best," he went on excitedly; "to man, where one
should find high purpose and noble desire if anywhere."

"First-rate," I cried; "just my own thought! I
have always believed that great men show us the
highest purpose of God; the growth of the soul in
man is the only revelation of the divine."

"Ha, ha!" he laughed; "let us test your divine
by facts.

"What do you see in man? Take the commonest
truth, the most universal. It is a proverb in a
dozen languages that the very tall man loves the
very small woman, and that the little bit of a woman
admires a man six feet six. Have you ever thought
why? Because mediocrity is the purpose of God;
the whole pressure and urge of the world is to produce the mediocre. God loves mediocrity."

I looked at him in astonishment.

"In everything the same," he went on; "in mind
as in body; wisdom is won by childish coquetry, and
purity adores a notorious libertine. Marcus Aure-
lius, the noblest pagan, falls in love with the prostitute Faustine; the most reasonable of men, Socrates,
selects the barking shrew, Xantippe; Goethe marries
his cook; Shakespeare, a woman half as old again
as himself, whom he detests and leaves, choosing

instead a wanton, who deceives him with his dearest
friend. Think of it! Goethe and his drunken
cook, a woman who preferred a sodden sleep to
thoughts that wander through eternity.

"The love of opposites points to the same purpose always: very big men marrying shrimps of
women; mediocrity the aim and end and purpose of
the world.

"At length I came to the heart of truth: 'God
Himself must be mediocre.'"

"Evil thoughts do come," I began when he
stopped speaking, 'and there is some ground for
them; but still there are glimpses of hope. If
mediocrity were indeed, as you say, the whole purpose and end and aim of things, then the Christs
would have been forgotten at once; they would have
passed out of our minds like the weak and the wastrels: but they do not; the finest all survive like
beacon-lights—Shakespeare, Goethe, Hugo, Balzac,
and the rest."

"Like marsh-lights," he broke in sharply, "to
lure you astray. Why won't you see the fact that
is before your face?

"Suppose," and he turned to me, holding out
his hands, "suppose that you have written a story;
would you be content with it? would you go on
making replica after replica of it, by the million, by
the hundred million, by the thousand million, year
in year out, through all eternity? Of course
you wouldn't; you said as much: not even for pay
would you repeat yourself even once.

"You must admit that the creative artist who repeats himself is an ass. And what does God do but that? Countless myriads of commonplace men and women—whole generations of them—all mediocrities, all, all. Throughout all the ages God is in love with mediocrity, with the common: 'was uns Alle baendigt, das Gemeine!' (that fetters all of us)"

"But they do not survive," I said; "and the great ones and their influence do survive."

"For all the good they do," he answered, laughing, "they might as well be dead. Jesus, who always spoke for the poor and the humble and the outcast, for peace and love and gentleness, has brought war and hate into the world. But let us keep to the idea of the creative artist. That will show us God in His true light.

"God created the sun to rule the day and the moon to rule the night. But why only one sun, and why in pity's sake only one moon? Why not a dozen suns and a score of moons lamping it every night?—moons of every shape and colour, so that a girl could look at her lover and say: 'That night you kissed me first and made me conscious of my body the moons were like primroses in the sky'; or some Cleopatra would remind Antony of the night when to celebrate their marriage she bared her beauty to the moons that flamed like orchids here in red, and there in yellow; and a youth would cry to his mistress: 'When you looked at me with love that night our moon was like a passion flower set in the purple Heaven, and when we went home afterwards a great marigold lit our steps.'

"Now, alas! the moon in waning or in waxing must always be the same—ivory light or silver light—something for the poets—a sliver of cheese in the illimitable vast. God a creative artist! There never was a creature more devoid of the creative impulse if creation means originality; if creation means mediocre, fishlike productivity, then you are right. He is prodigious; a gigantic Conan Doyle.

"Ah, you listen and so I'll confess to you.

"I was an artist in the beginning and tried to paint my dreams. In one picture I put three moons with astonishing effects of light and shade, and everyone who saw it laughed and jeered—the idiots.

" 'Nothing like that in Nature,' the critics sneered.

" 'Sure,' I answered; 'don't you wish there were?' Oh, the fools!

"Don't you see, man, God hates originality; that's the first truth. And He is immoral; that's the second great fact. Ha! that makes you gasp. And I will prove it, show you how.

"If suffering were to be any good in life it would have a moral purpose, would it not? You would suffer in exact proportion to the injury inflicted on the organism. But no! Tear your nail to the quick and you will suffer more than if a knife were driven through your heart. Pain has no relation to morality; you are pained gratuitously, suffer agonies for nothing: a scratch hurts more than a death wound; it is all chance and senseless. Moreover, God is cruel! He loves to punish without reason and beyond measure."

I found almost nothing to reply. "Pleasure, too, is disproportionate?" I said half to myself.

"Sure," he cried; "sure. Pleasure is a lure to disease as pain is malevolent cruelty. Pleasure is as immoral as pain. God knows nothing of morality, cares nothing for man or man's welfare. Think of man's miserable state: one organ for pleasure and a dozen for suffering. One small palate to taste with that gives both pain and pleasure, but a stomach, liver, spleen, lungs and useless yards of intestine and God knows what besides, all to give pain and no pleasure at all!

"Pleasure the rare exception, pain the rule. Everyone knows that our nerves feel pain and suffering ten times more keenly than pleasure or joy: how often does one scream with pleasure or go mad with joy? God is a Sadist who delights in our suffering!

"Look at the world to-day. . . .

"Men are like God. Look at the cities they build; dreadful places, hideous. A big meaningless street or two and leagues of hovels and festering animal dens, all sordid, squalid, commonplace.

"If I were the master of London or Paris or New York I would build a city to delight the soul; beautiful houses all different and all healthy. Why,

I'd have a children's park that would be a paradise for the young, where paving-stones should gather themselves into big rockeries to mirage mountains for the tots and there should be sandy beaches and lakelets for the girl children to play by.

"I would have a comic street too, of course, that would be a delight to all of us—a really comic street, where the chimneys would lean over the eaves and listen to what went on below; where lamp-posts instead of being ranged stupidly at equal distances (they measure them to be exact!) should be distributed about like lilies pensively reflecting on the light they shed in dark places: here one should stand in the middle of the street with head bent over as if the neck were too weak to bear the weight of light, and there one should lean against the wall weak-kneed as if drunk, with a flickering gleam to mimic the intelligence floating in a drunkard's eyes.

"And the side-walk. It should surely wander into the road at places and return when you least expected it; and the houses should all have character: here a marble palace should lean against a frame shack as if for support as in real life. Oh, oh! I would build a City of wonders.

"But now every street is dull and sordid, for men are as mediocre as the God that made them. I hate God and I hate His dull commonplace world, and I hate most of all the myriads of cruel, greedy, ferocious men and women He has made, the slimy spawn of selfishness——"

"There, there," said a voice, and as I looked up I saw a man of middle age, who had come out of the wood behind us, touch my companion on the shoulder. "Don't you go exciting yourself, Mr Scroper. God's all right, I guess, It's your wits that are wrong."

The keeper turned to me: " 'Tain't good for 'm, sir, exciting 'isself like this. He do 'ave strange ideas though, don't 'e, sir, and 'e do talk 'em fine."

All the light had gone out of my companion's face. As he was led away he would not even look at me. Was he insane? I could not believe it.

After a moment's pause I hurried after him:

"There's nothing wrong with you?" I cried; "nothing."

He turned to me with a wan smile:

"Thank you, thank you!"

"But why are you here?" I burst out.

He lifted his hand with resignation:

"The mediocrites," he said gently, "are our masters."

IN CENTRAL AFRICA

IN CENTRAL AFRICA

I

I HAD gone to Zanzibar and hired carriers for a hunting expedition and then pushed into the wild alone—for uneducated natives are not companions. Week after week I had marched, rising steadily towards the great lake, killing game only when food was needed, going wherever the spirit moved, in perfect lawless freedom.

One evening the great mountain Kilimanjaro etched its mass against the opal sky and I made up my mind to climb it, or at least to get to know it, and a week later we were among the foothills. One day the negro captain I had put in charge of the men told me the carriers were all frightened, for a great chief lived on the mountain, and he was a slave-dealer and might send them away in chains to die far from kith or kin on the further side of the sea.

I asked his name. Suleiman, I was told; and for curiosity's sake or for adventure I resolved to visit him. Two days later, just as we were breaking camp, three men from Suleiman presented themselves with a letter asking me to halt my men and accompany the messengers to the Great Chief. In spite of the captain's warnings I took my English servant and went with them.

All three were fine specimens; the leader, a chief of the Swahili, must have been six feet three and was broad in proportion, and two of his tribesmen, both above medium height, were stoutly built and armed, as I noticed at once, not with assegais or clubs, but with cheap repeating rifles.

"Where did you get them?" I asked the chief, pointing to the rifles.

"Chief Suleiman," was his reply. Evidently Suleiman, in his eyes, was a sort of god, for he mouthed the word like a challenge.

That first morning the march lay through scattered clumps of trees and bushes of thorn and was steadily upward, I remarked, for towards evening the air was at once lighter and cooler.

Next day we got into the forest itself and marched along a narrow winding path, which ran like a black ribbon through the gloom. Often I had wondered who first made these winding ways through the forest trees and thorn bushes; wait-a-bit thorns the Boers call them, and indeed if you get caught in them you are likely to wait a bit and be uncommon glad to get free with a whole skin, for the thorns are often as thick and long as a man's little finger and as sharp as a steel fishhook, and these hooks are set at all angles on tough branches. I'd rather brave a German barrage and the worst barbed wire than that murderous, elastic entanglement.

All that day I walked behind the big chief and learned from him half a hundred Swahili words;

savages, I found, are very like children, and love to give themselves airs as teachers.

Early in the afternoon he stopped suddenly and pointed into the thick bush on the right—"Buffalo."

I looked, and after a while distinguished the beast's head, chiefly because he kept moving his ears to ward off the flies; but for the life of me I could not see his body.

"Shall I shoot?" I asked the chief.

"If you can kill," he replied shortly.

I thought the doubt ridiculous at ten yards' range; besides, I had a double-barrelled ·450 Rigby and felt that if one shot failed to kill, the second would not. I knew the chances, knew that if he were not killed the great beast could rush through the thorn bushes as we would go through rushes, whereas we should all be kept to the path, and as he could move twice as fast as we could, in ten minutes he would have killed us all. But I felt sure and, besides, I was excited. The beast was looking right at me, so I aimed just below the horns and between the eyes and fired. With a grunt the buffalo pitched forward on his knees and rolled over, dead.

In a trice the Swahili tribesmen had cut their way through the thorns and we were standing over the dead body of a fine young bull. They all made much of the shot, though in truth it was not a good one. Either I had aimed a little high or the rifle had thrown high at the short range, and only the force of the nitrous powder had driven the steel-pointed bullet through two inches at least of the bossed horn into the brain. As a matter of fact the whole head was traversed, for we found the bullet in the skin of the neck.

That evening we halted in a clearing and I saw an African feast; it began about six in the evening and went on till after midnight. Each man stuffed down ten pounds, at least, of buffalo meat, and with a bottle of Cape "smoke" they soon became half delirious with excitement, mimicking my shot and the fall of the buffalo a hundred times. The chief, too, though less excited, was just as enthusiastic. I was immediately christened "Rahala," or the man who kills dead.

Next morning the chief told me that we had nearly reached our destination, and I found that every quarter of a mile or so we had to turn out of the path and make a detour in order to avoid some murderous trap or snare. The whole forest was mined for some three miles deep. I began to have a high opinion of Suleiman's power and cunning.

I was soon to have convincing evidence of it. A little after noon we came through the forests into the open and found ourselves in cultivated fields of maize and vegetables. I did not pay much attention to these surroundings at the time, for there was a broad road rising steadily, and half-an-hour or so of rapid walking brought us out on a grass-covered slope and in front, a mile above us, there was a collection of kraals, and people moving about like bees before the hives. Beyond the grassy slope again the mass of the mountain rose in almost a cliff at least a thousand feet in height and thickly wooded; the kraals were all together near the foot of this natural bastion.

About a quarter of a mile away from the Big Kraal we were met by some messengers who came to conduct us to the presence of the Great Chief. We found Suleiman seated alone in front of his kraal, with at least two hundred Swahili warriors about him, all armed with repeating rifles; the source of his power was obvious enough.

Chief Suleiman impressed me; he was an imposing figure, with large head, beaked nose and hawk-like eyes, evidently an Arab, or Semite, if you will, of pure race. Usually his eyes were half closed, peering at once and reflective, with a myriad of tiny wrinkles about them, as if he lived in the Great Desert, where men have to shield their eyes from excess of light. Some remark would interest him and suddenly his eyes would flash wide open and the imperious hawk-glance would shock you. He was somewhat above middle height, forty-two or forty-five years of age; his thick black hair and beard were slightly grey already and he was rather stout. An air of high courage and command seemed to emanate from him. He rose from his chair to meet me, took my offered hand, put me in a seat on his right and sat down. While this was going on all the men about him bowed with their hands on their hearts and profuse "salaams." It was evidently peace.

Though he talked Swahili at first I soon found

that Suleiman knew English and French, and talked both much better than I could talk Swahili. Strange to say, as soon as he spoke English he put off some of his pride of place and became more human and friendly. I learned that he had been born near Tangiers and had lived for ten years near Biskra: like most successful men he preferred the English to the French. He was curious to know in what way I represented the British Government, and when I assured him I had no official position whatever, he was still more curious to find out why I had come at the risk of my life to Central Africa. I told him I loved the wild freedom of the life and loved to watch the habits of wild beasts and birds, and even to note the characteristics of native customs. "It rests me," I said, "to live as a hunter and watch life as it was a hundred thousand years ago."

"Do you collect ivory?" was the next question, for ivory is the road to wealth in Africa.

"No. I have a pair of enormous horns just for specimens, and that is all."

"How do you protect yourself from wandering bands of warriors of this or that tribe?"

"I have a dozen well-armed men," I replied.

"As well armed as mine?" he asked, and I nodded, smiling; no conception of the seriousness of the question even dawned on me.

We talked more than an hour, and then he invited me to dinner in his kraal. The food was very good indeed, but the wine was a sort of native product, and I contented myself with tasting it. After

the meal we came out and sat before the kraal, and
suddenly a dozen girls came and danced before us,
Arab fashion.   Some were negresses, but one or two
were Arabs of the famous Ouled-Nail tribe, heredi-
tary dancers by profession, as graceful as possible,
sylph-like, indeed, for they all exercise assiduously
and train themselves as strenuously as our prize-
fighters.

The show amused and interested me, for the girls
were of different colour and very different type, but
all had been selected by no mean judge for their
beauty.   The Arabs were, of course, white, but
there were two or three golden-brown girls, whom
Suleiman spoke of disdainfully as Copt-Christians,
and in contrast with these the shining bronze of the
natives, with their pearly white teeth and flashing
dark eyes.

The natives were only clothed in the "moocha"
tablier about their waists; but the Copts and Arabs
were swathed in silk veils that floated about the slim
figures, now revealing, now concealing rounded limbs
and curves.   The music was a slow chant of the
girls' voices, punctuated by the beat of the tom-tom.
Large fires had been lighted, because at sundown a
chilliness came into the mountain air.

It would have been impossible, I thought, to have
imagined a more primitive or a more picturesque
scene.   The girls danced between us and the fires,
their figures and waving limbs etched, so to speak,
against the red glow, while all around the natives
sat or hunkered down as a living frame.   Gradu-

ally the girls left off, the natives first, and then the Copts, while the trained Arab professionals continued to show all their powers, from the famous *danse du Ventre* to posturings and abandonments, such as the Almas of India display. The fires had died down and the round yellow moon had climbed high above the trees.

"Bedtime," said Suleiman. "You will find beds and servants yonder," and he pointed to a kraal near by.

"You have given me a royal entertainment," I said. "I am infinitely obliged to you."

His eyes flashed and, as we parted, he summed up:

"Power and women. What else is there in life?"

I laughed and made some remark about wishing that I could show him equal hospitality and that I would do my best when my carriers came. He waved his hand to me: "To-morrow is another day."

Next morning I was a little surprised to find all my men grouped round the kraal Suleiman had allotted them. The Chief told me he thought I should be more comfortable if he hastened to bring up my baggage and stores. I could only thank him for his foresight. At the same time a doubt of his good faith occurred to me, but I showed no sign of any suspicion; in fact I scarcely felt enough for the apprehension to become articulate.

I had armed a dozen of my best men with Springfield rifles and automatic pistols, and Suleiman, I found, was very eager to know how far the pistols could carry and whether they would kill or not.   I soon proved to him that they were more trustworthy and far deadlier than his "trade" rifles, which often burst or jammed.   Seeing his admiration of the automatic pistols I made him a present of one and remarked casually that when I returned to the coast I'd send him up a hundred; his face lit up at the promise.   Before leaving me that morning he pointed out a kraal some distance away which he had allotted to my carriers and baggage, but, fortunately for me, my armed guards always slept about my kraal, and so I told him.   The Chief bowed, smiling (he was really a born diplomat), and went away after saying he would send food in for me.   Fortunately, again, I asked him to lunch with me, as I had some champagne.

We had a great lunch and Suleiman, though a Mohammedan, drunk much more than was good for him, and indeed was not to be seen for the rest of the day.   But about nightfall one of the Arab dancers whom I had admired the evening before presented herself, declaring proudly that she had been sent to me as a present by the Great Chief. I laughed and shook my head, telling her she must return to the Great Chief's kraal, as women were not allowed in my religion.

She seemed much hurt, told me she could serve me in many ways, and began unwinding her swathing veils.   When I stopped her showing her beauty she would have me touch her arms and breasts and hips

to prove that she was firm everywhere, as a trained
boy might have been.   Were it not for her too large
nose she would indeed have been a model of rare
beauty.   But I could not assume the responsibility
for her, so I sent her back pitilessly, and as it turned
out I could not have acted more wisely, for I thereby won a priceless ally.

The third or fourth day I had been Suleiman's
guest two or three things happened that gave me
pause. Tapp, my English servant, came to me,
saying he could not find his automatic pistol, and
when I questioned him I found that he had been
flirting with one of the Arab dancers, and he believed she had taken it. Tapp was a Cockney
youth, undersized and ugly, but wiry and healthy,
extremely clever with horses and, strange to say,
with machines also, willing to make himself useful in
any way, brimful of the spirit of adventure, yet
quick-witted in life and extraordinarily loyal. "I
thought I ought to tell you the story, sir," he said,
"because that Chief Suleiman's a slippery sort of
gent, and in my opinion he's up to no good; he's
put our carriers slap-bang in the middle of his sol-
diers, where they're no use to us," he added significantly.   I told him to keep his eyes and ears open
and report anything suspicious, and I assured him
that I was on the look-out, though I didn't believe
in any danger.   I had a couple of automatic pistols
that were not being used, and I knew the value both
of a small gift and large promises.

The next afternoon Suleiman came and told me

that he wanted me to come to his kraal to see his
daughter. I looked surprised, and he added, "My
only real child. The others don't matter; but
Rachel is beautiful. I was married to her mother
in Algiers," he added. "She was of the great tribe
of the Ouled-Nail—the tribe in which all the women
are dancers from generation to generation." An
hour or so later I went over to Suleiman's kraal,
and I took with me the automatic pistols; his people
would perhaps cease stealing them when he got a
couple for nothing. But I forgot what I came to do
when Rachel, his daughter, came towards me out of
the gloom. She was short rather than tall, with
very fair skin, and showed hardly a trace of her
Jewish origin. Her nose was slightly aquiline, but
the eyes were blue—at once candid and cordial eyes
that met yours fairly, and lent her a sort of innocent
air, at variance with her quiet, self-possessed manner. There were contrasts in her that piqued
curiosity. "I wonder if you know why I am glad
to meet you?" she asked, after father had introduced us.

"No," I replied, a little astonished at the unusu-
alness of the greeting. "No, I can't imagine, except,
perhaps, out of loneliness."

"I have books," she replied, "and am not lonely
—at least not very," she added truthfully. "But
I wished to meet you because my father said you
knew French and had lived in Paris, and because—
well, because you sent Micah back to him—the
dancer, I mean," she added hastily, for the Chief

seemed about to break in, as if he wanted to complete her thought. "He thinks Micah a miracle of beauty."

"She's certainly pretty," I said, "and has a lovely figure; but she speaks only a very few words of French, and I thought she'd be happier with her companions than with a stranger of another race."

Rachel clapped her hands together with a little crow of delight. "I told you so, father," she said; and then to me: "You were quite right; she snores dreadfully; what could you expect with that nose! But won't you be seated? What's in the package?" she added, pointing to the parcel in which I had the automatics.

"Something for the Chief," I replied, and I took out the pistols and handed them to him. Suleiman started and the hawk's eyes stared at me. I saw at once that Tapp's suspicions had been well founded. I should have to take care.

"I had a couple of these pistols over," I added significantly, "and I thought you might like them, Chief, and if you do, and find them useful, I can write to London and get you as many as you wish."

He was trembling with eagerness. "I'd like to try them myself," he broke in, "then I'll talk to you."

"Sure, sure," I interjected, putting the parcel with the cartridges into his hands. "You have five hundred shots there, and fifty will tell you all about them."

In a trice he was out of the kraal, his usual dignity thrown off in his excitement. As we sat down Rachel looked at me.

"You are very clever," she said thoughtfully, "and I like clever people. But how did you know?"

"Know what?" I asked.

"Know," she replied, "that my father is crazy to have all new weapons. His power," she added, "is founded on his rifles."

"Oh, that's nothing," I replied negligently. "The Chief has treated me well. I wanted him to have the pistols."

"When you write to London for more," she said quietly, "I'd show him the letter and let him send it. It'll get to Mombasa quickly," she added, smiling.

I noted the advice and gave Suleiman the letter the morning after. Meantime I went on talking to Rachel. For some reason or other she interested me. She moved gracefully and was beautifully formed—as, indeed, all the women of her tribe are apt to be; for as dancers they have developed in the centuries the perfect dancer's figure. They are nearly all slight and round, with small breasts and fine limbs. Most Arabs, I think, have small wrists and ankles, and Rachel happened besides to have an interesting, pretty face and the curious, frank ways of one who has always been in authority, so to speak, and had to consider nothing but her own pleasure.

Almost at once she asked me: "Are you married?"

and when she heard I was free she rounded her
shoulders and hugged herself, so to speak, in a funny
little gesture, very expressive of intimate pleasure.

At once, too, she asked me about Paris. I had to
tell her what women did there, and speak of theatres
and dances and jewellery and dresses—dresses
especially. "How did they dress in the evenings?"

A little maliciously I told her how low the dresses
were being worn, and her eyes made pictures of all
I saw and all I left unsaid as well.

"Do you like those low dresses?" she asked, and
I confessed that I did, that the Paris Opera House
was a splendid sight with the myriads of nude
shoulders set off by the diamond and pearl necklaces.

The music, too, interested her, and she got up and
went over to a sort of musical box, which presently
wheezed forth *Voi che Sapete* and *Caro Nome* and
half-a-dozen other favourite airs. Rachel had
musical talent and could hum (and did hum in and
out of season) more tunes than I had ever heard of.

In many respects she was a child of nature, and
if my talk did not interest her, she usually began
humming or singing some tune to herself in a way
that set all my nerves on edge. What pleased her
must evidently please everyone else, and she had
no voice, poor girl!

I soon found that she thought over everything I
said and acted on it very ingeniously.

Suleiman asked me to dinner a day or so later
and told me Rachel was going to be there, and sure
enough she appeared in a dress without shoulder-

straps, as I had said, and cut far lower even that one would find in Paris. But her figure was almost perfect, and she was as pleased as a child when I praised it.

When the dancing girls came in she drew back, and we talked together in the mouth of the kraal. She asked me again whether "she was pretty this way," and she touched her low dress. I told her she made one want to kiss her, she was so pretty. "Why not?" she asked simply, and our intimacy began.

After my gift of the automatics and my letter to London ordering a hundred more pistols of the same calibre Chief Suleiman became very confidential, and gradually I learned all about him and his pretty daughter. Whenever I was in any doubt as to the Chief's motives Rachel enlightened me and unconsciously, at the same time, discovered her own character.

Suleiman was a Mohammedan, and while studying him I found I was getting an astonishing insight into his religion; for his faith was merely the garment of his spirit. He was of an incomparable, a brutal sensuality; he could imagine no heaven without houris, and his individualism was just as marked. Mohammed's view of life was that of the Arab sheik; he wanted "justice" for all men, kindness to dependents and those of the true faith; but there he stopped. Suleiman had no conception that the claims of other weaker human beings were as valid as his; Socialism was clean beyond his horizon; he

thought it as silly as an American banker thinks it
or a French Bourbon. And Rachel was as self-
centred as her father, as resolved to get what she
wanted out of life. All this dawned on me gradually through the intercourse of many days and
weeks and shall be told in the next chapter. Here
and now I just want to say that as Suleiman grew
friendly he showed a wonderful hospitality. He
devised a great game-beat for me, where I feasted
my eyes for days and nights on all sorts of strange
beasts; he taught me, or one of his conjurers did,
that snakes talk, and often I spent the night listening to the "mambas" or cobras making weird
noises, which the conjurer often interpreted rightly.

He always knew, for example, when they were
going to separate; the curious way they rubbed their
bodies and heads together before they parted taught
me that our human "good-night kiss" may perhaps
be found all through nature, even in the rustling
of the leaves.

But feastings with dances afterwards constituted
the chief element in Suleiman's hospitality, and one
incident illumined the man's whole being to me in
such an astonishing way I must give it as it took
place.

I had asked him about African cooking, I remember, told him I wanted a distinctively African
meal, and he promised he would have one prepared
if I cared to provide the "sweet, foaming wine," as
he called champagne.

In a day or two the feast was arranged, and as usual now Rachel took her place at the board. We had an ostrich egg on a sort of native spinach, and then a small roast that looked like a leg of lamb or kid. I should have thought nothing of it if Suleiman had not expatiated on its merits even before it was brought on the table.

"What sort of meat is it?" I asked casually; "what do you call it in French?"

"Taste it," he said, putting a large slice on my plate. "Taste it and tell me what you think; this is the best meat in the world, the sweetest and most tender, and agrees with everyone; a fever-sick man can digest it."

I looked at Rachel and she nodded, smiling encouragement. She evidently thought as much of it as her father. But now my curiosity was roused; I turned the meat over; it was very close-grained and evidently tender, though it was dark in colour.

"What is it called in English?" I asked. "Surely you know its name in French or English, or at least you can describe it." And I filled their glasses and my own with champagne.

Suleiman saw he could get me no further, so he began: "It is the best meat on earth; that is, tenderer," and he pointed to the pear-like joint, "than lamb, sweeter than kid or chicken. If you won't taste it till you know, then learn that it is the thigh, properly kept for a fortnight and smoked, of a young girl about thirteen years old——"

"Did she die?" I asked, cold with horror.

"Sure," he said with a loud laugh, "that's not alive, is it?"

"Was she killed?"

"In a row," he remarked, waving his hand. "She was in a slave-gang and got in the way of a Swahili's spear when her mother fainted."

The whole scene flashed before me.

"Good God!" I cried, and poured down my glass of champagne while drawing back from the table.

They both laughed. Suleiman said: "Look at the effect of mere prejudice, stupid prejudice. Try it, man, and you'll get the same liking for it we have; won't he, Rachel?"

Rachel agreed, but I got up and went to the door of the kraal. God's sunshine even seemed unreal to me—from that moment on I began to think better of some prejudices.

II

I have often wondered since how I came to put myself into Suleiman's power without hesitation or suspicion. And even more curious it seems how I learned to know the dangers of my position bit by bit and just in time to save my skin.

After my letter to London, ordering one hundred automatic pistols for him, Suleiman promised me a wonderful entertainment.

"I will show you all Africa can show," he said, "in beauty."

Naturally I thanked him, and we were still in talk when a sort of headman, Abdulla, "salaamed" before him, calling "Sultan."

This Abdulla was a Bajoon, a tribe of mixed negroid and Arab descent, a mixture which gave him intelligence above the average. He was very short and broad, evidently powerful, and though probably not more than thirty always had his head shaved— shaved, as I found out by chance, with a piece of broken bottle-glass. Abdulla was the Sultan's right hand in all ways, and deserved to be. He was not only intelligent as Europeans estimate intelligence, but a master of slave-craft and bush-craft as well. He came, it appeared, to announce to the Sultan that a herd of elephants had been located on the other side of the *shamba* (the Swahili word for a native clearing). Abdulla's excitement was contagious, and when he wound up with *Wananame labuda,* "Males too, I heard!" I saw that Suleiman was keenly interested.

"A troop of elephants, isn't it?" I asked.

"Yes," replied Suleiman; "males and females in a herd. Do you love shooting, like most Englishmen?"

"No," I answered. "But I'd love to study a mixed troop on the feed without being seen."

"Without being seen," repeated Suleiman disdainfully, "is easy enough: elephants have poor sight; but without being smelt is another thing. Besides, the males seldom feed with the females. Elephants are hard to kill," he went on significantly, "and a wounded elephant is more dangerous than a buffalo in bush."

"Our modern rifles kill elephants as easily as deer," I replied carelessly.

Suleiman flashed his hawk-glance on me, in surprise I thought, and his daughter's phrase came into my head that her father's power was "founded on his rifles."

He was probably even more desirious of getting fine rifles than automatic pistols. But for the moment he said nothing, save that he would have the elephants kept in the same bush till next morning. Abdulla assured him that was easy, for the forest was full of rubber bushes, and the elephants loved the fruit.

That evening I met Rachel as usual between the kraals and went with her for a walk. She spoke of the elephants.

"Of course, if you'll kill elephants for father he'll do anything you wish," was her way of putting it.

"But you said he was rich," I put in lamely.

"No rich man is ever rich enough," she remarked shortly, as if announcing a universal truth. Probably because she felt she had been abrupt she added: "Riches give power. But why do you object? It surely isn't the danger?"

"No, no," I replied; "the contrary is nearer the truth. Modern weapons and scientific knowledge have made killing wild animals too easy and too safe to be exciting. Besides, I hate taking life——"

She shrugged her pretty shoulders. "Why not

do what is safe and easy?" It was evidently useless to argue, so I changed the subject.

About three in the morning Abdulla woke me
with the news that there was one big solitary bull
elephant as well as the herd of smaller animals. I
felt little scruple in killing an old "rogue," and consequently in about half-an-hour we had entered the
bush preceded by Abdulla. Tapp followed me with
my ·404 Rigby, while I carried a ·450 Westley-
Richards. Suddenly Abdulla stopped and showed
us the footprints of the herd; most of them were
round and not more than twelve or fourteen inches
across, significantly he pointed to an oval spoor fully
twenty-one inches in length—"the big bull."

After feeding, the old solitary had walked fast
for a couple of hours, for it was nearly six o'clock
before we found warm droppings, and then, moving
cautiously, came on the bull lying down and apparently asleep, though one huge ear was mechanically
fanning the air to his trunk, so that even in sleep
he could get the scent of any intruder.

"Shoot, shoot before he wakes!" whispered
Abdulla in great excitement; but I saw that it was
easy to get a better view by moving a few yards
to the left. Holding my hand up for warning I
crawled round and soon got the head quite distinctly.
I had never seen such horns; but all my attention
was concentrated on the saucer-like depression in
the forehead of the great beast just between and a
little lower than the eyes. Aiming at the bottom of
the depression for fear the rifle should throw high

at the short range, I fired. To my astonishment nothing happened; nothing, save that the ear stopped moving. I saw the bullet-hole. Was the beast dead or only stunned? Should I fire again? The next moment Abdulla came to me: "Shoot again, quick!" I shook my head. I wanted the credit for killing the bull with a single shot. "He's dead," I said, and the event proved I was right.

Luck was favouring me persistently. I was not a good shot; yet even Selous, who was a fine shot, had bagged many elephants before killing one with a single bullet. And the horns of this one were very large, weighing over one hundred and sixty pounds, and splendidly regular, except that the tip of one had been broken off years before. . . .

I knew about Suleiman to guess that the more he wanted my rifles the less he would say about them; but before noon he came to ask me if I wanted the bull's horns, and when I said "No," he announced a great entertainment for that evening. "My daughter says she will be dressed like the Paris ladies," and he added, smiling through half-closed eyes, "the dancers will not."

At first Rachel did not appear; but instead a great troop of Swahilis, mimicking an attack on a village and the carrying off of the women. The whole thing was staged with a prodigious realism and excellently acted. Then a dozen Hottentot girls moving to the slow melancholy beat of the tom-toms; they were hideous I thought; short steatopygous figures of the most extravagant proportions. I

found that if a girl sat down she could only get up
by turning over on her face and rising with the help
of her hands.

Then a crowd of natives of various tribes and
half-breeds danced with the Arab professionals. It
interested me to notice that some of the natives had
as fine figures as the Semites and danced as well.
In particular, one mulatto not only had an excellent
figure but a bright, vivacious face to boot, and
danced as lightly as any sylph. I asked her name
and found she was called Leah and much liked by
Rachel, her mistress.

It was fascinating to watch these hundreds of
half-nude girls mimicking before one the vagaries
of savage courtship, for all the dances were in essence seductive symbols of love and desire, and
Leah, for example, had caught all the tricks of the
Arabs and used them with an astonishing artistry.

I called her over to me and could not but admire
her. She was tall, with surprisingly regular
features; the skin was citron-coloured, but soft and
clear, the eyebrows pencilled and the large brown
eyes were simply startling. Looking closely I found
that their beauty came from the fact that there
were golden specks in them radiating light and
warmth. Her figure was all grace, though somewhat fuller and rounder in outline than the Arab
dancer type. Leah was very quick and intelligent,
and caught the meaning of my Swahili in spite of my
grotesque blundering. While talking with her,
Rachel surprised us.

Leah moved away as Rachel came to the entrance of the kraal. Her dress was of shimmering blue and draped about as low as the European full dress, but tightly swathed about the hips, Indian fashion. It was very becoming and set off her fair skin and shapely figure.

"You're late," I said.

"I hate to see those creatures," she replied, indicating the little fat, crab-like Hottentots; "they seem to me caricatures of humanity. What a pity Leah is coloured, isn't it? If she weren't, she'd be quite pretty, don't you think?"

"She is more than pretty as it is," I said, "and has a lovely figure to boot. I think she is lovelier than any of the dancers."

"Really!" rejoined Rachel, a little piqued. "Perhaps you told her so."

"No," I rejoined; "I'm sorry, but my Swahili does not go that far."

Rachel broke in: "Do you like my dress? Is it right at last?"

"Perfectly right," I replied, "and extremely becoming; you are *en beauté* this evening." Smiling, she made me a little curtsy for my praise.

"I'm glad," she began, after seating herself at my side; "every woman likes to know she's looking her best." After a short pause she went on: "You've covered yourself with glory again I hear, and the horns are really fine. Won't you tell me about the hunt?"

"There is nothing to tell," I answered, "and I'd much rather talk of you."

"Let us go to my room then," said Rachel, rising. And now I must explain what the room was.

Almost midway between our kraals and a few hundred yards down the grassy slope was a clump of trees with little clearing in the middle, and here Rachel had made her pet withdrawing-room—only a roof, leaf-covered and supported on four stout poles. Beneath its shelter a wooden flooring raised six inches above the ground was covered with rugs and cushions. On moonlit nights the place was nearly as light as day, but without the moon it was ghostlike, eerie in dark glooms and silence.

The natives all believed that the grove was spirit-haunted, and not one of them, not even Abdulla or Leah or the Sultan himself, would willingly come near it. With glee Rachel had told me how she had heightened this dread by smearing phosphorus on the posts one afternoon, and then visiting the place at night, accompanied by Abdulla, Leah and some of the dancers. When they caught sight of the posts they all fled shrieking, and afterwards spread such tales of what they had seen that Rachel's resting-place was free of spying eyes and curious ears for ever. Hither we went that evening almost in silence. The edge of the estrade was in the full light of the moon, and there we seated ourselves.

"I hated to hear you praise Leah's figure," Rachel began; "it's stupid of me to say so, I know, but I

just can't help it. Why do you think her figure the
loveliest of all?"

"I don't," I rejoined; "I haven't seen more than
half-a-dozen. How could I say hers was the
loveliest?"

"Were her shoulders prettier than mine?" she
went on earnestly.

"No, no," I replied, after apparently weighing
the question; "and your skin," I added slowly, "is
milky white, which gives you the advantage."

Suddenly she stood up, and in a moment, as with
one gesture, unveiled herself to the sandals.

"Is her figure prettier than mine?" she challenged.

"No, no," I cried, seizing her in my arms, and
delighted to find that she was as firm and lithe and
shapely as the prettiest of the dancers; but the next
moment she had wound herself out of my hands and,
with a quick turn, had swathed herself again in the
soft Indian silk. She sat down and I drew her
to me.

"You shame me," she said with quivering lips.
The next minute she added hotly: "I'm a fool,"
shaking off the emotion in proud revolt.

I soon comforted her, however, and my enthusiastic warm praise quickly brought her back to her
usual good humour; indeed I think the little fever
fit did her good, shook her out of her habitual mutism. She became really affectionate and prodigal of
caresses, and for the first and only time showed
pretty fancies.

"Do you know why I was so jealous and am now

so happy?" she asked with shining eyes. "Because
I dreamed of you last night, and the first man a girl
dreams of will meet her soul when on its way to the
Judgment!"

"Is that a Moslem belief?" I asked in wonder.

"Do you like it?" she countered.

"It's charming," I exclaimed, "quite charming;
but I never heard it before."

"The tribe I come from, near Fez," she went on,
"believes, too, that all a man's good deeds turn into
a lovely girl, who meets his spirit to give it courage
and hope in the dread hour. The better man he
has been, the lovelier the angel. The woman's lot
is different. You find an ideal of beauty, whereas if
we have been good, it is the first man to whom we
give ourselves, even in desire, who appears to com-
fort us on the dark way."

"I thought that in Mohammed's teaching," I exclaimed, "no woman entered Paradise——"

"How awful!" she broke in; "you are all wrong,
wrong. Ayesha, the Prophet's wife, is highest
among the holy, and Zahra Fatimah, his daughter,
sits by his feet in heaven. Think, even after bearing two sons she was called the Virgin. Everyone
knows that. Every Moslem believes it." I was
amused by her earnestness and delighted with the
pretty imaginings. It was the first touch of poetry
I had found in this child of nature, and it really gave
my liking for her a fervour of spiritual intensity
entirely lacking before. And this deeper feeling
made me bold, and I took her on my knees and

began kissing her with glowing lips and praising her.

"You are lovely, lovely," I whispered; "but why didn't you let me see you longer and imprint your beauty on my heart?"

"Hush," she said prettily, putting her hand on my mouth, "and tell me why you love beauty so excessively. We women don't."

"One of our poets, named Spenser," I responded, "has given the true reason." I repeated to her the lines:

> "And every spirit, as it is more pure,
> And hath in it the more of Heavenly Light,
> Lo! it the fairer body doth procure
> To habit in——"

"It isn't true," she interrupted. "I know a—— If it only was true, what a wonderful world it would be. Oh!"

I had stirred her at length, and she kissed me now as I kissed her; but soon she pouted and restrained me, and in my vexation I quoted another couplet to her, wondering whether she would understand it fully:

> "She partly is to blame, who has been tried,
> He comes too near who comes to be denied."

But that sort of wisdom is within the ken of every girl, and she just shook her head.

"To put off is not to deny," she pouted, and I

kissed her for the word; but when I sought to detain her, she said simply:

"Lady Moon is going to bed. My father will wonder; and surprise and suspicion are of kin, you know," she added, "and just now I don't want to vex him.

"My father's beginning to think you're a wizard or magician," she went on, smiling, "for your shooting surprised everyone. He told me to-day that he liked you; he is willing to have you as a son-in-law."

She said it quite casually, as if the whole thing were fixed and arranged. I was more than astonished. I had flirted a little, kissed and paid compliments as one does to a pretty girl; but matrimony—straight off—without more ado—I was not prepared for it. I grasped at the first straw of excuse to gain time.

"Marriage," I cried, "is a costly business, and I'm a poor man—very poor."

"Father'll make that all right," she replied; "he's rich enough for anything."

"But I mustn't take your father's money," I replied. "I don't like being a parasite."

"What matter who has got it," she remarked, with a superb indifference, "so long as we can have all we need. Kiss me and don't talk nonsense."

I did as I was told, but the curious command in her word and voice stirred me to revolt. I can't explain why, but I began to look at Rachel critically from that moment.

She was certainly pretty, and the face with its
ivory skin, candid blue eyes and rounded chin, had
no suspicion of hardness; but the imperiousness in
the girl was extraordinary.   Perhaps I resented it so
strongly because I had always been used to taking the
lead myself.   Suddenly as she moved the moonlight
fell on her chest in ivory radiance and showed up a
dozen or so small, curling, black hairs.   It was the
first time I had ever seen hairs on a girl's breast.
I don't know why, but at once a suggestion of negroid or Indian intermixture came into my mind
and my critical observation became depreciatory.

When she reached the kraal, ten minutes later,
Rachel clapped her hands for a servant; she wanted
to know where the Sultan was, and when told he
would be back soon, she wished to prepare his
chibouque.

I noticed now that she was short; in ten years
she would be stout; she was just an ordinary pretty
girl with a domineering character.   As she resumed
her seat she began to hum Mimi's song from *La
Bohême*: "Mi chiamano, Mimi."

Involuntarily I shrugged impatient shoulders.
Interminable evenings of boredom intensified by
badly hummed music came over me in a wave.
Rachel had no gift of conversation, knew no literary
language, took no interest in the best that was
thought or known in the world.   Nine hours out of
ten she was uninteresting.   In the tenth, however,
she showed rare qualities.

Ever since the word marriage had been spoken

she let herself go and she showed me her real nature. She was curiously passionate and even magnetic; she seemed to know all the ways of love by intuition, and her heat was contagious. At the same time she was reticent in speech to an extraordinary extent and would give no account in words of her feelings or sensations.

"Why talk of it?" she used to say when I questioned her, and with a *mon petit homme* she would close my lips with a kiss. She was always eager to talk French and to learn French phrases. Paris was her Mecca.

Now, telling love's secrets is half the joy of intimacy, and her persistent silence at first annoyed and then exasperated me. I think she might have won me had she given up her mutism or even tried to relax her rule and please me now and then by a frank confession. But her imperiousness was the very soul of her. She was not only unwilling to constrain herself in any way, but apparently incapable of understanding any desire but her own, and absolute reticence was natural to her.

She didn't even recall the past, as lovers are accustomed to do, and retrace the flowered steps by which love came to his dominion. If I told her how I first discovered this, that or the other trait in her she would listen, it is true; but never respond in like manner. She was as dominant as an empress, and through her I realised that small and ill-furnished minds and hearts can be even more despotic than great and rich natures.

Bit by bit I turned against her, and as my affection died out I set myself to master my desire. After all, the body is easier to subdue than the heart. "I am not going to marry Rachel": that was a definite irrevocable decision, and when I returned to the present I found her still humming the intolerable hackneyed tune, as if to confirm my resolution.

Next morning, when dressing, I asked Tapp how he was getting on with his courtship. "Like a house on fire, sir," was his frank avowal. "They don't let the grass grow under their feet, these Arab girls."

"What do you mean?" I asked.

"Leah says we'll be married when you marry Rachel," he explained.

"Leah is very pretty," I remarked, "and dances wonderfully. Are you in love with her, Tapp?"

"In love," he repeated. "Every man's in love with a pretty girl when she makes up to him. Leah is very clever."

"Do you want to marry her?" I probed.

"Does a man ever want to be tied?" Tapp countered, with a grin.

"Well, if you wait till I'm married," I concluded, "you'll wait some time."

"Miss Rachel means business, sir," warned Tapp seriously. "She has sent to Mombasa for her wedding dress, veil and orange blossoms."

"Good God!" I cried, "who put it into her head that a veil and orange blossoms were necessary?"

"Me, sir," replied Tapp unblushingly. "I

thought you might want a little time, so I mentioned
the orange blossoms casual like. You ought to take
care, sir," he went on; "that Abdulla is crazy after
Miss Rachel, and before you came along he had a
good chance, Leah tells me."

The idea of Abdulla as a rival killed my affection.
I looked on him as an inferior, as a mere servant.
Had there been passages between them? I must
find out. "I wonder," I began, "if Leah would tell
you how far the courtship had gone?"

"Sure," replied Tapp unhesitatingly, "me and her,
sir, is that thick she'd deny me nothing. Leah is a
good sort," he added; "and beautifully made, sir,
isn't she? A perfect picture, but I don't care for
'em so dark myself."

"Find out what you can, Tapp," I concluded,
"and let me know if we can get away without
trouble. I don't mean marrying, that's certain."

"There'll be bad trouble," said Tapp, "when
Miss Rachel finds that out; but we needn't cross
the stream till we come to it. When will the automatics reach Mombasa, sir?"

"How did you know about the pistols?" I asked.

"The Sultan tells everything to Abdulla and
Rachel, and she and Leah are like sisters; they're
always talking. She asks Leah whatever she wants
to know; Leah is a sort of help to her. Suleiman
meant having all our pistols when he brought us up
here, only you promised him more, and now he's half
frightened of your rifles; they all think there's magic
in 'em. They're a honeducated lot."

"Well, keep your eyes and ears open," I counselled, "and let me know if anything important happens. I'm not afraid of Suleiman, but we don't want to fight if we can get away peaceably."

"We could get away all right," rejoined Tapp, "and with our guard too, by all going on some hunting expedition; but how to get the carriers and baggage and rifles out of the Sultan's clutches will be a job, especially if Miss Rachel is against us."

"Do your best with Abdulla," I replied. "I might arrange with the Sultan to go to the coast for his guns with Abdulla and bring back my marriage licence."

"That might work," cried Tapp. "Abdulla will help, I'm sure. Leah says he would have tried to kill you long ago, only he fears your magic. No one ever killed an elephant before with a single shot; that's frightened them all. Even the girls put out a finger when you come near, Leah tells me —afraid of your devil.

"But are you sure, sir, you don't want Rachel? She's very pretty."

"Prettiness alone soon loses its appeal," was my reply.

"That's it, sir," cried Tapp; "these girls are all right for a week or a month, but I likes 'em more refined if I have to live with 'em." He had said it in his way.

From this time on I began to think what pretext I could devise to get away. I was not anxious, for, after all, European wits, I knew, are better than African.

A little later Suleiman drew me aside to consult when the marriage should take place; the dresses could be delivered in a month. Would some date a couple of months ahead suit me?

"The truth is," I replied, "I haven't money enough to keep myself, let alone a wife."

"Leave that to me," said the Sultan. "Rachel will not go to her husband empty handed."

I felt I was on the wrong track. "Besides," I added, "I shall have to go to Mombasa too."

"Why?" he interrupted.

"To get a licence," I rejoined lamely; and then, as I saw I had made no impression, a brilliant idea occurred to me. "A consular officer, you know, must be present as a witness, or there is no marriage in England or France or any civilised country. I must get a consular officer as 'witness,' and a licence, or Rachel would not be accepted anywhere as my wife. Why, I haven't even a Prayer Book," I cried, as if shocked.

His eyes narrowed and the wrinkles all showed; but the suspicion or apprehension of the unexpected was only lulled, not stilled. I set my wits to work, and then remarked casually but seriously: "I think, too, you should have at least a dozen modern rifles. I had no idea how bad your guns are, or I'd have ordered for you rifles like mine instead of automatic pistols. Abdulla says you never kill buffalo, let alone elephant, with a single shot, and you've seen that I always do. It's the rifle does it. With a dozen rifles like mine in the hands of men like Abdulla and yourself you would be invincible for the next twenty-five years."

I had won. I saw it in his eyes and manner. "If you'll do that," he exclaimed, "I'll do more for you even than I promised Rachel. I'll send a slave-gang, not of five hundred, but of one thousand, with you to the coast, and sixty thousand pounds of ivory is a fortune, you know," he remarked regretfully, not a thought in his head of the poor human beasts of burden carrying each sixty pounds of ivory, besides yoke and food and scanty belongings, through that awful tropical candescence. His inhumanity confirmed me in my purpose. Bad men make us worse, just as good ones make us better.

I had won if Rachel could be fooled as easily.

Of course I saw Tapp and talked it over with him.

"Beat it into Leah's head that a consular officer as 'best man' is necessary," I said, and made him repeat the phrase "best man" over and over again.

"Abdulla is keen to get you away from Rachel," Tapp responded. "He let out to Leah the other night that she hasn't kissed him once since you came, and that he was really resolved to murder you when Leah put it into his head to get you away instead. We'll have no difficulty with him, sir."

"Did he really say Rachel used to kiss him?" I

asked, jealousy stabbing me with the memory of her wonderful kisses.

"Sure," replied Tapp unhesitatingly. "Leah says they were as loving as we are, and if that's true, Miss Rachel didn't deny him much."

"That's how she learned the magic of her caressing," I said to myself. "She practised with Abdulla—perhaps that's the reason, too, of her mutism," I went on infuriating myself. "He couldn't have been very articulate."

Jealousy is the only passion that feeds on itself and grows rank on its own maleficence. As soon as I became calmer I recognised that Rachel's silence was more wilful than any man's could be, and more obstinate; it was native in her, invincible.

That evening, or a little later, I was with Rachel again. She sought now naturally to be alone with me on all occasions, and so we went straight to her "room." Usually she turned to me with burning lips, but the evening after I had made my proposal she was astonishingly cool. She wished to understand the whole position, and I let her talk and draw me out, knowing that the conclusions thus reached would be more effective than anything I could say. It is well to let small secretive natures persuade themselves in their own way; then they are immovable in their mistakes.

She probed skilfully, and I answered as if I were reluctant to go, reluctant to leave her. "I want to kiss you," I broke off, but when I kissed her I found her totally unresponsive; she evidently was intent on making sure first that it was necessary for me to go, and then that I was sure to return.

"Is a licence and 'best man' necessary?" she asked.

"Who told you of a 'best man'?" I questioned, with feigned surprise.

"Never you mind," she replied. "I know a great deal more than you think," she added; and I immediately thought of her relations with Abdulla.

"Very likely you do," I retorted bitterly, and my unfeigned feeling convinced her better than any acting.

"But is a 'best man' necessary," she persisted, "to a European wedding?"

"In every marriage," I replied, "a licence is needed, and in any marriage outside England a consular officer as witness; but I think I could get an officer who would also act as 'best man.'"

"Would that be legal?" she asked.

"Oh yes," I remarked; "but what does the marriage matter if we love each other?"

"Love's all right," she said, "but marriage gives security, and that's what a woman wants above everything.

"You'll see," she whispered, "how I'll love you when you're my husband," and she wound her arms around my neck and put her lips on mine. In one moment they were hot, and she began then to ruffle my hair with quick, impatient hands, small symbols of her keen desire. As in turn I took and kissed her she sighed and relaxed, yielding to my embrace. However self-interested and tyrannic she might be, she was certainly a wonderful lover.

I now pretended that I did not want to go to the coast. "I'm in no haste," I said to Rachel. "I'd be content to stay always just as we are. What do you care for a dress? And what's a 'best man' to me?"

She appeared to agree with me, though now and then she would say that the sooner an unpleasant thing was finished and done with the better; but I noticed that the Sultan and Abdulla steadily hastened our departure, and Tapp informed me from Leah that Rachel was secretly helping the whole movement.

Meanwhile she showed me more unreservedly the passionate side of her nature, evidently trusting altogether to the sex attraction to pull me back to her at the earliest possible moment.

I sometimes wondered if she had any further or higher conception of love; and now, looking back, I question it. No doubt a certain motherliness would have come into her love if ever she had children, but as a girl she was singularly free of it—a lover and nothing more.

The æsthetic sense in her was fairly developed. She knew a lovely woman's figure from a common type; knew that Leah's shapely slim form was more beautiful Micah's, and that Micah in turn was finer than the negroid type. The conventional appealed to her strongly. As soon as I spoke about the black hairs on her chest, they disappeared. She tweaked them out ruthlessly, though she made her chest sore by her roughness. I was astonished to see how angry and inflamed the place became, but I treated it with wet pad of boracic acid, and it healed up in a day. "He just put his hands on her breast and a little water on a rag, and next morning it was well: great magic, his," Leah told Tapp, and that report brought me hosts of patients. But that's another story. For music Rachel had a distinct gift, but there her talents ended. Love to her was a matter of sex, and spiritual companionship had little or nothing to do with the matter.

It was Rachel who taught me to see the ordinary girl without glamour or romance. As soon as I drew away from her I began to study her, and with study came understanding. I could soon read her like an open book, and her ignorance would have aroused my pity were it not for her hard obstinacy of temper. In spite of her passionate kisses we drifted steadily apart, till I could see her and her father in fair perspective as Semites and Mohammedans. Their self-centred imperiousness threw light for me on that religion of Mohammed that captivated, as by a sirocco or cyclone, the whole Semitic race and still sways more than two hundred millions of people. There is little of gentleness or meekness or broad humanity in that creed, with its paradise of lovely houris and sensual delights. Man's duty to his brother man is summed up in kindness to one's dependents if they are of the true faith. It is the religion of rank individualism and unrestrained sensuality.

But there is just a touch of higher things in Mohammed el Amin, or The Honest, as he was called—an æsthetic sense at least. In the Koran I find this great injunction: "If you have two loaves, sell one quickly and buy a flower, for the soul, too, must be fed." This love of beauty was typified to me in Rachel's pretty fancies and in her love of music. She represented to me the very soul of Mohammed at its best.

At length the great moment came. The slave-caravan under Abdulla would be ready next morning, the Sultan said, and my carriers had been warned to be prepared.

The caravan taught me all the horrors of the African slave-trade: over a thousand men and women, yoked by pairs and loaded down with sixty or eighty pounds of ivory each. The younger girls and boys had been reserved; only the older folk were used as carriers to the coast; but many of the women were not more than twenty or twenty-five, and I was horrified to find that three out of every four of the men and many of the older women were suffering from recent wounds.

Suleiman had organized two or three slave-raids in order to get his carriers. I was relieved to find that the caravan was to take another road. We should be close to them, Abdulla informed me, but not with them. In the half-hour they were grouped in front of the Sultan's kraal I saw such brutalities that I was glad to lose sight of them for ever, and to try to forget. I may as well give here one incident that struck me at the time and hardened my heart for the separation and deception.

While I was talking to Abdulla one of the pairs of women came towards us, and I saw that one of these was a mulatto, pretty and young. She stretched out her hands to Abdulla imploringly and fell on her knees, beseeching him. I caught the words "Sultan" and "forgive, sorry, sorry, I love him," and then a flood of tears and sobs shook her slight, nearly nude frame.

Abdulla glanced at her indifferently:

"Get back," he ordered harshly.

I was surprised. "Does she want the Sultan to forgive her?" I asked. "Surely he will? Why, the poor girl can't be more than sixteen."

"She was a fool," remarked Abdulla sententiously; "she didn't want to yield to the Sultan at first, and he never forgives that sort of thing; that's why she's in the slave-gang now and is to be sold at Mombasa."

As the girl looked from one to the other of us, seeing, I suppose, some hope in my pity, Abdulla grabbed her by the left breast, dragged her to her feet and threw her back in the row.

"Get back," he growled, "and keep quiet or you'll have a hot back to-night."

With lips parted in a gasp of pain and staring wild eyes of fear, the poor girl stood drooping, held up by her yoke-mate.

I don't know why, but the whole scene sickened me. Abdulla's act was so unconscious in its brutality, the girl's fear and pain so unaffected, that I turned away and could hardly speak when a minute later the Sultan came out of his kraal to give the final directions. I hated all of them and wanted to get away.

Sultan Suleiman and Rachel in her French frock, accompanied by a guard of honour, went with us through the belt of forest by a way until then unknown to me—a broad road well defended. At the edge of the clearing they halted and we said "Good-bye!" Sultan Suleiman's eyes shone with a certain kindliness, and Rachel did not hesitate to put her arms about my neck and kiss me again and again.

"In a month I shall be here expecting you, my husband," she whispered. Not a word of love—"my husband"—strange pride of possession.

Two hundred yards lower down the road wound round a clump of trees and bush, and we waved them "Farewell"—the last "Farewell."

I never saw either of them again; but all through the trip, which took me to the shores of the Great Lake and afterwards down the Nile to Khartoum, the memory and image of Rachel pursued me. Often I'd awake with her blue eyes looking into mine and hot kisses on my lips.

THE EXTRA EIGHT DAYS

THE EXTRA EIGHT DAYS

LÉON FORNAGEOT had lost his place as a notary's clerk; he had been proud of his position, and really dressed the part. He always wore a frock-coat and a white tie; his short whiskers, too, cut English fashion, gave him, he thought, an air of dignity. But once out of work he fell to pieces very soon.

Madame Fornageot now dressed him and fed him, and did not forget to tell him so even when pouring out the glass of water for him, with which he had now to content himself. She was always reproaching him; in a crowd she did not hesitate to push him. He would turn on her: "Amelie! do not be brutal; I cannot be quicker than I am going; there is someone in front of me." "Yes," she would reply angrily, "there's always someone in front of you."

The rage of Madame Fornageot, with her spirit of economy, can be imagined when Grabiche, a cousin of her husband, presented himself one evening at seven o'clock and invited himself, if you please, to dinner. They had not met for twenty-five years. Young Grabiche then was fat and joyous, and used to sing songs in a café concert—naughty songs, disgusting songs, according to Madame Fornageot. "A pretty family yours!" she sighed afterwards to her husband.

But now here was a new Grabiche, a Grabiche of fifty-five years of age—fatter than ever, redder than ever, and under his right arm an immense paté and under his left a bottle. "We will have a jolly dinner," he cried. "Uncle Cyprien gave me your address."

Madame Fornageot smiled, because she had noticed that although the tweed suit of Grabiche showed marks of wear, still across his immense stomach there was a beautiful gold chain, and on one rather dirty finger a large diamond.

"Do you still sing at la Chaussée Clignancourt?" she asked.

"No!" cried Grabiche. "Oh no! It is the others now who sing for me."

He explained that he had seen how the directors employed singers and got the chief profits for themselves, so after ten years of economy he bought an establishment of his own, "Le Cri Cri," and baptized it "The Music-Hall des Rigolos" (those who mean to enjoy themselves). "Now, my children," he added joyously, "I gather in my thirty thousand francs a year without any trouble.

"The essential is never to have any trouble. My father and mother gave me a salt mouth: I do not drink because I like it, but I drink because I am always thirsty. I live well and save nothing. I am not married and have no children—indeed, Fornageot, you are my only heir, and if I kick the bucket before you I will always leave you enough to drink to my health. . . . Do not shake that bottle, man, that's good wine!"

After the dinner he took them to his music-hall: a dreadful clientèle—men without collars and women without any hats. The director put his relatives into a box, and the young fellows in the audience in front of them kept making fun of them, especially of Madame Fornageot, who had put on some little curls.

"They like to amuse themselves," explained Grabiche. "They will not throw anything at you. I know them nearly all"; and suddenly noticing one of the guttersnipes who was making fun of Madame Fornageot's head-dress, he cried:

"Look here, Calves-liver, you shut up or I will come and talk to you!"

In the *entr'acte* he took Léon Fornageot behind the scenes. They came immediately upon half-a-dozen women in every state of undress, three or four playing cards in a corner waiting for their turn.

Grabiche introduced them: "My English dancers: Rosa, Carmen, Bijou and Mélindie. Do not get up, my dears!—only a relation." Fornageot bowed gravely to Monsieur Ernest, a comic, and Mademoiselle Laura Ponestier, who seemed to be able to walk about on her hands as easily as on her feet. He bowed also to Chung-Li, a Chinese juggler, who had the accent of Montmartre, and to the Kreitzer family, newly imported from Vienna.

Grabiche ordered drinks, and as soon as they came, "This is the life that pleases me," he cried to Fornageot. "I change the entertainment every eight days, but whenever I find a little girl that I like, instead of sending her away I keep her a week longer—that is a little present I make to myself. She is like the manageress for a whole week, never more. Both my public and myself like change. At the end of a fortnight she must go: they can cry or groan, I pay no attention.

"That is why whenever I change the bill here they ask, 'Who is going to get a week longer?'"

"Grabiche!" Fornageot cried reproachfully. "Grabiche!" But Grabiche did not even notice the moral reproach.

When they came back they found Madame Fornageot very vexed, troubled too, a little. She kept looking at her husband to see the effect that had been produced upon him. But Léon had his old air of a head clerk who was impenetrable. All he said was: "I was never behind the scenes before; it is all excellently arranged. The lady artistes were playing cards." . . .

From this moment on, every Sunday Grabiche paid a visit to Fornageot. He always came provided with food and rich wine. Madame Fornageot was once able to recommend a sentimental song to him, and he always said afterwards she was born for the theatre because the sentimental song had a success.

One Sunday when Grabiche came Fornageot noticed that he was redder even than ordinary, and could not walk straight. Instead of wine, too, he had brought a bottle of old Cognac.

"I am not well," he said. "I need to be screwed up a peg or two. I am going to watch you folk dine, and I shall just be content with a glass or two of old Cognac in which I dip a crust; that is my remedy for all ailments."

"It would perhaps be better——" insinuated Léon Fornageot.

But Madame Fornageot cried: "Leave your cousin alone; he knows best what is good for him."

"You are right," cried Grabiche. "I am too well, my blood is too strong, that is the terrible part of it; but I'll pour out a little of this Cognac. I have a sort of vertigo—a noise, too, a rumbling in my ears. I'll have a glass of this Cognac and I shall be all right."

The Fornageots noticed that the first three glasses turned him to violet instead of red, but Madame Fornageot helped the soup and they began to eat. Suddenly Grabiche put out his right hand and closed it in the air.

"The bottle is by your side," cried Madame Fornageot. He tried to reply, but it ended in a sort of groan. His face became blue instead of violet, and he fell forward on the tablecloth.

"He is drunk!" cried Madame Fornageot.

He was dead. . . .

.   .   .   .

There were long formalities, but at the end of

three or four months, thanks to M. Fornageot's
training as a notary's clerk, the couple came into
possession of the Music-Hall des Rigolos and of
about five thousand four hundred francs in cash.
The music-hall was not easy to sell, but it was evident that with a little care it would bring in twenty
or thirty thousand francs a year. It was a fortune
for the Fornageots, and they did not hesitate to
grasp it.

Madame Fornageot put herself before the cash-
desk and engaged a strong man to turn out any
riotous spectators, and Fornageot carried on the
music-hall.

Monsieur Fornageot's whiskers became more
important than ever. He was always now in a
frock-coat and perfectly new white tie. And before long his temptation came. There was a little
Italian dancer whom he pinched as she passed him
and who smiled so sweetly at him that he made up
his mind he would follow the example of Grabiche
and give her—an extra week.

But he found it difficult to tell Madame Fornageot, for Madame Fornageot now had put on great
airs. She constantly wore her jewellery. He noticed, too, that she rouged her cheeks a little, and
that she always put on artificial curls. But the
charm of the Italian dancer was invincible. M.
Fornageot determined to speak plainly. So the
same evening he went to the cash-desk where Madame Fornageot was arranging all the moneys:

"That little lace necklet suits you, my dear," he said; "I want to propose something——"

But Madame Fornageot interrupted him: "You know the tight-rope dancer, he is very successful; he has made a hit, and as it is the custom here, when the proprietor is content with the performance, I am determined to give him an extra eight days."

M. Fornageot found nothing to say!

THE GREAT GAME

THE GREAT GAME

WHEN Dick Donovan was about seven he had a novel experience. One of the boys in the street called him an "orphin" and jeered him because he had no father, and when he clambered up all the stairs to the seventh floor and asked his mother what an "orphin" was, she said:

"Your father was a pólisman (may God be good to his sowl!) and was killed fallin' into a ship's hould wan slippery marnin' on the docks."

Soon after this Dick was packed off to the primary school, but as his playmates were going too that did not make much difference to him. He was naturally quick, and had a good memory.

Bit by bit in the next two or three years his mother's tears and complainings told him that they were going down in life. She often got very little washing to do, and sometimes she was too ill to do it. Dick had to carry the washing to the various houses and bring home the money, and soon grew an adept at getting small coins on his own account. He knew every cent in a dollar better even than his prayers.

He got through the primary school at about thirteen, and though his mother was ill she insisted that he should go on to the high school, which Dick thought mere waste of time and energy.

A little later when she was coughing worse than usual Bill Butler came to see them. Bill was a big longshoreman, a friend of the boy's father, and he offered to get Dick a job under Long Dan O'Connor, the head of the longshoremen, to run errands and do light jobs at Pier No. 9.

Mrs. Donovan protested feebly: "The boy must get his schoolin'"; but Butler insisted that he was growing quite a man and "the very spit of his father," and Dick, seduced by being called a man, begged that the proposal might be accepted, so that he could earn four dollars a week and have done with that beastly old school.

The next day, in charge of Bill Butler, he went down to the docks and began what he always regarded as his adult life. He was just thirteen.

Every day for the next four years Dick worked at the docks—ran errands, did whatever they told him to do—and at the end of that time was proud to bring home his eight dollars a week, that kept the house going.

As Dick's earnings grew larger Mrs. Donovan's health improved, and when he reached eight dollars a week she kept her room far better than Mrs. Rubin kept hers.

The Rubins were wops from near Trieste who had just moved into the next room and shared it with another Jewish family. Mrs. Donovan did not like them. She thought it wasn't "dacint" for two families both with boys and girls growing up to be living in one room with only a chalk line on the floor to divide them.

But Dick thought Maggie Rubin the prettiest girl he had ever seen, with her black eyes and hair and her air of disdainful self-possession.

When Dick got to know them the Rubins were dreadfully poor and seemed likely never to be richer. In the summer Mr. Rubin got a living out of his push-cart with fruits and ice-cream, but in winter his earnings fell away to almost nothing. His wife did her best to keep the house going, but there was something reckless and extravagant about her. Some said she was a gipsy, and it may well have been true, for Dave, her son, was tameless as a hawk, and even as a lad took to gambling and bad company, and Maggie never could resist pleasure, though her mother was always preaching to her the necessity of getting rich.

"Take warning by me," she used to sigh. "It is just as easy to marry a rich man as a poor one, and oh! the difference afterwards." Maggie's school chums all taught the same gospel.

Maggie liked Dick, for she saw that he admired her, and he was tall and had fine grey-blue eyes and worked hard and—she just liked him.

Then came a bitter winter and on top of that the great strike. The longshoremen, led by Bill Butler, would not accept a cut in wages and Dick was out of a job. His mother looked very grave when he told her the news, but determined to make the best of it.

For a long dreadful week, Dick was at a loose end, and for the first time in his life a prey to absolute fear. He could earn something; he could get wood enough from the houses that were being torn down and rebuilt and coal enough too from the docks to keep a fire going and the room warm, but he was out one whole day without earning ten cents, and no two people can live on ten cents a day in New York.

Dick's next discovery was that his mother loved to deny herself, but when he found her eating potatoes for the second meal and giving him the meat he couldn't stand it.

"I don't want the mate," she said when he reproached her, "and me doin' nothin'."

"Then I won't eat it either," Dick replied, and forced her to take her share.

After this Dick went out determined to get work somehow or other, and the first person he struck was Dave Rubin.

Rubin was full of resources and knew New York like his pocket. After talking a few minutes he told Dick that he could get him a place in Heenan's saloon on Maple Street where, after a week or so, he would get five dollars a night for boxing and an extra buck slipped to him besides if a gentleman drew blood or knocked him down.

With his mother's economies pinching his heart Dick jumped at the chance.

"Take me along," he said; "sure they won't kill me anyway." And that night, being Wednesday,

Dave kept his word and about eight o'clock presented Dick to Heenan's partner, Ricker.

"If he can't box," said this worthy, "take him to the boys and let him put the gloves on at once. I am afraid he is too young and lathy to be much good."

Dick found that at Heenan's there were two large rooms on the ground floor flanking the bar-room: one was kept for serious matches and bouts; it had a twenty-four foot ring roped off all complete; the other was where the boys boxed and talked and drank and smoked like men—up to any devilry.

Dick was inclined to be shy and quiet, but Dave was evidently free of the place in the widest sense of the word. The two boys who had been boxing when they came in broke off for a moment of introductions, but were soon at it again hammer and tongs. Dick's eyes grew wide in admiration of their skill. He confided as much to Dave, but Dave thrust out contemptuous lips:

"You ought to beat them both at the end of your first week," he said; "they are only beginners."

Dick's eyes widened still further. He thought them both wonderful, though rather small.

Suddenly Ricker broke off the contest: "Go down and bring me a drink," he said to one lad, "and you, Jones, come here and put on the gloves with this dub."

In a twinkling, under Dave's orders, Dick slipped off his coat and vest, drew his belt tighter round his middle and put on the gloves for the first time in his life with Ed Jones, an undersized youth of twenty or so who had already passed out of the feather-weight class.

As soon as he saw that Dick was a complete novice Jones seemed to take pleasure in telling him how to hit and how to guard, and from the first Dick took to the new sport with enthusiasm. True, Jones showed him more than once that he could hit faster and harder than Dick had any idea of, but he had learned his first lesson of life on the docks, and he took the hard blows with the light ones without showing any pain, and at the end of ten minutes or so he began divining the heavier blows, either guard-ing or getting his head out of the way of them. Ricker's final "green as grass" only made him re-solve to do better. Dave told him it was a rather good sign, for after all Ricker had stood by to see him begin.

As Ricker left the room Dave went with him, and when he came back seemed rather anxious. "I'll put on the gloves with you," he said, "and give you a lesson or two." And then he began to show Dick how to hit quick by throwing his fist, and how to guard and slip blows, and kept on with him for nearly an hour, till Dick was wet with sweat and be-gan to get slow.

"You're tired," said Dave suddenly. "You'll have to begin again to-morrow."

He confided to Dick on his way home that he had to beg Ricker a little and promise to come himself one night because Ricker said that Dick would need more than a month's practice to get into the boxing enough to be any good to the house.

Of course Dick was full of his evening and wanted to talk of it, and by chance they met Maggie with a man in the hallway and out it all came.

Maggie was interested, but she told him that he musn't get thick ears or have that nice nose of his broken. Dave assured her that Dick showed signs of being very quick. "He has a long reach," he said. "I shouldn't be surprised if he does things; he is quicker than he looks."

Dick glowed with pleasure and went up to tell his mother all about it. But Mrs. Donovan wouldn't hear of fighting as a profession. "All thim fighters," she said, "get dhrunk and look fierce. Sure, we can wait a wake or two till ye get honest work."

But Dick knew better—knew that there was no time to lose; that already the portions of meat at supper had grown small and stringy. So he just resolved to keep his own counsel and do his very best; and, boylike, he lay awake a long time thinking of how he could strike and get his head out of the way, because Dave had rocked him once with an uppercut that hurt.

.   .   .   .

Now began for Dick a wondertime. By nine o'clock next morning he was at Heenan's, made his way to the back room and went over to Ed Jones, who happened to be talking with two other boys.

"Feel stiff?" asked Jones.

"No," replied Dick, "but I had a bit of a head-ache last night."

"That will wear off," said Jones. "Do you want to put them on again?"

"Sure," said Dick. And in two minutes they were hard at it; and after Jones he took on another boy, and a little later another.

Dick was toughened by hard and constant work, but he soon found that there is no taskmaster so exacting as one's own desire. He boxed that day till he ached from head to foot, and yet when new-comers came in and wanted a round or two he was always willing to put on the gloves and try to learn something new.

At noon he went out and got a sandwich, and when he came back he was so tired that he fell asleep and slept through all the hubbub till nearly four o'clock. Then he got on the job again and soon found out that it was better to slip blows than ward them off, for by slipping them he had both hands free to hit with.

That very first day Dick began training his head to slip to one side or the other, and soon his head began to guard itself by getting out of the way automatically.

There was no dreaming and wondering for him that night. As soon as his head touched the pillow he fell asleep.

The days passed in a whirl till Sunday, when Dick was so tired that he slept right on till past noon, exhausted nature taking its revenge. He had a little chat about two o'clock with Maggie, who told him that Dave had made five hundred dollars on horses; then he went out for a walk right up to the park and fell asleep on the grass. But on Monday he was at work before nine o'clock and as keen as ever. To his delight he found that he had improved out of all recognition. The rest had enabled him to realise his knowledge.

The first boy he boxed with was a feather-weight called Jack Geary, and he found that he could nearly hold his own, and after the bout was over he got an approving nod and a word of good advice from Ricker.

"Don't mix it, you boob," said Ricker, "when he is short and strong. Keep him out. Use the length of your arms."

It was true, Dick felt, and he put the tip into practice. When Ed Jones boxed with him that afternoon he was astonished at his progress. "You will make some fighter," he said, "if you keep on. When a man tries to come in remember he's as likely to come round your left arm as inside it, so always be ready with your right fist."

That day brought Dick several new lessons and he profited by them. He was soon well liked by most of the fellows in the place because he was always willing to box with any of them, and in fact he did more work in the next week than all of them put together.

One day Mr. Ricker brought a gentleman in and Dick soon discovered that he was twice as quick and could play with him; but after the first round Ricker drew him aside. "You don't want to hit him," he said, "you want him to hit you. If he knocks you down he will pay. Tell him he is hitting so hard that it hurts. They love to hear them things."

Dick went home that night with six dollars, which hugely increased his zeal, though his mother was not satisfied till she had daubed all his face with arnica.

In a month Dick was one of the regular boys, willing to mix it with anyone and not likely to come to much injury, while his pay had risen to be twelve or fifteen dollars a week.

One day Ed Jones asked him if he would go over to Philadelphia with him. There was a house there where they were giving ten and twenty dollars a night, and Ed thought they would have no trouble in coming back with a hundred dollars or even two for a week's work. "I want the dough," said Jones; "my girl wants to doll up all the time and that takes coin in New York."

They went to Philadelphia, but in spite of Ed's coaching Dick had a very unpleasant experience.

After two or three fairly light bouts he was matched to box Harry Wilkins for two hundred and fifty dollars, a gold watch, and the feather-weight championship of Pennsylvania for boys under eighteen years of age. The promoters had advertised the match very cleverly; the feather-weight championship under eighteen limited the competition to a very small number, and it was told to the boys that the prize was really one hundred dollars, and a gold watch worth one hundred and fifty dollars, which an enterprising firm of watchmakers had supplied for the advertisement.

Dick had never seen his opponent till he entered the ring at Oddfellows' Hall at nine o'clock that night, but from the thundering applause that greeted Wilkins when he appeared there could be no doubt that he was a popular favorite.

Dick measured his adversary with a glance and thought he might be a tough customer, and Ed at once advised caution: "He's quick and strong and the old hands all say that he's full of tricks, so take care."

At first the lads felt each other out cautiously, but almost at once Dick's long stabbing left hand seemed to disconcert his opponent, and Dick began to hope for an easy victory. Ever afterwards he laid one proverb to heart: "Easy beginnings often have hard endings." Very early he noticed that Wilkins was clever in dodging with his head, and in the third round he only just stopped him from getting to close quarters by a half-arm jolt with his right and a lightning step back. Still Dick was very confident from the beginning that he could win, and win easily.

This confidence in prize-fighters is often misjudged by the outside public. The truth is that fighting men are trained so severely that they enter the ring in the very pink of physical condition. They feel so well, so strong and lithesome that they can't imagine defeat. A boy of one hundred and ten pounds feels that he could fight Samson or Goliath—that no blow could hurt him; it's only long experience teaches him that his confidence is the mere conceit of perfect health.

The fourth and fifth rounds both went to Dick, though he remarked that his opponent managed to slip or guard all his really heavy blows and the light ones didn't seem to make much impression on him.

At the sixth round Dick stepped toward mid-ring with the resolve to get home with at least one heavy blow. With this in mind he put more weight than usual into his left leads, and Wilkins shook his head over one as if dazed; at once Dick followed it up with a hot left and right. Both missed by an inch or so and Dick's own impetus brought him into a clinch.

"Break away there, break away," warned the referee, stepping forward; but before the two could be separated Wilkins had screwed himself round Dick and given him a half-arm punch in the side and small of the back. In a moment they were parted, but the "kidney punch" had gone home and Dick began to feel sick and weak, as if all the vitality had been suddenly drained out of him.

"Spar with him, keep him away, side-step him," called Jones in a frenzy of fear, and Dick did his best to follow the advice, but he had all he could do to evade his adversary, and never in his life did he find a round so long. When he got back to his corner Ed was very helpful; he rubbed the sore spot gently, gave Dick a mouthful or two of brandy and assured him that if he could only keep up the defensive for two or three more rounds he might yet win.

Dick did all he knew. Bit by bit the faint, sick feeling vanished and he felt the constant stabbing with his left was again beginning to tell; but for the life of him he couldn't put vim enough into his work to win the fight. Still his pluck gained him a good many friends who knew nothing of the foul blow, and when the fight was proclaimed a draw, and the purse divided, Dick was glad to take the gold watch as his reward, though its real value was probably less than the one hundred dollars which fell to Wilkins.

That fight taught Dick a painful lesson in the importance of caution and humility.

When he returned to New York after a couple of weeks he had cleared one hundred and twenty-five dollars in cash, and as luck would have it found his mother out shopping, so he knocked at the Rubins' door.

Maggie was crying and Dick was delighted to caress and make up to her. What was the matter?

"Dave has lost all his money," she said, and to console her Dick slipped her the extra twenty-five dollars he had made. She threw her arms around his neck of her own accord and gave him a long, long kiss on the mouth that awakened all his senses.

That night a surprise was awaiting him at Heenan's. For the first time he saw Zu Lenward, the bantam-weight champion, box with three or four of the boys, and was astonished at his footwork. He not only got his head out of the way, but his body as well. Dick had begun to find out that a punch in the wind, as they called the pit of the stomach, was even more unpleasant than a jolt to the jaw. Then, too, when Lenward struck the weight of the blow came from his hip and back as well as from his arm. Dick saw at once that Lenward could beat Jones because of fast footwork, and he got still another lesson.

At about ten o'clock Mr. Ricker brought in a funny little old man, introduced him as Patsy M'Gee, and said he would have to keep order, because it appeared there had been a good deal of drunkenness and free fighting the night before.

At the idea of Patsy keeping order Dick laughed, for in truth he was a comical figure. His head was almost over his left shoulder and the left side of his face was all wrinkled up. Dick made some such remark to Jones about him, but was astonished at his reply.

"A light-weight champion once," said Ed, "but he was knocked out badly later and got a paralytic stroke; very useful with both hands and a rushin' in-fighter, like them Irish usually are."

In a short time Dick and Patsy became firm friends. Perhaps because the boy was Irish, Patsy was never tired of teaching him and giving him advice.

One day, during a prolonged bout with Jack Geary, who was going to fight for the feather-weight championship, Patsy took Dick in hand: "Keep him out," he said; "use your long arms. If he comes in stop him or side-step him; but try to keep him out. In two or three rounds he will be shaken; you will have knocked all the pep out of him. Use your natural advantage, boy. You have extraordinarily long arms; use them."

And after the bout nothing would do but Dick must stretch out his arms to their full length and have them measured. "Sure," affirmed Patsy, "what did I tell ye? Instead of seventy inches, stretch you have seventy-five inches. Arms two or three inches longer than anyone of your weight in New York."

After a week of Patsy's training Dick passed into the championship class. He was already making twenty-five and fifty dollars a week, and his mother began talking about a house at Mamaroneck which she had once seen on a Sunday trip with her husband.

"We could get the whole house and garden," she said, for a couple of thousand dollars, and I could keep chickens and a pig and make ye more comfortable. Ye don't need to be up early to get to Heenan's by ten or eleven o'clock."

The truth was the little woman was frightened of Maggie and her influence, and she knew as well as if she had been told that while Dick always gave her twenty dollars a week, the rest of his money went to Maggie, and she wanted to get Dick out of her clutches.

When Patsy M'Gee heard of Mrs. Donovan's wish he made up a party for the next Sunday and took her and Dick out to Mamaroneck. They had a great day and saw the house; it overlooked the Sound and had two acres of ground around it—a lovely little place. Mrs. Donovan was in ecstasies, but the price put on it they found to be five thousand dollars, and that frightened Mrs. Donovan, though the agent said he would take one thousand dollars down and the rest in three years. And when Dick opened his eyes at the one thousand dollars Patsy told him the great news, that already he had been mentioned for the next good fight and he might make five hundred dollars out of it.

A week later, with Patsy as chief agent, Dick was matched to fight Jack Geary, who had already been mentioned as the most probable American feather-weight to box Cock Robin, as he was called, the English champion who was coming across with a great reputation.

Dick had nearly a month to prepare and in this month Patsy M'Gee showed himself to be a trainer of the first class.

"You must strengthen your back muscles, my boy," he told Dick, and presented him with a pair of heavy dumbells. "They all use the light ones," he went on, "but I want 'em heavy for you. You are young and are coming to the end of your growth; you will have lots of extra pep to put into your back muscles now and that is where you want weight."

Then he taught Dick how to swing Indian clubs, and again he insisted on these being heavy.

Dick took to it all with his usual enthusiasm,

and he found that the dumbells and clubs strengthened his back and biceps from day to day; in fact he grew so rapidly in weight that in a week Patsy began to wonder whether he could keep down to the weight, and started him off on a long fast walk each morning to take down any fat.

About a week before the great night Patsy introduced Dick to Sid Harriman, a betting man, whom the boys thought to be a millionaire. Strange to say, Harriman, after looking him over, was pleased with his chance, and when he saw Dick box once or twice he was more pleased still, though Patsy admitted that he was not certain enough to bet much money on him. "You see," said Patsy, "it takes a cert before they put down the dough."

A week later Dick had his first real trial. At first it looked as if he must be beaten. In the third round Jack Geary managed to get in and do what he would; Dick could not get rid of him, and Jack punched him in the body again and again till he felt sick.

In his corner Patsy was full of advice. "Sidestep him," he said; "side-step him and keep him out; you can only wear him out. Don't let him mix it. If he gets in again, clinch."

And so with varying fortunes the fight went on, round after round. One round went to Dick because he was able to keep his adversary out or sidestep him and his long arms did their work; other rounds went to Jack because he managed to fight his way in and used his body blows tellingly.

About the sixteenth round Dick began to feel that Geary was not hitting as hard as at the beginning, and when he came back to his corner he found Patsy of the same opinion.

"Go in and win," he advised. "Hit him with the left and follow with the right as hard as you can on top of it. One good punch will finish him."

Patsy told the truth. Dick half feinted, half struck, and followed it up with a heavy right, and Geary went to the floor and took the count.

Dick felt sorry for him, but Patsy whispered: "That's the house at Mamaroneck. I'm going home with you to tell your mother; it was a great blow entoirely." And Patsy said it full of admiration, just as if he hadn't suggested it himself.

To Dick's astonishment he found that he had won not only five hundred dollars, but one hundred dollars more that Mr. Harriman had left for him.

Patsy talked all the way home. "Cut out the booze and the wimmin," he said, "and you'll be the first fighter in America."

"What was it knocked you out?" asked Dick at last.

"Both," answered Patsy. "But it was the booze that made me a cripple. Sure, I was half drunk when I went into the ring. I could almost see two fighters agin' me instead of wan."

Mrs. Donovan was delighted, and asked Patsy in the nicest way whether he would not come out to stay with Dick and help him always with his advice;

and Patsy said that was exactly what he wanted to do if she would take board-money from him.

They resolved at last to buy the house if it could be bought and go out at once with Patsy as a lodger. But the mother noticed that Dick was not keen about this. She noticed, too, that fifty dollars had disappeared next morning and that Maggie had a new dress on and a new hat that must have cost all of ten dollars. "The slut!" she said to herself.

A night or two later she had a real talk with her son.

"I only want your good," she said; "ye are all I have in the world. I would give ye all the girls in New York if it would do ye any good; but Maggie Rubin is not a good girl, and if ye want me to I can prove it."

But Dick didn't want any proof. He kissed his mother and told her she was the best mother in the world and then went out to fight his first soul-battle alone.

That week he was with Maggie more than ever, perhaps because of the new dress and hat. Towards the end of the week, after a round or two with Ed Jones, Patsy took him seriously to task.

"Why is it you are not so fast to-day?" he said. "It isn't booze with you. Wimmin's the divil!" he went on; "the bad ones are ruination and the good ones won't lave a man alone."

Dick scarcely needed telling. He, too, had felt

when sparring with Jones that his blows lacked speed; he sometimes saw the opening almost as soon as his hand took advantage of it, whereas before his hands were always quicker than his eyes.

A little later the crisis came. When he got home he found his mother waiting for him, and she spoke briefly and to the point:

"The girl's out with a salesman from Macy's," she said, "and I heard him say he was going to take her to a roadhouse for the night, and that's not the first time, I'll be bound," she added.

That was the worst night in Dick's life. To say he was awake all night would be nothing like the truth; he was mad with jealousy and rage, and when it got light his mother knew that he was crying in his bed at the side. She had stretched burlap from the ceiling between the beds so as to give both all possible privacy. Her heart was as sore as Dick's and she suffered with him.

When Dick got up he went straight to Heenan's and sought out Patsy. "Let's go out to Mamaroneck at once," he said; "to-day if you like."

But matters could not move as quickly as that.

Before he went he got a note from Maggie, who had somehow or other heard of the intended moving, begging him to see her.

"Dick, you must forgive me," she said, kissing him. "I love you, you know, dear; but I've got to get money to keep the house, Dick. Dave brings in nothing, and my father's only good to be a Rabbi and say prayers and mother and I must live. Mr.

Williams is the head salesman at Macy's and gets one thousand dollars a month now and a commission. If you had such a place—oh, Dick, it's too hard, for I love you," and she hugged him; "but what's a girl to do. After all one must have money to live. Dick, say you'll always care for me—won't you, dearest?"

Dick nodded his head; he could find no words. He was numbed and for the moment felt nothing, and when afterwards the pain began again he found it was lessened by Maggie's assurance that she loved him best, so strong is vanity even in passion. And Maggie probably believed her protestations of affection, though in the back of her little head she knew that Mr. Williams was "a dandy dancer," as she phrased it, and took her to dine and dance at swell places Dick had never heard of, though Williams didn't slip her fifty or one hundred dollars as Dick did, and was not so loving. Still his position was sure, and he had told her he'd be rich one day and already he had twenty-five thousand dollars in good securities laid by, and that seemed to Maggie a fortune.

Take it all in all, Maggie was rather relieved that the Donovans were going to move, for Dick's propinquity and passion were tempting, and she knew instinctively that Williams wouldn't forgive an infidelity as easily as Dick did—"dear Dick!"

In concert with Mrs. Donovan, Patsy got Dick two contests at Philadelphia, which took him away for a while, and when he returned to old New York he found his mother and Patsy already settled in Mamaroneck.

. . . . . .

With one exceptional happening Dick's career in the next two years could be told in a phrase. He fought Cock Robin, the best English fighter of his weight, and won after a hard battle of eighteen rounds, mainly because the fight with Geary had taught him how to keep his man at arm's length and use his height and length of reach. Height helps a man; you can hit down heavier than up, and length of reach, too, Dick found, helped him, as a longer sword used to help a duellist till it was forbidden and the swords were equalised to an eighth of an inch.

Thanks to the open-air runs and the constant exercise with clubs and dumbells, reinforced now with all sorts of stomach exercises under Patsy M'Gee's superintendence, Dick grew rapidly in sheer muscle weight, and with all the glory of his victory over the English champion about him, was matched to fight Zu Lenward for the bantam championship of the world.

Zu, Dick found, was short for Zulu, because Lenward had coloured blood in him. Anyway, according to Patsy, he was a real opponent and "up to every trick in the game, but a little ould; he must be thirty if he's a day."

A week before the fight Sid Harriman drew Dick aside. "What will you make by winning?" he asked.

"The purse is for two thousand dollars," replied Dick simply.

"You can have ten thousand dollars," said Harriman, looking him straight in the eyes, "to lose in the eleventh round."

"How do you mean?" asked Dick.

"Let yourself be knocked out," answered Harriman. "I will tell Lenward, and the punch you will get on your jaw won't do you any harm, and you can flop about like a fish on the floor as well as another man I suppose."

Dick looked at him. Sell the fight? Not he. But he went to Patsy with the news, and to his astonishment Patsy was delighted with the offer: "Ten thou.!" he cried; "that's goin' some."

"But I can't take it," said Dick; "I'd be ashamed to sell a fight——"

"You can't buck against the game," Patsy admonished. "Nobody can be honest in this life. Suppose you go on bein' honest and beatin' everybody, no wan will bet agin' ye. You won't get a match, man; they'll avoid ye like the plague. All the excitement is in the doubt.

"Take the ten thousand dollars for being knocked out or you'll regret it. It will increase the interest for your next fight, and if you win that there'll be more dough still in being knocked out the time after. Don't be a fool. Sure, no wan will bet on you if he does not win by you.

"Take the ten thousand dollars, boy, and put it in

your kick. You make glory by winnin' but the dough by losin'."

Dick could not stomach this advice. Sid Harriman did not come near him though Patsy was evidently on his side. A day or two afterwards he returned to the charge.

"You're young, Dick," he said, "and you scarcely know what a foul is. You're a clean fighter; but nobody can be honest in this game, Dick, nobody. You are very good, but as good as you or better can be found. Put the money in your jeans, man, and don't be a boob!

"I know what life is. You have only five years at this game. At the end of that time you'll either be a rich man or you will be knocked out and poor, perhaps paralytic. Dick, if you were my own son, I'd tell you the same thing. Let me go to Mr. Harriman and accept his offer. I'll get you two thousand in advance—as much as you'd get by winnin'—and eight thou. after. What better can ye want?"

Dick shook his head. He was obstinate, though honesty to him was only a word. In his cruel doubt he went to his mother for counsel. "You dassen't act dishonest, Dick," she cried, "and yer father a polisman; but Patsy," she added inconsecutively, as Dick thought, "is a good man and a friendly." Something obstinate in Dick made him stick to his first resolution.

Was it Dick's fancy when the great day came, or

was there really an air of doubt in the room before the fight began?

Zulu was much stronger than he looked. All his weight was behind the shoulders. His legs were very thin and betrayed the coloured blood in him; but he was twenty-six or twenty-seven at least and, like most prize-fighters, he had lived a life of alternate hard training and mad dissipation, so that, as Patsy phrased it, the real "pep" had gone out of him. Still, he was an awkward customer and Patsy preached caution.

"Keep him out; keep him out," was his advice in every round, and towards the tenth round he began to get insistent. "Keep him out and watch him. Mr. Harriman's not coming round again is a bad sign, Dick! Watch him and hit like hell. Watch him and do all you know."

In the eleventh round Dick's blows and his long reach and height began to tell. Suddenly Zulu feinted and drew Dick's left. As the Zulu rushed in Dick stepped back and hit hard with the right, but the Zulu ducked it and threw his arms round him.

"Break away! break away!" cried the referee, stepping forward to the fighters. But before Dick could break away the Zulu had struck up against him with his knee, and the whole room swam with lights, floor and people all rocking in his agony. Zulu jumped in like a wild cat, hitting again and again, and when lying on the floor Dick heard the referee counting—seven—eight—nine. He tried to get up, but couldn't. The next moment Patsy had burst into the ring and carried him out to the dressing-room.

A doctor came and they gave him brandy, which only seemed to intensify the intolerable pain. He was fully conscious now and sick as a dog. He heard the doctor say: "He's young and there's nothing burst; he'll be all right in a week. Was it a blow?"

"Zulu's knee," said Patsy, sobbing with rage. "I never warned the boy. I thought he could keep him out."

Dick never knew how he got to Mamaroneck; in fact he was ill for nearly three weeks and it was a month before he came again to Heenan's, and as luck would have it the first man he met was Sid Harriman.

"You didn't want the two thousand or the ten thousand dollars either," said Harriman, sneering, "but you took the knockout in the eleventh round all the same. It doesn't pay to be a d—d boob."

All Dick's anger at the sneering tone vanished. "I guess you're right, Mr. Harriman," he said. "It doesn't pay to be a boob." But he registered an oath to himself that the next time he met Zu Lenward he would take it out of him.

But he didn't know even then how being honest in life weights the dice against you. He found it hard to get a match, and without Patsy it might have been impossible.

He proposed to fight this man or that, but everyone turned him down. At length he asked Patsy for the reason and Patsy gave it to him with a certain reluctance.

"Put yourself in the other man's place and think," he said at length; "that's the way to understand it right.

"Why did Harriman offer you ten thousand dollars to lose that fight? Because he had some big bet on——perhaps for one hundred thousand dollars ——that you would lose it, and perhaps another bet at long odds that you'd be knocked out in the eleventh round.

"Now when you refused what had he to do? First, he had to tell Zu Lenward to knock you out in the eleventh round; but he had to pay for that. Zulu said ' 'twas only certain by a foul.' 'Then you must foul him,' said Harriman, and he'd have to pay much more for a foul. Besides in case of a foul the referee must be squared, and that costs a mint of money; then the foul may be seen by the onlookers and cause a scandal, and therefore he bears you malice for making him pay out p'r'haps five times as much as he had reckoned on paying. See!

"Well, thin it's all over and you're K.O. And later your name comes up before the promoters and Harriman says: 'Not that guy; he's honest or stupid or——' And so you're finding it hard to get in the swim agin, but you'll get in. I know how to do that. Harriman won't let anger button his pocket; lave it to me."

The chance came sooner than Dick thought possible. Two or three months later he fought with Walt Thompson and that gave him the right to fight Lenward again for the championship. This time he made no mistake. He had measured his man. In the first two or three rounds he hit him so heavily that the result was not doubtful. A pitiless devil had entered into Dick and he was transformed. He fought as he had never fought— not to win, but to punish—and by the tenth round Lenward was incapable of any tricks. He was beaten to standstill, and in the seventeenth round was knocked clean off his feet and through the ropes. The cool savagery pleased the onlookers, and Dick went out of the ring a fighting man willing now to take his orders and put the dough in his jeans. He realized that being straight led only to ruin.

The next time he fought it was all arranged. Sid Harriman told him that he was to be knocked out in the fourteenth round and in the fourteenth round he gave his opponent an opening and got it on the jaw. He flopped about on the floor like a fish till even Harriman was delighted. "Some actor," he cried. "By God! I thought for the moment you were knocked out."

Patsy, too, was delighted, for Dick's bank account had jumped up five thousand dollars, and there was more excitement about his next appearance than there had ever been before.

The next two years were filled with alternate victories and defeats, and it seemed curious to Dick,

but it was the defeats that brought in the money—
twenty thousand and fifty thousand dollars at a time
—and no risk—even of a foul. The certainties
gave the cash.

．．．．．．

Gradually the place at Mamaroneck was improved and extended. One year Dick bought ten
acres of adjoining land and the next spring built a
walled-in bathing place and a little pier for the time
he'd be able to afford a steam launch, the desire of
his life.

Towards the end of the third year he outgrew
the weight, and though for six months or so he
could still sweat himself down to it by hard exercise
he preferred to give up the championship even while
he was too light to enter the light-weight class with
any hope of conspicuous success.

Bu he had no difficulty in getting a vaudeville engagement at a thousand a week for boxing with Ed
Jones a quarter of an hour each night, and he soon
found that the rest and absence of championship contests improved his health and strength in the most
astonishing way. Of course he described the im-
provement to Patsy, and as usual Patsy, who could
hardly write and never cared to read, understood
the phenomenon and had reasoned it out for himself.

"Sure, it's plain," he said, "every athlete has to
take a rest before he comes to the trial; even a
jumper or runner has to have a day's rest annyway
before he tries to beat the record. That's why I
never let you box for a couple of days before goin'

into the ring. And a tough fight takes it out of a man more than annything else in the world.

"Take the great fight between Sharkey and Jeffries, the greatest fight ever was fought; they both went into the ring perfectly trained, yet Sharkey, who had two ribs broken, lost thirteen pounds in weight in the fifty minutes the fight lasted and Jeffries lost eleven. Think of it! eleven pounds lost in an hour by a man trained fine and hard. A fight's a dreadful punishin' test, even if you win.

"A man," he went on reflectively, "has only a certain amount of reserve vitality; it's like a balance in the bank; he should never exhaust it or draw it down too low, for it's that gives him strength. When you increase the size of yer muscles you do it through using some of this nerve-force, and you must rest in order to let it accumulate again. Rest's a great thing," Patsy summed up, "and so's exercise, and you need both to be perfect. This vaudeville stunt for a year or so will be the making of ye, if ye keep away from wimmin an' booze."

   .   .   .   .   .   .

But the stream of Dick's life was not fated to run as smoothly as Patsy hoped. Men are the dupes of their desires. Dick had a pronounced success on the stage; he was good-looking and lightly built, without the bunchy biceps and knobs of muscle which most strong men display and most women dislike. He boxed with a certain grace and his footwork in especial was magically swift and catlike. His Celtic sensitive nature made him a natural actor, and from his first appearance he got letters from women and girls who wanted to know him.

Along in the first summer he and Jones were filling a week's engagement at Newark, N.J., when a rich woman, a Mrs. Faber, invited them to a garden-party, and arranged that they should box for the amusement of her guests. Both men took the invitation as a mere joke; but the grounds were crowded with fashionably dressed young people, and the performance was a huge success. After the boxing Mrs. Faber, struck by Dick's looks and quiet manners, introduced him to some of her guests, and notably to a Miss Woolcombe, who set Dick's blood in a turmoil. The first glance from her dark eyes and Dick's heart seemed to stop; he had to gulp down the fever of emotion, and indeed Kate Woolcombe was pretty enough to have seduced a less impressionable nature. In ten minutes Dick found that she had a very keen sense of humour; a sort of natural gaiety danced in her hazel eyes and lit up her whole face. And her personality was as marked as her beauty. When he spoke of his home at Mamaroneck and the joy he took in the waters of the Sound he was delighted to learn that she lived there too, not a mile away, with her father and mother. "May I call?" Dick risked; but the little lady treated the question quite as a matter of course. "I think my mother will be glad," she said, "and my young brother will be overjoyed; in fact the eldest, Harold, who is just seventeen, will make a hero of you at once, I'm sure," and she laughed charmingly.

When they said "Good-bye," and she gave him her hand, he had to look at in in surprise, it was so tiny.

Dick went back to his hotel walking on air; the vision of the mutinous lips and laughing eyes went with him everywhere; in bed, when he tried to sleep, they were photographed on his brain in colour, lifelike. At first it was the sheer bodily beauty of her that enthralled him, the little round lissom figure, the lovely face; but soon this vision grew less distinct, while the impression of her whole personality seemed to grow deeper.

As soon as Dick got back to New York he called at the Woolcombes, and found they lived in a big colonial house bowered amidst gardens and overlooking a wide reach and the shore of Long Island. Mrs. Woolcombe was kind to him, with a shade of restraint, and the banker father condescending at first, but the two boys, Harold and Fred, soon broke the ice by their enthusiastic interest in "the great game" and hero worship of the champion whose feats they had read about.

Then a new life began for Dick. Miss Kate read a great deal and spoke French fairly and had more than a bowing acquaintance with French literature.

She was learning Spanish, Dick found out, and this pleased him as putting her too with him in the class of learners. His naïve admiration of her wisdom and knowledge made her laugh outright, but at the same time flattered her deliciously, and the acquaintance ripened rapidly, thanks mainly to the two boys.

Dick gave Harold boxing lessons, and soon his sister heard nothing but "Dick does this" and "Patsy says that" till the two households became intimate. Mrs. Donovan was unaffectedly proud when Mrs. Woolcombe came to see her, but had the natural tact and good manners of the Celtic race, and the better-taught woman recognised at once her native good sense and amiability.

The year before Dick had realised his dream and had bought a high-powered launch, and Fred soon learned to drive it as well as the owner, and so the four made continual excursions. It was a book and a moonlit night that finally brought Dick and Kate together.

They had gone for a long trip in the launch, had taken food with them and were returning rather late. Kate had lent Dick *Slippy McGee,* and Dick wanted to know whether the heroine had realised that Slippy was in love with her first. Did she hold aloof from him because he had been a burglar? "No," Kate thought, "that had nothing to do with it."

"You know," said Dick simply, "that's why I'm afraid to tell you how I love you, for fear you'd think a prize-fighter too common to care for."

She sat there beside him in silence, as if thinking, and he went on with love's instinctive cunning:

"It's for all my life. Oh, Kate, I'd be content to wait on you hand and foot and serve you all my days if you'd just let me," and he stole his arm round her waist. "I know I'm not good enough for you; I knew that when you just said 'Good-bye' to me at Mrs. Faber's and gave me your little hand. Sure, look how small it is beside mine," he continued, taking it in his own brown paw; then lifting it he kissed it again and again and looked up. Kate's face was very earnest and her eyes flooded with emotion. "I love you, darling," he went on, and somehow their lips met.

Dick never forgot that kiss. It was more than a kiss; it was a consecration. "I'm not good enough," he went on. "I wish I were better. I'll try," he ended simply.

"We'll both try," the girl said. "You mustn't run yourself down. . . . You're good enough for me, Dick," she added, "for I love you."

They sat hand in hand in a sacred silence and next day agreed to say nothing about their love for a little while, as if such a secret could be kept.

But the course of passionate love never yet ran smooth; smoothness is not in the nature of a torrent, and Kate's awakening came very soon.

The rest and the long trips in the motor-launch had made Dick put on flesh, and one day Patsy weighed him and was horrified to find that he was beyond the light-weight limit. He measured him too, and found that he had grown nearly an inch and was now five feet ten and a half inches, with an arm-stretch of nearly seventy-six inches. At once he set Dick to work: long walks and runs every morning; potatoes and bread and all sweets were cut out of the diet, and instead of a lounging day steady exercise increasing in severity, especially exercise on the mat.

"You are strong enough for annything," said Patsy, "but now I want to get thim belly muscles as hard as iron—strong enough to protect that plexus of yours. Sure you put your big shoulder in front of yur chin fine; nobody will get you on the chin; but you are inclined to lave yourself open about the body, and a punch on the spleen would make you go groggy."

Dick realised the truth of this, and as usual went in for the new exercises with enthusiasm, Patsy assuring him that the stomach muscles were the strongest in the body and that he could make them like a wall of steel if he chose.

In three months, when Dick had brought himself down to the requisite weight, Patsy went into Heenan's every day and soon made up a fight between him and the light-weight champion, Benny Rossiter.

Benny was the best man that Dick so far had ever met. A New England boy, brought up on a farm, he had gone to Princeton and there fallen in love with the game, perhaps because of his extraordinary excellence in it. Almost as soon as he began to box he seemed to know everything by instinct. Patsy and Dick went one afternoon to see him box, and Dick was impressed by his speed and

strength.   He was very dark; some said his mother
was a Jewess.   While only five feet seven or eight
in height he was more strongly built than Dick, and
carried, they said, a terrible punch in his right hand.
But what Dick especially admired about him was
the natural way he ducked and slipped, even in
practice boxing; it was uncanny the way he could
get down and avoid blows.

"That man is better than me," said Dick, as they
went away.

"Better'n nothin'," replied Patsy; he's naturally
quick and he has learned the game like them ama-
toors, but you have learned it bit by bit and paid
for your knowledge again and again.   I tell you
he will live with you only about ten rounds, perhaps twelve, and then he'll go to pieces."

The announcement of the fight made a great
sensation.   There was nothing much doing in 1919
and the papers seized on the two men as repre-
sentative Americans; would-be literary men wrote
them up incessantly, and the reporters told everything about their daily lives and practice that they
could get hold of.

Benny, the college boy, was of course the favourite in better circles, so Dick was not surprised
when Harriman came round to watch him exercising
one day and afterwards said to him:

"This thing must be staged in Madison Square
Garden, and there ought to be a big wad in it.
If I give you ten per cent. of what I make clear
will that suit you?"

Dick looked at Patsy. "Sure," said Patsy; "sure, Mr. Harriman. Dick will fight according to instructions."

A day or two afterwards he learned that he was to be knocked out in the eighth round.

He regretted this for one reason in especial. Both the Woolcombe boys were crazy to see him fight and had begun to bet on his winning, and one day Kate said to him shyly: "I would like to see you in the real ring, though I am afraid it will be very brutal."

"Oh, you mustn't come this time," Dick blurted out.

"Why not?" she asked.

"You know," he said, putting his arms round her and drawing her to him, "I told you long ago I was not good enough for you"; and then love's humility being strong upon him, with the need for confession and the urge to tell the loved one the very worst about himself, he went on:

"I'm going to lose this fight. Benny Rossiter is very good"; and seeing her look of amazement, added, "and I'm a little out of practice—and—I shall probably make a lot of money by losing."

"What do you mean?" asked the girl, with parted lips and wide-open eyes. "What do you mean, Dicky?"

"Just that, he said bitterly. "He is champion, and it pays a fighting man to lose some fights. I'll get another chance later and then maybe you can

come to see it. If I lose then it will be because I
am not good enough to win."

They were entering her house when he began
speaking and she gave him no chance to talk further
to her that day, and the next day he got a letter
from her in which she said that she could not believe
what he had told her; could not believe that he was
going to let himself be beaten in order to win money
unfairly—"because that was what you said, Dick:
no one but yourself would make me believe it of
you."

He had feared just this and now the catastrophe
was overwhelming. He wrote begging for an in-
terview, and when she kept away a couple of days
without answering him he confided in Patsy and
sent him to her. Patsy shook his head when he
knew what was expected of him.

"All wimmin is crazy," was Patsy's verdict;
"they're all looney. Does she expect a prize-fighter
to be an angel; why doesn't she feel for your wings?
Does she think a boy like you could have one hundred and fifty thousand dollars in the bank and a
place like this in four years by fighting on the
square? Why, it ain't sense! Let her go and ask
her banker father how he made his fortune; sure,
she'll find that he has done things that would make
Beelzebub blush, if he tells the truth, but he's too
cunning."

But Dick prayed him to do his best as mediator
and sent him off, and the result of Patsy's inter-
cession was that the day after he got another little

not from Kate: "Have you told your mother? Does she approve?"

So Dick had to tell his mother the same day. When he told her that he was going to lose the fight and that it was by losing that he had made all his money, she looked at him horror-stricken, almost like Kate, and cried out: "Oh, wirra, wirra, to think of that and you a son of a p'lisman."

Dick felt inclined to smile, but it was on the wrong side of his mouth. There was something pathetic in Mrs. Donovan's hero-worship of her policeman husband as a defender of justice and a champion of right.

The next three or four days were filled for Dick with suffering of a new sort. In many Celts there is a vein of absolute pessimism, and as Dick did not see how to conquer this difficulty the natural melancholy of his nature awoke and he simply tried to make up his mind that he had lost everything, that life was like that; it would give you this, that and the other, and then snatch the cup of happiness from your lips and spill the golden liquid in the dust.

"It was to be," he said to himself with Celtic fatalism. "I suppose it had to be."

But now Patsy got after him. He was falling off in his speed and strength, and as a ring-general Patsy would not permit that. In his misery Dick at last told Harold all about it, and although he did not know he thereby played a winning card, for Harold, boylike, saw very little in it and went to his father, and when his father heard that Dick would probably win one hundred thousand dollars, and not be hurt by losing, he said before his daughter that he hoped a man would not fool enough to throw away such a chance of a fortune. His daughter turned on him, but her mother immediately sided with the father, and Kate began to feel outlawed in her righteousness. In her heart she was glad to acknowledge that perhaps she had been too severe, and off she went with her brother to meet Dick.

The reconciliation was a renewal of love. In her desire to atone she showed her lover all the warmth in her nature. She threw her arms round his neck and said: "I won't dispute any more. I think life horrid. But one thing I am determined on. I want you to leave off fighting altogether. Surely after this big lot of money we'll have enough and you can get a vaudeville engagement as you had at first."

Dick was jubilant. "I will lose this fight," he said, "but within three months the fight for the championship will be staged again, and if I win it I'll fight no more. I've had enough of it. I'd like to travel in France and Ireland and perhaps learn something and be more worthy of you."

And for the first time he ventured to touch her breasts and show his passion. To his delight she responded and kissed him with hot lips. And when he put his arms round her and held her to him closely she was all yielding softness, and his desire for her grew to madness.

The fight at Madison Square Garden attracted an enormous crowd. The place was crammed from floor to ceiling at unheard-of prices and the betting was insane.

Dick measured his man as well as he could without trying to beat him, and in about the eight or ninth round came to the conclusion that he could beat him. Nevertheless he took the right and left on the jaw in the twelfth round and went down for the count.

The audience went crazy with delight. The best people in New York were there, had all bet on the college boy, and the college boy had won. It had been a clean fight and their joy knew no bounds, and the Irish who followed Dick to a man took their beating philosophically. "It always needs a batin'," they said, "to wake our man up. Sure, Donovan will come again, and the next time we'll get our money back and more."

And that turned out to be very near the truth. Another fight for the championship was staged in Newark, N.J., and once again the papers boosted the fight just as if they had been paid for the advertisement, when they got nothing by it except enthusiastic readers.

Before the training even began Dick had a long talk with Harriman.

"We'll begin," said that gentleman, "by handing you these for the last fight," and he gave Dick four cheques for twenty-five thousand dollars each;

"that's about eleven per cent. of what I made."

Dick thanked him.

"And now," Harriman went on, "I want you to do me a favour. Can you beat him?"

Dick nodded his head.

"Are you sure? I can only get odds of about five or six to four against you. Dare I risk eight hundred thousand dollars on it? Will you bring me my money home? If you do I'll quit promoting and retire to my place in the Adirondacks."

"One can never be as sure of winning as of losing," Dick replied, "but I am satisfied I can beat him and I intend to."

A few days afterwards the announcement came out that an agreement had been signed; the prize would be one hundred thousand dollars, sixty thousand dollars to go to the victor and forty thousand dollars to the loser. Nine out of ten newspaper readers in New York believed that Rossiter would be the victor and that Dick would again be beaten.

This time the whole Woolcombe family came to the fight. Harold and Fred had interested the father and mother, and even Kate was carried off her feet by the excitement.

The fight was very like one of the old Roman gladiatorial contests. Harriman and his friends had built up a great amphitheatre that would hold nearly sixty thousand persons.

At three o'clock on the appointed day the two men faced each other in the ring. Half-an-hour before Harriman had said to Dick: "If you beat

him before the tenth round I will owe you another
sixty thousand dollars"; so Dick went in under the
eyes of his love determined to fight as he had never
fought before, but like an old ring-general determined, too, not to risk anything.

The first two rounds went to Dick, but the third
went to Benny. He had slipped Dick's lead and
ducked under his right arm with catlike speed, and
in infighting he was more than Dick's match. But
Dick's stomach muscles had become indeed bands of
steel; no body punch of Benny's had the smallest
effect on him. Again and again Benny drove in
his right like a battering pile and again and again
Dick took the blow and countered on the jaw. The
third and fourth time he countered so heavily that
Benny reeled back. At once Dick was on him, rain-
ing down a hurricane of blows, right and left, with
all the power of advance and the spring from hip
and shoulder in every blow. Before the torrent
Benny went down, and though he got to his feet
again before eight was counted, it was only the gong
sounding at the end of the round that saved him
from being knocked out in the third round.

The fourth and fifth rounds he fought very cautiously, avoiding everything and ducking all Dick's
blows, waiting evidently to get back his strength.
But Dick took Patsy's advice and crowded the fight;
he jumped in, hitting right and left with tremendous
speed and force, following his man to his corner.
In the sixth round Benny was overwhelmed. His
blows had lost both speed and force, telegraphing

thereby to Dick that his opportunity had come, and he used it quite fairly but relentlessly. Before the round was half through Benny's seconds threw up the sponge and the championship was won.

So perfect was Patsy's training that Dick had scarcely a mark on him and felt really just as well as when he entered the ring.

Mr. Woolcombe was delighted. It appeared that he was a friend and backer of Harriman, and this time Harriman had let him in on the good thing and he had made nearly a quarter of a million dollars betting on Dick.

They all went back in automobiles to Mamaroneck and the Woolcombes gave Dick a supper. After the supper the lovers stole out together and, to Dick's surprise and joy, Kate was incandescent, which, whether Dick knew it or not, was full of good promise for his married happiness. She caressed his bruised cheeks and fondled his hands with little cries of passionate tenderness. The varied incidents of the conflict, the dreadful risks, the alternate mad hopes and fears had whipped her blood to flame and held her enthralled, panting with excitement, and then the appalling swift attack, the grace, speed and strength of her lover had swept her off her feet, flooding her with a delicious triumph and afterwards the wild applause of the ringside and cheering of the crowd had broken her will to resist and made of her his creature—one with him for ever.

"Oh, Dick, Dick," she sobbed, "you wonderful

Dick," and tears streamed from her eyes; "but—but—" (striving to control herself) "I was sorry for Benny; you hit him dreadfully. It's the last fight, isn't it, dear?"

"Yes, indeed," said Dick. "The vaudeville manager told me he would give me fifteen hundred dollars a week, and that ought to keep us for the next year or two. I want to read and study and become worthy of you."

"You are worthy of any woman," she said, looking up at him with shining wet eyes. "Oh, Dick, the applause of the people and their cheering will be in my ears all my life. You're a hero, sir, to hundreds of thousands."

And perhaps, as heroes go, Dick Donovan deserved the title better than most.

THE TEMPLE TO THE
FORGOTTEN DEAD

THE TEMPLE TO THE
FORGOTTEN DEAD

I SUPPOSE I had a good conceit of myself and some apparent reasons for it. I had won a scholarship at Clifton and gone to Balliol and won first honours in "Mods." and "Greats" and got the Ireland scholarship, and thought myself a wonder. It was the year after Asquith had swept the university of prizes and, like Asquith, I, too, went to the Bar in the Middle Temple. I swotted the first term or two and then, having worked too hard, went for a walking tour through Surrey and Sussex. Cæsar had kept off headaches and sickness by eating little, walking much and living always in the open air, and I followed the same regimen—with equally good results.

At the end of the second week of my holiday I reached the outskirts of Brighton, feeling very fit. It was a lovely evening, bright and warm, and I was glad to see a "pub" almost as soon as the heath died away in the streets.

The landlord was a big man. When I asked him for a "lemon squash" he seemed surprised, but soon put it before me. While we were talking there issued from a neighbouring room to the left of the bar shouts of laughter and a great noise, as of glasses being beaten on the table.

"What's that?" I could not help asking.

"It's a Mr. Collinson," replied the landlord apologetically. "They have a sort of club there, sir, twice a week, and Mr. Collinson tells 'em stories."

"Stories?" I repeated in a question.

"Yes, sir," said the landlord; "and he does tell 'em surprising, sir."

"Might I hear one?" I asked. "I love a good story."

"This Mr. Collinson," confided the landlord, "is some'ut out of the common. He used to be a master, I have been told, in Dr. John's Grammar School, but he married an aunt of the doctor's that had quite a bit of money of her own and now lives with her in 'The Grange,' the house standing alone on your left as you go out of the door. She was a widow and is quite a few years older nor him; but they gets along very well, though they do say as she wears the breeches. You know what I mean, sir, don't you? No offence!"

I nodded. "Are you sure the other guests wouldn't mind my listening?" I asked the good-humoured host.

"No, no, sir," he replied cordially. "I often go in myself and listen when I've nothing better to do. No one will object, sir, I'm sure," and he came round the bar as he spoke and opened the door for me.

There may have been a dozen men in the room.

The story-teller, Mr. Collinson, was in the chair at the far end of the table. He was a man of perhaps five-and-thirty, nice-looking, with fair features, blue-grey eyes and almost black hair, worn rather long: he would have been very good-looking were it not for an outjutting, fleshy nose; the mouth, too, was a little large; but at first the impression was altogether pleasing, the eyes were so bright and quick and the smile so engaging.

"Here's a friend," said the landlord by way of introduction, "who would like to hear your stories, Mr. Collinson. Your name, sir?" he added, turning to me.

"My name is quite unknown to fame," I replied; "it's Clarke," and I spelled it out.

"Mr. Clarke," repeated the landlord, and Collinson rose and bade me welcome.

"Do you make up the stories?" I asked.

"Of course," replied Collinson reproachfully.

"He tells 'em wonderfully, sir," said one of the guests. "I never misses a Wednesday or Saturday evening. I——" And he shut up, apparently from excess of feeling.

"And he never tells two alike," said another.

"What will you all drink?" I asked. "I must stand something for the good of the house!" The proposal seemed to be acceptable, and after everyone had a fresh drink before him Collinson wanted to know whether I'd mind a half-religious story. Naturally I told him that I left him the choice, and he began at once:

"This story came to me in sleep. We all know the brain often works in sleep and solves problems even for mathematicians that puzzled them when awake, and performs other wonders, and this dream of mine was strangely vivid, in spite of its wild improbability. I dreamed I had awakened on an isle in the South Pacific that was shut off by electric clouds from all communication with the outside world. There I found a curiously high civilisation, a society of people extraordinarily cultivated, who had made their little island (it was barely fifty miles round) an artistic home, where everyone worked and all enjoyed the luxuries even of a simple life. They had a law that any stranger reaching their land by any chance should be condemned to painless death, and I was so sentenced, and in ignorance was walking to my doom when I caught the eyes of an astonishingly pretty girl. I could not but smile to her, she was so fine and seemed sad, and she turned and took me from my attendants. I learned later that anyone who came from a family that had been thanked by the State for services could exercise the right of mercy at any time, and so Irene, as I called her, saved my life.

"All this and more I learned gradually as I mastered the language, for Irene had taken me to her home and taught me every day, though she was the daughter of one of the governors of the island. I had been reading a little before how Diotima, the lovely, light woman of Athens, told Socrates all sorts of new things, and I dreamed into Irene a sort of ideal nature, and indeed she was very fine.

"She held herself curiously erect; she had large grey eyes, with long black lashes, and a rather rich mouth showing bluey-white teeth. There was something challenging in her good humour and smiling superiority of approach. Though still in the twenties she was very wise. In my dream we were together, this Irene and myself, in a garden. I had been impressed by her wisdom and her air of conscious superiority, and accordingly I put forward the Sermon on the Mount as the sublimest height of wisdom that I knew anything about. 'The Sermon on the Mount begins with beatitudes,' I said, 'or a sort of declaration of faith,' and I recited them.

" 'I see, I see,' said Irene, smiling, 'the sort of thing a young man gets off to convince himself of his own originality.'

"I was struck by the truth of her remark, but went on reciting. When I came to the verses:

" 'Agree with thine adversary quickly, whiles thou art in the way with him; lest at any time the adversary deliver thee to the judge, and the judge deliver thee to the officer, and thou be cast into prison.

" 'Verily I say unto thee, Thou shalt by no means come out thence, till thou hast paid the uttermost farthing.'

—Irene was indignant. 'I never heard worse

morality,' she cried. 'Am I to make it up with an enemy merely for fear of the consequences? It's degrading.'

" 'Listen,' I said, and went on to the end of the chapter, and when I had finished this was Irene's criticism—and I think it worth remembering:

" 'At first I thought it all bad,' she began, 'because of the judge and prison business, but soon I came to see that the whole sermon is a medley of thoughts put together at different times and representing very different stages of growth. The morality of the judge and prison is childish. If Jesus ever used the incident it must have been as a boyish memory; for it is expressly contradicted later when He teaches you to forgive your enemies and those who would despitefully use you and persecute you, ending with the noble words: "Be ye perfect, even as your Father, which is in heaven, is perfect." That's far enough away from the making up with your enemy for fear of consequences, far away, too, from the youthful, prig beatitudes. To be perfect is the real goal, but I don't care for the tag, "As your Father in heaven is perfect," for I see no striving after perfection in any part of creation.'

"When I asked Irene about her religion she told me that the popular religion of her people was as high, she thought, as the Christianity of the Sermon on the Mount, but very different; and one day, when I pressed her, she took me in her airplane to their Sacred City.

"It was a great wooded hill laid out in gardens and groves, and here and there were temples scattered about; she took me into one of the first of these and made me observe that there were realistic busts of men on all sides, with a kindred air of boldness and resolution.

" 'This temple is dedicated to courage,' she began, 'the youngest of all religions or, if you will, the oldest. Most of the worshippers here are boys and young men, and courage is commended to them as a sacred duty, and they are advised to imitate the courageous men whose busts are collected here.

" 'On the other side of the main road there's a Temple to Pity, and that's frequented by young girls and is to them the most appealing of all the creeds and the highest.'

" 'I see, I see,' I exclaimed; 'all the base of the hill is taken up with temples dedicated to various virtues.'

" 'And the preachers,' she nodded, 'are all picked because of the proofs they have given of pre-eminence in this or that quality that they talk about.'

"Slowly we made our way up to the top of the hill, to find it crowned by great colonnades interspersed with statues of every kind.

Suddenly I cried: 'All these statues lack something. See, that one is without hands and that there is eyeless. What does it all mean?'

" 'This,' said Irene, 'is the obverse of what you've already seen. Some of us worship in that temple at the foot of the hill, and some in another; but we all worship here, for this is "The Temple to the Forgotten Dead."

" 'Who was the first to invent the *wheel* and so reduce the work of man by one-tenth? No one knows. Who was the first to make a screw? These are the Unknown Benefactors of Humanity, to whom we are all indebted and whose very names are lost in the whelming flood of oblivion. And our wisest suppose that these heroes and seers are forgotten because they lacked this quality or that, and so these statues prefiguring them all lack something, now an eye, now a hand.

" 'In my opinion they were content to give of their best and pass into the shrouding darkness without a word——'

" 'Wonderful,' I broke in. 'I shall not soon forget the Temple to the Forgotten Dead; but is that all there is in this Holy City?'

" 'One thing more,' said Irene, 'and perhaps the chief thing,' and silently she led the way through the colonnade into a large grove of flowering, perfume-ladened trees.

"In the middle there was an open space and in it a great statue of a woman with both hands uplifted. I noticed, too, that her eyes were sightless.

" 'What does that prefigure?' I asked.

" 'Our Rulers,' replied Irene, 'have given us that as the very soul of religion; they wish to tell us that woman is nearer the heart of things than man, and her hands are uplifted, as you see, in yearning desire, but her eyes are sightless, for she knows not whither she goes or to what bourne. Her aspiration is without a goal——'

" 'A lame and impotent conclusion,' I cried, and Irene, agreeing with me, hastened to add:

" 'I told you I would show you our popular religion. I did not say it was perfect. The real religion of the best among us is made of two parts: the first is our duty to ourselves and is summed up in complete self-development; the second is all in the duty we owe to others, to help everyone born and especially the best to the utmost of our ability. We mortals don't know much, do we?' She broke off, with brooding, sad eyes."

Collinson's voice ceased.

"So that's the end?" I half asked, and Collinson answered a little defiantly, I thought:

"That's the end in one mood; but, fortunately, we men are allowed to have contradictory moods."

I'm quite aware that I've told the story badly. To hear such a story in a common public-house almost took my breath away. And then Collinson told it inimitably. He made you feel that Irene was at once an English girl in looks and wiser than Diotima in reality; the bounds of the possible fell away as he talked. The myriad inflections of his voice, his dramatic pauses, the abrupt changes of tone, all were used to make the extraordinary probable and of everyday occurrence.

I hardly knew what to think and was very eager indeed to know what another first-rate mind would think of this story-teller.

I thanked Collinson warmly and promised to come on the next Saturday evening and bring a friend, an Oxford professor of rare talent, York Fowell, who would be infinitely pleased to applaud so gifted a story-teller. Fowell was already in Brighton, and I intended to see a good deal of him. Collinson smiled pleasantly, told me he'd be glad to meet any friend of mine, was very amiable; but he seemed just a little tired, as if telling the story had exhausted him somewhat. Thinking it over afterwards I began to realise that he was not very strong.

Well, the Saturday came in due course and I brought York Fowell to the public-house and introduced him to Collinson. After the usual courtesies and fresh drinks I asked Collinson would he tell us another story like "The Temple to the Forgotten Dead." He immediately wanted to know whether we would mind a story of Art-life in Chelsea. Of course we told him at once to go ahead, and without more ado he began:

"This story is about the artistic life in Chelsea. I call it

'THE STRAIT-WAISTCOAT'

"I don't know that I ought to tell this story. I don't even know that I can tell it, though I lived

cheek-by-jowl with it for years and know intimate
sides of it that are now completely forgotten.

"Everyone has heard of John Craven, the Royal
Academician who made a great name for himself
early in life as an artist.

"He was a very agreeable man.   I had to inter-
view him once or twice for *The Daily Herald* just
after he did his famous picture of *The Cup-Day at
Ascot*.   It was very realistic and astonishingly
effective; all the leading figures of the day and
society queens were in the picture, and so it made
a huge sensation.   Crowds thronged to see it as
they never throng to a masterpiece.

"Craven took it all as a matter of course, but
Mrs. Craven was delighted with the notoriety.   She
was a very pretty woman, Mrs. Craven, perhaps at
this time about thirty years of age.   The Cravens
had no children, but she was very, very sympathetic,
and Lord Leith's brother, Eric Falconer, evidently
thought her the Queen of Fairies.

"I wrote about the picture and Mrs. Craven
enthusiastically, and she asked me to dinner at 'The
Red House' in Chelsea, which was very wonderfully
furnished; in fact everything in it was very well
done.

"In time I got to know the Cravens well.   I must
say I had no inkling at first of any disagreement between Mr. and Mrs. Craven.

"The garden at the back part of the 'Red House'
had a big studio in it, where Craven used to work.
And one day whom should I meet at the door but

Miss Stannard, a famous model and extremely pretty girl in whom I was very much interested.

" 'Fancy you here, Leslie,' I cried. 'What are you up to now?'

" 'Mr. Craven wants me for his next picture. You know what a success *Ascot* has been!'

" 'They had to rail it off,' I agreed, 'but it is a poor picture, I think.'

" 'Rotten,' she replied. 'Everyone who knows what pictures are, thinks it worthless. John August says it's only a coloured photograph, and bad at that.'

" 'He may be a little jealous,' I suggested.

" 'No, no,' she exclaimed, 'he knows.'

" 'Don't forget it was put on the line in the chief room by painters, Royal Academicians,' said a voice close to us, and out of the studio, in front of which we had been talking, stepped Mr. Craven. Naturally we both backed down at once. Leslie said August was very young and of course mistaken. She was an awfully kind sort, was Leslie. But she did not think much of Craven's painting. She had been knocking about studios for years and she knew pretty well who were the good painters and who the bad. I always thought Daisy Raffles had taught her a great deal, and everyone knows that Daisy Raffles is a genius as a critic!

"I think Craven's change of attitude came from this picture, *Ascot,* and from Daisy Raffles. It all happened strangely enough. One day a whole party accompanied the Cravens to the Royal Acad-

emy Show to see his picture—the picture of the
year. While he was standing in front of it two
students passed, Walter Rainforth and James Simson. Rainforth said: 'Don't look at that botch!'
Simson replied: 'It's pretty tawdry, but I have always thought he might be a painter some day.'
They went on, but Craven had heard them.

"A little while later he had taken Daisy Raffles as
a model. He told Daisy what the students had said
and she told him they were quite right—dotted the
'i's' and crossed the 't's' for him. She really knew
and had any amount of cheek.

"Daisy was a curious product of the studios: an
orphan brought up by an aunt and sent out at twelve
as a model. She always said it was her youth that
saved her. By the time she was a woman she had
not only learned all the painters' slang, but also
their morals, or rather their amorality, and this
knowledge, reinforcing a natural fastidiousness,
kept her straight. She was nearer thirty than
twenty when she became interested in Craven; she
saw at once that he could both draw and paint, and
bit by bit she developed in him a new mentality. I
can't explain how she did it, but she certainly did
draw him out in the most astonishing way. And
women, as a rule, I've noticed, are apt to like those
whom they can help and who are dependent on them
—the mother instinct in them, I suppose. But there
was nothing more than friendship between her and
Craven for a long time—indeed until his wife threw
him over and took sides against him.

"As soon as he took Daisy on as a model Craven began to paint in a new way. In the first year he had no success at all—in fact I don't think he showed a picture. But a year or so afterwards he exhibited his model, Daisy Raffles, painted 'in the altogether'; she had evidently by this time got into his blood.

"Nearly everyone thought the picture ugly; nobody wanted it, but painters said it was surprising; it had quality in it. From that time on Craven's downfall began. He painted pictures that nobody wanted; they were not even pretty; and gradually, bit by bit, he lost his money and began to be hard up.

"This much of his private history everyone knew. His wife tried again and again to get him to paint in the old way, but he wouldn't, or perhaps couldn't.

"According to Daisy Raffles his wife had always been in love with Eric Falconer, and certainly they were now very thick. When a woman of thirty or thirty-five falls in love she takes it badly, and Mrs. Craven took it worse than most. She was with Falconer or Falconer was with her morning, noon and night; their names began to be coupled together, and everyone knew it except Craven.

"I always wondered how the *exposé* came.

"Daisy Raffles said that it came about money, that Mrs. Craven got it into her head that Craven was mad. And indeed there was a good deal to be said for that theory. He had made thousands and thousands of pounds by his early pictures, then suddenly he began painting pictures that nobody wanted and no one would buy.

"One day I met Leslie Stannard with Daisy Raffles and had new light on the subject.

"Daisy Raffles swore that Craven was doing very interesting work; told us that his wife was a fool, and the sooner she got a divorce and married Eric Falconer the better. Daisy was quite pretty when she got excited and everyone knew she had the prettiest girl's figure in London.

"Craven, she declared, was going to be one of the great painters. 'You will see,' she said: 'the studies he has made of me will be worth a fortune yet'; and I remembered that Simson had said that he had the painter's hand if not his head.

"In some way or other Daisy had given Craven a new view of art and life. Before he met her he was a photographer, so to speak; she made him an artist—taught him that it was not the object in itself, but the impression the object made upon him that was important. His portrait of Daisy as Salome was a masterpiece; it gave the essence of her: the sensuous, slim body and the supersensuous soul, like a flame triumphing over Death; there was something unearthly in the spirit-beauty of it. She believed, with Nietzsche, that all great art is produced in a sort of ecstasy, an intoxicated heightening of all the faculties.

"I was very interested in the whole thing. I never liked Eric Falconer and Mrs. Craven had always seemed to me rather pretentious.

"The catastrophe came suddenly. Falconer laid the trap, I am sure, and Craven fell into it.

"Craven thought, naturally enough, that people were down on him. They had swallowed all his earlier work greedily, had given him a great reputation, had filled his pockets with money. And now, when he was doing far better work than he had ever done, no one wanted it, no one would pay for it, no one seemed to appreciate it or had a good word to say for his striving. No wonder he became a little bitter. If it hadn't been for Daisy he'd have been worse.

"It was on that bitterness of Craven that Falconer founded his plot. He encouraged Craven in his belief, made him think he was really hated and persecuted, and then one day he brought in the celebrated surgeon, Sir James Tripper, to meet Craven.

"Craven happened to be exceedingly bitter that day; the Academy had returned a picture to him; they wouldn't even give it wall-room; yet it was a beautiful little study.

"Tripper drew Craven out a little and made up his mind at once that he was suffering from the mania of persecution. Doctors believe in the prevalence of disease, as saints in the universality of sin.

"A few days later Falconer brought Mr. Wisley, a friend of Tripper's, to see Craven. Wisley, of course, came to the same conclusion as Tripper, and was fully convinced besides that Craven should be shut up and treated to a strict regimen.

"About this time Daisy Raffles had gone to

Brighton to take care of her aunt, who was ailing,
and Craven, all alone, was shutting up his studio
one evening when two keepers and a warden came
in and arrested him. He asked them to show their
warrant and they showed it. It was in order: a
London magistrate had signed it on the affidavit of
the two doctors. Tripper, of course, had a great
name.

"Craven, poor devil, wanted to go home to tell
his wife, but the warder would not allow it. He
was taken down by train and put in a private asylum
in Surrey, kept by a Mr. Waterman. Waterman
had evidently received his instructions from Wisley,
so when he got his patient he pretended that Craven
was violent and put him in a strait-waistcoat and
threw him into a padded room. But he left the window open, and so the flies got in and wandered about
Craven's face and buzzed in his hair and moustache.

"They woke him up too every night by frequent
visits of the warders. Daisy Raffles said afterwards that this was a well-known way of driving
people mad, particularly excitable, strong men.

"Daisy was a wise little thing. When she came
to the studio a week or so afterwards and found it
all shut up, and heard that Craven had not been
there, she began ferreting round, and soon ascer-
tained that Craven had gone away with three com-
mon-looking men. I do not know how she came on
the idea that he had been arrested, but she went
and interviewed his wife and they had a regular
slanging match, it appears, and the wife must have

let out something, because Daisy told Miss Stannard that his wife knew all about Craven's arrest; knew, too, that he had been taken down to Waterman's private asylum in Surrey.

"Miss Stannard came to me about it. Daisy, she said, was in a fearful state and I must devise some way of getting Craven out of the asylum. I soon found out that it could be done by a writ of habeas corpus. To cut a long story short we all swore that Craven was quite sane and got out a writ to have him examined publicly and by independent doctors.

"In the meantime something had happened at Waterman's asylum. Dr. Girton was the visiting doctor. After Craven had been about a week in the asylum Dr. Girton, according to law, had to see him and report on his case. Girton reported that Craven was suffering from persecution mania and was violent. But before the magistrate the case took on a very different complexion.

"Dr. Girton gave his evidence very emphatically, but Craven was plainly as sane as anybody in the court. He took the case into his own hands almost at once. 'Your Worship,' he said to the magistrate, 'they did all they could to make me insane; they put me in a padded room and would not let me sleep, but when Girton came in one morning, he found me perfectly quiet, and he was so surprised that he asked me how I had borne it so well, because to have flies eating your face while you are unable to protect yourself is somewhat exasperating.

I told him the truth: no persecution, no prison, no want of sleep, no strait-waistcoat had any effect on me, for I have been an artist in England.'

"The phrase made the magistrate smile and won the day.

"The end of it was that Mrs. Craven got her divorce unopposed, and when she married Falconer Craven married Daisy Raffles and began to produce the wonderful pictures that are now making him famous in the highest sense."

This story taught me what a great talent Collinson possessed; he mimed the voice and accent of every character, managed in this way to convey subtle nuances of the personality that are utterly lost in the written story. For example, he showed you Miss Stannard as a sort of tall English beauty, and Daisy Raffles as a little dark-eyed, fair-skinned creature, whose soul had been drawn out by this painter and by that, till she had attained an extraordinary culture. Is there any education of a woman which can compare with the companionship of gifted men?

In some way or other, perhaps by cunning inflection of voice, Collinson managed to suggest that Craven was Daisy's complement, that the two, to use an old phrase, were made for each other, and that their union was rarely perfect.

The more I thought of it the more I liked Collinson's little tales. In this one he had given us a sort of picture of that artist-life in Chelsea flashed out on a dark background of calumny, vilification and hate.

I was astonished to find that York Fowell was even more deeply impressed. Suddenly he spoke to Collinson: "You know that Clarke, here, had already told me your story of 'The Temple to the Forgotten Dead.' I dare not say it made a deeper impression than this; but it was surely an extraordinary story or, if you will, an extraordinary idea. No one but Goethe has ever tried to add anything to the Christian ideal, and his pagan attempts in the *Wanderjahre* are not very successful. But your 'Temple to the Forgotten Dead' has really something in it; we should cultivate piety and reverence for those who have gone before us, as you call them, 'The Unknown Benefactors of Humanity.' To have succeeded even partially where Goethe failed is honour enough for any man. I congratulate you with all my heart. And this Chelsea story might have written by Maupassant. It is enough for any man's measure to touch Goethe on the one hand and Maupassant on the other."

To my surprise the warm praise affected Collinson greatly; his whole face quivered, his eyes filled with tears. "I never expected," he said, "to be compared with Goethe; but ideas come to me sometimes that I love; they don't seem to be mine," he added deprecatingly. "They come to me—at their will and time—"

"You have got," said York Fowell abruptly, "what I would give ten years of my life for—the creative spirit. I've toiled and studied, but never

had any such divine visitation.   You are very lucky,
I think.   But why don't you write these stories of
yours?   They'd make a reputation for you and
you should be known."

"I can't write," said Collinson abruptly.   "You
overpraise my little things; but it's very kind of
you," and he stretched out his hand impulsively to
York Fowell, who took it, smiling amiably.

A little later we went away together and to my
wonder York Fowell praised Collinson enthusiastically.   "We must draw him out," he concluded;
"we must find the hidden source of those charming
imaginings.   Fancy the little master of an unknown
school living on such heights of thought!   What
does he read?   Do you know?"

I had to confess that I knew nothing really about
Collinson, but Fowell's enthusiasm affected me and I
resolved to get to know him."

But the next Saturday came and Collinson
wouldn't tell a story—had none in his head, he said;
and when we questioned him he told us he had an ordinary grammar school training, had learned German and French and Italian on his own, and, curiously enough, had gone as by instinct to the very
greatest spirits.   Heine, we found, he knew nearly
by heart; he used to call him the first of the moderns.
And in French, Villon and Balzac and Vauven-
argues, and in Italian, Leopardi.   He had got to
the heights through literature.   He was a Socialist
without knowing the modern concept of the word—

thought the land should belong to all the people and all public utilities should be nationalised, and stopped there.

Curiously enough Collinson was passionate about the need of nationalising coal-mining. I found out that he had once paid a visit to a friend in Merthyr and had been horrified by the degrading slavery of the miners' life. "Humane living," he exclaimed passionately, "is impossible under such conditions! It must all be lifted and ennobled."

Little by little I came to know Collinson. One evening we walked to his house and he said timidly: "I'd ask you in, but my wife hates me to bring any-one unless they are known here socially, and she always objects to men without their wives. She was a Paget, you know, and is in love with all conventions."

"Why did you marry her?"

He shrugged his shoulders: "I had a turn of bad luck. I found it so hard to teach kids who didn't want to learn and I had a couple of boys of sheer genius who interested me intensely. The 'Head' gave me notice just after I had met Mrs. Livinstone. She had married an officer in the 10th Cavalry; he drank himself to death, I believe. Anyhow, she was a widow and pleasant and always inviting me. I told her one evening that I thought of going to London to get a new place and—some-how or other—I don't know how it was—I found she wanted me to marry her, and I was—a coward.

I hated to go to the agencies and pay and beg a
place; it was humiliating, with 'thoughts that wander through eternity'—thoughts make aristocrats of
some of us.   And so we were married.   But I hate
her society friends; that's why I began going to the
'pub.'   It's common, and most of the *habitués* don't
understand me or my stories, but after all they don't
look down on one like the society crew.   I'm quite
happy when I can meet someone like you and York
Fowell; he's very able, isn't he?"

"Very!" I nodded.   "They say in Oxford he
knows more than half the Faculty—an extraordinary
power of assimilation; he learned everything as a
sponge absorbs moisture."

"And he compared me to Goethe, didn't he?"
said Collinson with jubilant eyes.

"Indeed he did," I replied, "and when we were
alone he thanked me for bringing him to the 'pub';
said he had never had so great an evening.   He's
coming again; but you disappointed him the last
time when you would not tell us another story."

Collinson turned his clear blue-eyes on me with
an expression of humility I never saw in anyone else
and cried: "I hadn't a good story in my head; but
the next time I'll do better than my best for you,
you'll see"; and his eyes seemed to veil themselves
in a mist of thought.

And in truth the next Wednesday he was better
than his best.   As soon as we came in he began:

"The other evening I had a wonderful night.
I dreamed I was in some city in India, near the

gates; it must have been Delhi, and I was a public story-teller. As evening fell, and the people began to drift into the country from their work in the city, I came out and sat at the door of my house in the deep shadow, with a great copper pan at my side for offerings. At first I told stories of Gautama Buddha, when he was a prince, and bit by bit the crowd gathered, and one asked me how I knew the prince.

" 'By likeness of nature,' I replied boldly. 'We can all know those we love, and I love the prince, who gave up everything—honour and riches and pleasure and joy and all the good things of this world—to go and live with his pain-stricken brethren and teach them how to attain Nirvana, where there is no suffering, because desire is dead.'

" 'But how can you know Gautama's life as a young prince?' another questioned, and a strange answer came to me in my dream. I said: 'You know that there is a star near the Southern Cross so distant that it takes nearly two thousand seven hundred years for light to come from it to our earth; the tiny spark of radiance we see and name left it before the birth of Gautama, and in my imagination I knew someone living on that star, and he had watched the light ray that started from earth in Gautama's youth and had taken photos of what the light brought him, and so he showed me pictures of Gautama even before his soul opened to the truth. Think of it! nothing is lost in this wonder-world. Light is still carrying the pictures it received ten thousand years ago, and it should be possible to reflect them again as easily as those of yesterday or to-day. Time is only relative; space a condition of our thought.

" 'I have begged my star-habitant to return to me out of the realm of sleep and one of these nights bring me light-pictures of the young Jesus as He walked and spoke when His mother and father found Him at twelve years of age teaching the Rabbis in the Temple.

" 'Fancy, if I could get the whole history of His life in photograph after photograph—when He first collected His disciples and drew them with Him to Nazareth, and how the townsfolk were indignant at one they knew giving Himself out as a prophet.

" 'Don't we know Him?' they cried; 'are not His mother and His brethren here with us? How dare He pretend to such authority?' and they went about to kill Him and He had to hide. His mother, we are told, declared He was mad; perhaps that was the reason He said afterwards: 'This is my mother and these my brethren who do the will of my Father.'

"And think of the picture of the woman taken in adultery, when Jesus at first did not know what to say, for He realized that He had not come to fulfil the terrible law of Moses, with its 'eye for an eye,' but was full of a new and diviner message: 'Let him that is without sin among you first cast the stone.'

"When this was said I saw all prisons vanish and all judges and judgments become ridiculous, for hospital wards took the place of prison cells, and doctors and nurses came instead of jailers and executioners. We have both now, side by side in our silly life, the prison here and the torturers, and the hospitals there and the healers! What madmen men are with Secretaries of State for War and no Secretary of State yet for Peace anywhere, though Jesus is dead these two thousand years!

"Think of it and remember that only one disciple records this story of the adulterous woman. Matthew, Mark and Luke saw nothing in it; but John remembered and recorded it: that explains to me why John was the beloved disciple.

"And remember, too, what Jesus said to the woman: 'Neither do I accuse thee.' What does this mean? Surely that He too was a sinner and had no more right to condemn than anyone else.

"Ah, the Sacred Story! One of these days we shall have all of it divinely illustrated and illumined, for the New Commandment of Jesus is the porch of the modern world, the door into the New Life!"

There was something inspired in the man. Even the tradesmen who sat around the table were moved by the unearthly passion of the vibrant voice, and York Fowell's eyes were a confession of astonished admiration. I don't know how we came away, but I shall always remember how York Fowell thanked Collinson.

A day or two afterwards I was called up to London and got that appointment at Durham which changed my whole life. I never saw Collinson again and York Fowell died untimely in the next autumn; but Collinson has left a memory as a story-teller that I have sought to perpetuate.

MY LAST WORD

There is an end of time and an end of the evil thereof: when delight is gone out of thee and desire is dead, thy mourning shall not be for long.

Grief, thou fearest, shall remain with thee now that an end of thy pleasure is come: but grief likewise shall not abide with thee.

At the beginning a little sorrow was ordained thee, and a little joy as well: but there is nothing of thine that endureth.

Yet the adventure of life was glorious and the magic of moments of love and pity and understanding beyond description or thanks.

In a sun-haze of exquisite memories I, too, like a God, look upon the world and say it was all "good."

FRANK HARRIS.

NICE, 1923.